ALSO BY JANE SMILEY

Fiction

Perestroika in Paris

The Last Hundred Years Trilogy:
Some Luck, Early Warning, Golden Age

Private Life

Ten Days in the Hills

Good Faith

Horse Heaven

The All-True Travels and Adventures of Lidie Newton

Moo

A Thousand Acres

Ordinary Love and Good Will

The Greenlanders

The Age of Grief

Duplicate Keys

At Paradise Gate

Barn Blind

Nonfiction

The Man Who Invented the Computer

Thirteen Ways of Looking at the Novel

A Year at the Races

Charles Dickens

Catskill Crafts

For Young Adults

Gee Whiz

Pie in the Sky

True Blue

A Good Horse

The Georges and the Jewels

Riding Lessons

Saddle and Secrets

Taking the Reins

A Dangerous Business

A Dangerous Business

JANE SMILEY

ALFRED A. KNOPF New York

2022

THIS IS A BORZOI BOOK
PUBLISHED BY ALFRED A. KNOPF

www.aaknopf.com

Knopf, Borzoi Books, and the colophon are registered trademarks
of Penguin Random House LLC.

Library of Congress Cataloging-in-Publication Data
Names: Smiley, Jane, author.
Title: A dangerous business / Jane Smiley.
Description: First edition. | New York : Alfred A. Knopf, [2022]
Identifiers: LCCN 2022007952 (print) | LCCN 2022007953 (ebook) |
ISBN 9780525520337 (hardcover) | ISBN 9780525520344 (ebook)
Subjects: LCGFT: Detective and mystery fiction. | Novels.
Classification: LCC PS3569.M39 D36 2022 (print) |
LCC PS3569.M39 (ebook) | DDC 813/.54—dc23/eng/20220224
LC record available at https://lccn.loc.gov/2022007952
LC ebook record available at https://lccn.loc.gov/2022007953

Jacket image: Folio Images/Offset/Shutterstock
Jacket design by Gabriele Wilson

Manufactured in the United States of America
First Edition

*I would like to dedicate this novel to all the copy editors who,
over many years, have steered me down the path
to an understandable and readable book.*

"Between you and me, being a woman is a dangerous business, and don't let anyone tell you otherwise."

—MRS. PARKS

A Dangerous Business

TWO MONTHS AFTER her husband died on November 12, 1851, Eliza Ripple stopped writing letters to her mother back in Kalamazoo. The reason was both simple and complex. Her mother had written her three letters, all of them lamenting and lamenting and lamenting Peter's demise, but, apart from the shock (which was perfectly understandable, given that he was shot in a bar fight in Monterey), Eliza was more relieved than upset. They had been married for a little over two years—she was eighteen when her father handed her over to Peter, who was thirty-eight. Eliza had hardly known Peter at the time, as he was new to Kalamazoo, visiting a cousin he had there. He had presented himself as prosperous and well mannered, an experienced traveler with connections and funds. Eliza had offended both of her parents by becoming fond of a boy her age, from Ireland (County Cork), who worked in a lumber mill, though not the one her father owned, was tall and handsome, spoke with a lilt, hadn't a penny, and was, of all things, Catholic. All of the members of her family, staunch Covenanters, were convinced that the Irish, especially those from Cork and Dublin, were soulless sinners. Her father had pointed to a freed slave who'd run across the Ohio River to Cincinnati, and then made his way north, and said, "Better Josiah Grant than that bog trotter."

Peter never told her parents he was a Covenanter, or even a Presbyterian, but he had the right name—Cargill—and was happy to be married in their little church in Kalamazoo. And the only thing Eliza could think of while the ceremony was taking place was the sight of Liam Callaghan standing on the corner of Lovell Street and Park Street, the red autumn leaves fluttering above him, staring at their carriage as they drove to the church.

Perhaps her parents assumed that Peter would settle down in Kalamazoo, buy himself a sturdy house, and produce the grandchildren her mother was ready for, but once the snow melted off in the spring, Peter was already preparing himself for California, the gold rush, his future wealth. And whatever wealth he had was all in the future—by the Christmas after they were married, Eliza knew perfectly well that the wealth he had wooed her parents with was a mirage. And Eliza, of course, was to come along as his servant. That was clear, too. It was not that Eliza's parents disagreed with the idea that Eliza was born to be Peter's servant, but they did not act out their beliefs. In actual fact, her father was her mother's servant, and had been as long as Eliza could remember—they slept in different rooms, he was to knock if he wanted to enter (because, if he came in suddenly, he would give Mother a headache), he was to let her decide what was to be done with the house or the garden or the horses or Eliza. At the end of each month, when he brought home his profits from the mill, he handed them to Mother, who divvied up the money to pay the bills and then sent him to the bank with what was left. Eliza was their only offspring—more evidence for Eliza, once she was married, that Mother called the shots. These sorts of things would never happen with Peter. Part of the reason Eliza didn't mourn him, and part of the reason she was now earning her living (and a good living!) in Monterey, was that he had made it clear that he intended to put it to her, whether she liked it or not, once or twice every day. Then, when she felt the quickening, he took her to a woman on South Pitcher Street, in Kalamazoo, who gave her some concoction and kept her overnight. She never saw the remains. After that, he regularly pulled out, and also bought a few rubber things that he used. When he got her to Monterey, he found a doctor who gave her her own rubber thing, a pessary, which she was to wash and insert and take care of. If there was anything that she was thankful to Peter Cargill for, it was the knowledge that enabled her to not be impregnated again.

Of course, the gold venture led nowhere. Once—say, ten years before—Monterey had been "somewhere," but now that status was conferred upon San Francisco, two days' travel up the coast. Monterey was a handsome and pleasant town, but there was no gold in the hills nearby, ships found the bay too big and the winds too variable, and the inland areas were intimidating, to say the least. There were fertile and productive places to farm, but they were cut apart by sharp peaks and deep slopes. There was plenty of lumber, but getting the pines and the oaks to a river was a fearsome task. There weren't many women—Eliza counted perhaps eight or nine fellows for every woman—and everyone got along well enough (Spanish, Portuguese, Rumsen, Ohlone, British sailors, American settlers, even the priests and the Presbyterians), but maybe that was because the more ruthless and ambitious fellows went elsewhere, as had the fellow who shot Peter—here one night, gone the next day, no one even knew his name, and his face, such as it was, had been covered with hair, so, Eliza assumed, all he had to do to hide himself was shave his mustache and his beard and clip his mop. There were no constables in Monterey—Eliza had heard about a "sheriff," but there was more talk about vigilantes. "Vigilante" was a Spanish word that Eliza hadn't known before coming to California. What it meant was that, if the community cared about the killing, some of them got together and snared the killer. No one, it appeared, had cared about Peter, and for that Eliza gave thanks.

And then, at Peter's interment in the public graveyard, a woman he knew, and had introduced Eliza to as Mrs. Parks one time when they were taking a walk up Pacific Street, approached her and said,

"Dear, if you find yourself in embarrassed circumstances, don't hesitate to come to me. I think I can help you." She pressed a bit of paper into Eliza's hand, with her name and address written on it in ink. Simpleminded as she was, Eliza had gone to her two weeks later for a bit of a loan, and understood, when she stepped through the door of a rather large establishment with a nice veranda in the front, that the place was a house of prostitution. She had swallowed her fears and offered herself, and the first fellow who came to her treated her much more kindly than Peter ever had. Of these things, her mother knew nothing. She also did not know that Eliza had changed her name, on the advice of Mrs. Parks, from Cargill to Ripple, a name that amused her and also reminded her of something pleasant. All the girls in Mrs. Parks's establishment had pleasant names—Carroll, Breeze, Skye, Berry (Ann, Olive, Harriet, Amelia)—and all of them English, too, even the girl who spoke mostly Spanish. They had been carefully trained in how to use the pessary and in how to discern whether a fellow might have an infection—sores or blisters on the prick, an ooze that stank or was an odd color. They kept themselves clean, and if a fellow was a mess, they pointed him to a basin of water that Mrs. Parks kept in their chambers. None of them lived at the establishment—only Mrs. Parks lived there, in a back room on the ground floor. But the others did make enough money to support themselves. That very first morning, Eliza had walked away with an entire dollar, a gold coin, which the fellow had given her. She handed it to her own landlady, who, looking at the coin, knew better than to ask where Eliza had gotten it. That was another way in which Monterey was agreeable—no one pried, no one asked unpleasant questions. Perhaps the reason for that was that there were few churches, and most of those Catholic. Down the road, in Carmel, there was a mission, but not a mission in the sense that, like the Covenanters, they were always talking in your face about whether you were saved.

Now it was April 1852. Eliza had heard nothing from her mother in two months and she had almost fifty dollars in the bank. Mrs.

Parks was strict about payment—the customers paid her when they came in, she maintained the books and the bank account. If they wanted to leave another payment for the girl when they left, that was fine with her. She was often paid in gold dust, but she paid her girls in dollars, which was fine with Eliza. Just now, she was not far from Mrs. Parks's establishment, and had just eaten a nice helping of mutton stew for her midday meal. She got up from her chair in the eating house she preferred, which was officially "the Bear Up," but which everyone called "the Bear," nodded to the owner, an agreeable man who sometimes betook himself to Mrs. Parks's, waved to Rupert, her usual server, and walked out into the street. The fog had lifted; there was a considerable breeze. She put her hand on her bonnet to keep it from blowing off, and decided to check on what she might have to do later in the day.

Mrs. Parks was sitting on her veranda with a friend of hers, Mr. Bauer. She gave Eliza a welcoming wave and stood up as Eliza mounted the steps. She of course knew what Eliza was after, and took her inside, where she checked her book. The fellow's name was Elijah Harwood, he would come at nine, and he requested that he might take Eliza to his house on Jefferson Street, keep her there for the night, and bring her back in the morning. Mrs. Parks looked at Eliza and lifted her eyebrows. Eliza said, "I've seen some lovely houses on Jefferson Street."

"Yes, indeed," said Mrs. Parks. "You may try it if you like. Some girls feel a little uncomfortable."

Eliza thought of Peter. He was the only fellow who had ever made her feel uncomfortable. Mrs. Parks said, "He is a rather elderly man. And not, shall we say, blessed. From what I understand, he does his best, but it wears him out. If he does it here, he's afraid he won't have the strength to return home."

Eliza said, "I suppose that going to his house is the kindest thing to do."

Mrs. Parks smiled. "Indeed. And the most lucrative."

So it was set, then. She did not ask Olive, who was also there, if she had been to the Harwood place. Olive was the friendliest of the other girls, and when Eliza had first started working for Mrs. Parks, she had exchanged a few words with her. Once, they had run into each other at the market and then walked along, chatting for a few minutes. Olive was two years older than she was, had grown up in western Massachusetts (which, Olive said, her father, who farmed, called "Massive Two Shits"), and liked music—she had grown up playing the flute (lessons every Saturday). But Mrs. Parks was strict about keeping all the girls apart: they were not to gossip about their customers, or say much to one another. Mrs. Parks told them that gossiping was like opening a door and leaving it unlocked—you never knew what might happen—so the girls were to be friendly but to avoid one another. They all lived in different boarding houses (two had houses of their own), and though all of them smiled or nodded to one another, they knew they were to keep to themselves. Eliza did not want to get fired, and neither did Olive, so, once in a while, they exchanged a word or two, and if they saw each other in town they were friendly, but they did not dare to become friends. Olive knew Eliza had come from Michigan, that she had no brothers or sisters (Olive had four of each), that she had been married (Olive had planned to marry, but the fellow had dropped her when a young woman showed up in Chicopee who was from a prominent Boston family—that chit had fallen for Olive's suitor and swept him off to the city). Apples and milk were what Olive's father produced on the farm. Eliza hadn't learned how Olive got to Monterey or how she came to work in Mrs. Parks's establishment.

On the way back to her boarding house, Eliza reflected upon the fact that one of her ambitions, to see the inside of a nicer house in Monterey, was about to be realized. The houses in Monterey were not at all like those in Kalamazoo, another thing that Eliza enjoyed about them. Many of them were adobe, and if they were not, then their style mimicked those. There was one place not far from her boarding house whose owners, her landlady, Mrs. Clayton, had told her, came from Australia, of all places, and brought all of the lumber for their house with them. It was quite large. Mrs. Clayton was a decent woman, perhaps the same age as Mrs. Parks. She didn't say where she had come from, or what had happened to her husband. She did say that her son was stuck with some farmland he had bought in Texas. He wished to leave, but was too indebted. Mrs. Clayton's place was where Peter had settled Eliza, a rooming house that, at the time, he could barely afford, and when Peter had been buried in the public cemetery, Mrs. Clayton had gone along with Eliza to watch, even, Eliza thought, to say a little prayer, but she hadn't questioned Eliza in any way afterward, or since. Eliza was happy to stay there. It was not far from the wharf or Mrs. Parks's. Her room was small but neat. Mrs. Clayton did not pester her or look at her askance. At one point, Mrs. Clayton had even patted her on the hand and said, "We all do what we have to do, don't we?" And she knew how to cook. At first Eliza hadn't liked the salted fish, but she did now, as long as she had some milk to go with it. Other boarders came and went— there were three rooms for them other than Eliza's. She was the only regular boarder, and Mrs. Clayton never said a word if she was gone overnight. All in all, how could she write back to her mother and successfully pretend that she was unhappy or in mourning? And her mother's response would contain a request, or a demand, that she return to Kalamazoo.

By the time Eliza returned to Mrs. Parks's establishment, the fog had smothered the town once again, and Eliza had had to wrap herself, head to tail, in a shawl she had made over the winter. A carriage was outside. An older man was sitting in the front room. He perked up when he saw her come in, and Mrs. Parks got to her feet and introduced them formally. She then followed them out the door, and helped Mr. Harwood down the steps, cocking her head toward Eliza, giving her to understand that she, too, was to help him about. Eliza nodded, took his hand. He untied his pony, got into the carriage. Eliza followed him, and they drove off. The pony knew exactly what he was doing, and took them straight to a certain house on Jefferson—he even went around to the back of the house, without being asked, and there was a boy there, evidently Spanish, who took the pony. Eliza followed Mr. Harwood through the back door—no steps. They walked to the front of the house. The first thing Eliza saw was innumerable tapers, all lit. From the odor, it was clear they were made from whale oil. Mr. Harwood said, "I do like light, my dear." He was friendly. He took her shawl and laid it across a small table. It was then that Eliza noticed, sitting quietly in a chair, an older woman, neatly dressed, evidently the same age as Mr. Harwood. Mr. Harwood turned to Eliza, and said, "Ah, yes. Eliza Ripple. This is my wife, Mrs. Harwood."

Mrs. Harwood lifted her hand, did not smile, continued to sit quietly while Mr. Harwood took Eliza to a room at the back of the house where there was a spare bedstead, a chandelier, and two hooks on the wall, one for her gown and one for his trousers. The tapers in the chandelier were lit. In Eliza's experience, most men preferred light, as they could then get her to walk around, or hop around, or even dance around in front of them while they fondled themselves, and then, when they were ready, they would come over, lay her down, and finish their business. Few of them stroked her or even looked her in the face. The younger ones did run their hands over her bosoms or backside—if she got a stray compliment, it was for her backside. Mr. Harwood sat on the bed, as there was nowhere else to sit, and stared at her. She stood quietly for a while, then turned this way and that, then walked here and there. She put her hands under her bosoms, ran them down her sides. He said nothing, only watched her with a bemused look. It was as if she was being tested for a job or a position, and her new employer was weighing her virtues against those of other applicants. The tapers flickered. Finally, Mr. Harwood's hand went to his crotch, rested there. She walked around again, then looked at him. He nodded, struggled to his feet, pulled down his underdrawers, stumbled as he did so, sat on the bed to get them off, sighed.

Eliza knew what she had to do—she sat beside him, stroked him gently on his leg, moving her hand up to his crotch, leaned against him. She tickled his prick, stroked it, remembering, as she sometimes did, how Peter had enjoyed referring to his own prick as "peter." When she suddenly felt the chill of the room, he put his arm around her, and that did the trick. No, he was not blessed, but neither was he damned—his prick was a prick similar to most of those she had seen in the last year. He put it to use, then reclined on the bed for a while until he stopped panting. Eliza lay quietly, thinking of the two dollars she would receive, wondering if there would be breakfast, and then, apparently, dozing off: she did not remember, afterward, Mr. Harwood getting out of the bed or leaving the room.

She saw, when she woke up in the morning, that he had forgotten to take his shoes with him. They were not boots, but chestnut-brown low, tied, malleable footwear with a darker-colored leather over the tip. Eliza picked one up. The leather was soft—possibly calfskin. They were very elegant. She set the two together, against the wall, then put on her drawers, her chemise, her gown. It was hard to tell what time it was, but, judging by the growling of her belly, time for breakfast. The house was utterly quiet. That was what caused Eliza to feel uneasy. Maybe she had never been in a house where morning didn't start with shouts and calls and bangings and evidence that the day's work had begun. The room had a small window, facing away from Jefferson Street. She pushed the curtain to one side and peeked out, but there was nothing to see other than some cyprus trees draped with Spanish moss (that's what they called it), some grass, and three crows sitting on the back fence. Even they were silent. Eliza gave a little shiver and decided that, in spite of the remuneration, she wasn't coming back to Mr. Harwood. She sat quietly for a while. The silence lingered. If the window had been larger, she would have climbed through it and walked back to Mrs. Parks's place, which was near the theater, only a few blocks away. She thought she could get her money, tell Mrs. Parks about how strange all of this was, and then go have a bite to eat.

There was a knock at the door of her room, and then the door opened. Why Eliza found this startling, she didn't know. Mrs. Harwood stepped into the room. She was wearing a navy-blue gown. Her hair was austerely pulled back, and she was leaning on a cane. She said, "Girl, there are some rolls on the kitchen table, if you care for one, and Raul will run you back to that place." She hobbled out of the room, dragging her right foot. After a moment, Eliza followed her. The house was not only empty—even though it was nicely furnished, it seemed as if it had been abandoned. It was empty of smell, of sound. Even the light, the beautiful Monterey light, had been blocked out, by heavy curtains. Eliza went straight to the front entrance, taking no rolls, not looking for Raul. She didn't feel at ease until she was halfway down the next block.

But she did get paid that day, and two days later, Mrs. Parks said that Mr. Harwood had asked after her—he hadn't asked *for* her, only wondered whether she was well, whether she had "been able to put up with him." Eliza replied that he was a pleasant fellow, evidently well meaning, but she said nothing about Mrs. Harwood or the house. Mrs. Parks turned and looked her in the eye. She said, almost sharply, "You need not go there again if you do not wish to do so, but let the other girls choose for themselves. He's a kindly man, with plenty of funds, and I would not like to lose his business." Eliza nodded. Mrs. Parks had never commanded her before. That, too, was strange, but, of course, understandable, given that Mrs. Parks's establishment was one of several.

THINGS WENT ALONG as usual for the next few weeks, which is to say that some of her customers were young, some of them were old, some were sailors, some were rancheros, some fished in the bay, some worked in the cattle business—skinning, drying, butchering, tanning. As part of their fee, those fellows might bring Mrs. Parks a roast or a haunch. But they had to bathe before they came. If she wrinkled her nose, they were unwelcome. One man—prosperous-looking, but a stranger, at least to Eliza—brought his son in. He was a shy, small boy. Mrs. Parks stood the girls up in front of him, and he gestured slightly toward Eliza, perhaps because she was the youngest and the smallest, so she took him to her room. As she passed Mrs. Parks, Mrs. Parks lifted her right eyebrow, which meant, "Go slow." But of course she would: no sense in frightening the boy. When they were in her room, and had closed the door, she sat on her bed and smiled. After a few moments, she said, "As you please."

The boy shook his head.

Eliza sat quietly. Yes, there was some way in which the boy reminded her of Liam Callaghan, though he didn't look like him and was much more elegantly clothed. She stared at him, but only from under her brow. He glanced around and tapped his boots on the floor. It was in the color of his eyes, she realized—large, open, as blue as the sky. She said, "Are you Irish, then?"

He started, then smiled, said, "My ma is Irish. Her name is Maggie O'Rourke. She had to run off with her folks because of the hunger."

"I had a friend that happened to."

Another silence. The boy's breathing settled. He moved slightly toward her, reached out, and put his hand on her knee. Well, it took forever, went on step by step, until he did finally bring himself to enter her. Afterward, she stroked his back while he lay facedown on the bed, recovering. They talked a bit. It turned out that he was nearly seventeen, still waiting to grow, that he was being sent back east to go to a school and would be gone for three years, and that his father was a strong believer in giving his sons (all three of them) sexual experiences. The boy, whose name was James, said, "My brothers said they liked it." This made Eliza laugh. James blushed, laughed, too, then said, "I liked it. I did like it."

One thing about the father was that he was patient. He sat quietly, reading a book, the whole time, and never pestered Mrs. Parks about a thing, slowly drinking a glass of ale. And when she paid Eliza, Mrs. Parks gave her an extra quarter for her evening meal.

As she walked home that night, Eliza listened to the gulls calling all around the bay. The only thing she regretted was that she hadn't been able to discover what book it was that held the father's attention for such a long period of time.

There was a rough one, too. He didn't look rough—if he had, Mrs. Parks would have sent him on down the street. He had a ready smile, was well dressed. But as soon as he got Eliza into her room, he pushed her against the wall so that she smacked her head. Nor did he apologize. He stepped closer and raised his hands with a grin. She reached over to her bureau and grabbed a candleholder. She didn't smack him—that wasn't allowed—but she threw the candleholder at her door, and a minute or so later, as Eliza was sidling away from the fellow, the door opened and Mrs. Parks appeared with her pistol in her hand. She walked over to the fellow, returned his funds, said he had the wrong place, and if he was into this sort of thing, he could go over to the brothel on Franklin Street. He backed out of the room and then ran out the front door. The best thing was that he stumbled down the steps and dropped his dollar coin, and when Mrs. Parks found it among the zinnias in the morning, she gave it to Eliza. Eliza hadn't known that there was a brothel on Franklin Street, and it turned out that there wasn't. Mrs. Parks had been talking through her hat, and she had done a good job of it.

Maybe a week later, Eliza was walking toward the general store that was across from Pacific House. She was looking about at horses and dogs and gowns and shawls, and she saw Mrs. Harwood come hobbling out of the door and down the steps. She also saw that Mrs. Harwood noticed her, but she was exactly as she had been before—stern, unmoved, indecipherable. Eliza watched her get into the carriage and go up toward Jefferson Street.

———

WHEN THE FIRST of "the girls" disappeared, no one thought a thing of it. Folks disappeared from Monterey all the time, mostly because there was more going on in San Francisco, or even San Jose. Or people took their families and moved down the coast because they thought they would find better hunting there, or some land with more rain. If they were lucky, they came back, gave up on the idea of owning their own farms or ranches, and went to work the way everyone else worked. In fact, Eliza knew that her mother would say that *she* had disappeared, and that thought was a bit of a prickle to her conscience, but not enough to get her to answer those letters her mother had sent. She thought there was a lot to be said for disappearing, and so she didn't think much of the disappearance of that girl, except to note the day, May 14, her very own birthday. Twenty-one now, and wasn't that strange?

But in the course of a few days of going to shops, eating here and there, sitting on a bench with a book in her hand, she noticed that people, especially women, spoke of this disappearance differently than they spoke of others—there was no "That family was only here for a few months—they might have waited it out and found something more productive," or "Good riddance! That fellow was always out of his head!," or even "Well, you bet they went back to Ohio! Wouldn't you, if you had the funds?" No, what she heard was "What it all comes down to is, those girls know what they are getting themselves into," or "I, for one, think we're better off! Luring our fellows into sin like that!"

Did the woman she overheard saying that know how Eliza herself made her money? Perhaps, though every time she left her rooming house, at least during the day, she made sure to dress modestly, never to eye any fellow, especially never to appear to recognize any of the men or the boys whom she had done business with. A brothel was not a secret, of course, but it had to pretend to be a secret. Mrs. Parks said nothing about the girl who had vanished, except that she worked for an establishment up by the Presidio, that she had been on the job only a few weeks, and that she said to the owner of that establishment that she'd come from Buffalo, New York. Unlike most of the girls, she had come on her own, by ship, and no one knew where she'd gotten the funds or what her original intentions had been. If Eliza had ever seen the girl, she couldn't say. Twice, when she saw Olive in the open area of Mrs. Parks's establishment, she tried to catch her eye and find out what she thought, but Olive avoided her gaze. Eliza did her best to put the girl out of her mind.

The talk went on, though. Monterey was curious about the girl, perhaps because there weren't many women around. Someone heard that she had a relative in the U.S. Congress who had pushed hard for the Compromise. As Eliza remembered it, when California had become a state, no one in the delegation had voted to become a slave state, but lots of folks in Alabama and Texas were determined to have access to the Pacific, and had pushed to separate northern California from southern California. But the south was all Mexican (some people said "Spanish," because that was their tongue, and anyway, California was not Mexico any more than Texas was), there were no slave owners, and Texas had some debts from when it was its own nation, so the government had paid those debts in order to persuade the Texans to shut up and leave California to decide for itself. At any rate, that's what Eliza remembered, and Peter, for all his faults, was very much against extending slavery to the west; what she knew about it, she'd learned from him. The girl, whose first name was Theresa, was a cousin, or second cousin, something like that, to this New York Congressman. After that went around, it was assumed that some renegade Southerner from Tennessee or Missouri had uncovered her and done her in for political reasons, as a way of getting back at her cousin, but after that it went around that her real cousin had the same name as that Congressman but wasn't the same person.

Over the summer, the gossip continued, but now it focused on whether any group of vigilantes in Monterey was going to pursue this question of what happened to the girl, and it appeared that no one was. What everyone said was that that was a shame, but resources were thin, life was chancy, the girl had no relations nearby, no one had stepped forward to advocate for her, and that was that. One evening, Olive did catch Eliza's glance, and they both grimaced, and then shook their heads, but no one talked about the event at Mrs. Parks's establishment. Mrs. Parks became even more careful about the customers she allowed, and she hired a big fellow, Carlos, to sit in the corner of the parlor, not far from the girls' rooms, as a guard. He said nothing, but he was visible to every customer. Eliza liked him. When the customers weren't around, he was friendly and relaxed, smiled often, and spent a lot of time improving his English so that he might eventually get a better job.

2

MRS. PARKS'S ESTABLISHMENT was busy—sometimes Eliza had two customers to deal with, one early in the evening and one late. She often didn't get back to her boarding house until almost dawn, and then she would sleep until noon, have a few slices of Mrs. Clayton's sourdough loaf, and while away her afternoon strolling around. She went back to work around seven. Most of the customers were sailors, some of whom were just glad to have made it to shore and were visiting the establishment as a celebration. A few of those tried their best, but actually only wanted a good night's sleep on solid ground. Eliza would sit near them, stroke their foreheads, or rub their feet. They might come back the next day for something more. One of them—Ralph, his name was, from England—came back four times in four days and declared that he was madly in love with her; would she marry him and go to England with him? She told Mrs. Parks this, and stayed away from the establishment for the three days before his ship left port again. Ralph was not one of the threatening ones, but his pursuit was tedious. She spent her three days off at her boarding house, knitting, finishing the two books she had started, and walking here and there, though nowhere near the docks.

AROUND THE EIGHTH of September—another date she noticed, because that had been Peter's birthday—another girl disappeared. She was Spanish—her name was Luna. The brothel she worked for also took away the girls' last names, not so much to make them seem pleasant, but, according to Mrs. Parks, so that their families, many of them from somewhere nearby, wouldn't be shamed. They were given names like "Estrella" or "Solana" or "Lucita." If there was gossip about this one, Eliza didn't hear it, because her Spanish was only rudimentary. The English-speakers that she passed or sat near or heard in shops said nothing, although the local paper did publish a short paragraph in English saying, "Luna was reported by her employer as having disappeared unexpectedly after completing her business and receiving her pay. She was seen walking down Scott Street early in the morning, but no one saw her return to her boarding house on the corner of Van Buren and Franklin." Mrs. Parks said only that she had warned the girl's employer to take care, but that woman, Mrs. Dominguez, had waved her off, apparently in the belief that whatever had happened to the first girl had nothing to do with the Spanish community. Eliza wondered if Olive would have anything to say (or communicate) about this incident, but she didn't see Olive, and decided that she must have adopted a different schedule.

On the very day when Eliza had wandered about town a bit, hoping to run into Olive, she sat down for a late lunch at the Bear. She asked for a small bit of beefsteak and some bread, to be followed by a piece of lemon cake. Hers was the last table in the dining area with a seat left, so it was no surprise when another young woman, whom Eliza judged to be about her own age, asked for permission, then sat down beside her. What was the surprise was that, when the customers at the next table got up to leave, this woman, who hadn't even begun her meal, stayed where she was. She was attractive, taller than Eliza, with dark, shining hair. Curly locks fell nicely beside her cheeks, setting them off. Still silence, and then the young woman said, "You are Eliza. Eliza Ripple."

Eliza said, "How do you know?"

The young woman said, "Don't be resentful! I'm in the same business! I work at the place on Pearl."

"What place? I didn't know there was one."

"The Pearly Gates. There are only four of us. We attend to the needs of ladies, not men."

Eliza said, "Ladies have the funds?"

The young woman said, "Some do. Others bring goods." She leaned back, opened her hands, and lifted her chin. "One of them made me this gown."

Eliza looked at it. Ten dollars, anyway. Not a bad exchange. Eliza said, "What do you call yourself?"

The young woman said, "Jean MacPherson."

That was the beginning of what Eliza felt was her first true friendship in Monterey (she decided that Olive was her "colleague"). Eliza had always thought of herself as independent, but she instantly understood that Jean was the sort of girl who really did do whatever she pleased. She might show up in rags at Eliza's boarding house to go for a walk, she might show up in that elegant gown, or, as she did one day, she might show up in a pair of men's trousers and a red shirt, with her hair tucked up under a straw hat. As Eliza did, she liked to walk about town and down to the docks, but she also liked to get into the woodlands. Monterey was known for its oaks, which reached out, with long, thick limbs that were gnarly, and spread into a canopy of dark leaves, but what Jean liked better was the pines, which were tall and fragrant. She would take Eliza up past the Harwood house into a beautiful pine forest that covered a hillside to the south and west of the Presidio (where many of Eliza's customers lived). On a Sunday, when there was no business, she thought nothing of walking to Carmel Mission, which was a good two hours each way, and the one time Eliza accompanied her, she thought she might die during the return trip, making her way up what they called Carmel Hill. Jean declared that she was well able to swim—it turned out that she had grown up on the other side of Lake Michigan from Kalamazoo, in a town in

Wisconsin now called Kenosha, and her parents had taught her to swim when she was quite young and the town was still called Pike Creek. It was a precaution, since the local children seemed drawn to the lake, and could not be stopped from going there, if only to look for bits of shell or arrowheads. And of course there was fishing, so being able to swim was a requirement. Even so, Jean had yet to try the bay. She often paused as they walked beside it, or above it, and stared longingly at the lapping water. She enjoyed the birds, too, and would point out a pelican or a hawk or even a condor—once, they saw one of those, silent and enormous, casting an unearthly shadow as it floated by.

As if by mutual consent, they said little about the details of their business, but they did exchange stories about the peculiarities of their customers. Many of Jean's customers were reticent, came often, and sometimes wanted no more than to be touched kindly, embraced, given a rest. Jean said that most of them worked much harder than she did, and for little remuneration. Most were married; some came with scars or bruises, but all of the girls behind the Pearly Gates knew better than to ask questions. Eliza related how the men who came to her with scars and bruises loved to go on and on about how they had earned them—which battles they had fought, and how well they had proved themselves. The best thing about having Jean as her friend, Eliza thought, was the number of times a laugh popped out of both of them at the same moment, whether one of them was telling a story or they were watching something in the street.

The only thing they disagreed on was the work of Mr. Poe, work Jean loved and Eliza didn't like at all, as it was too strange and gave her the jitters. Yes, said Jean, that was the point, and she never minded having the jitters. That, at least, was better than feeling down; it gave you a curiosity about things. Eliza admitted that she had read only two of his tales and two of his poems; of those, she could remember the one about the Raven a little too well. Many times when she saw a crow cawing and wished it would stop, she would say to herself,

"Quoth the Raven nevermore," then laugh. The story she remembered was about someone killing a friend, hiding him somewhere, then hearing his heart beat until, as she remembered, the fellow killed himself. Crazy at the beginning, crazy to the end—that was the one that put her off reading Poe. Jean said, "Oh, of course! 'The Tell-Tale Heart'! One of my favorites. Do you know that he died, I think a year and a half ago? What a shame. But haven't you known people who were that crazy? I have a cousin in an institution back in Wisconsin. Among other things, he is convinced that there are beings under the soil who see you coming, then make a hole for you to put your foot into so that you will break your leg, and they can enter your brain."

Eliza stared at her.

Jean shrugged and said, "My dear, if you don't have crazy relatives in this world, you are one of a kind."

Eliza thought of Peter, and wondered if those times he had locked her in her room qualified.

However, it turned out that Jean had a stack of old periodicals with stories by Poe, and the next time they met, for their midday meal and then a walk, she brought along an issue of *Graham's Lady's and Gentleman's Magazine,* some ten years old, from Philadelphia. Eliza had heard of it, but never seen a copy. She promised to take good care of it, and that evening, while she was waiting for her customer, she read the first half of a story called "The Murders in the Rue Morgue." It was hard going at first, lots of big words and ideas that Eliza didn't understand, but when the fellow telling the story got to the part about going to Paris and meeting his new friend, there was a way in which Eliza could relate to that. Of course, she could also relate to the way that the two men, the narrator and his friend, lived very private and secret lives, and this part, which she had gotten to just before her customer arrived, did resonate for the rest of the evening, because her customer was a rather well-known and you might say important fellow in Monterey, a judge who lived, she thought, somewhere up High Street, a place where she liked to walk. He came often; Mrs. Parks passed him around among the girls, because he said he liked variety, but when it came down to it, he did pretty much the same thing every time—undressed Eliza himself, slowly, then had her walk around the room, then had her stand by a window, hold a candle, and open the blinds. Then he would stare at her, feel himself all over his groin, and finish rather quickly. He was in no way unkind, but neither was he affectionate, as some of them were. It was not late when he left, so Eliza went to her rooming house, taking the magazine with her.

She liked the fact that the story was set in Paris. One thing she had learned from living in Monterey was that any place that was not Kalamazoo was interesting, and Jean seemed to feel that same way about Kenosha. However, the two characters, the fellow who told the story, and the smart fellow, Dupin, only liked to go out at night. They seemed to think that this city of Paris, about which Eliza had heard nice things, was a foul mess. She wondered what they would make of Monterey. Of course, things did happen here at night—Peter had been shot at night, and maybe if the fellow who shot him hadn't been drinking for three hours, he might have held his temper. And Mrs. Parks had once warned her to look about when she walked back to her room late, but she had never seen anything that truly frightened her. All of the men—whether they were American, Spanish, sailors, dockworkers—smiled and stepped aside when they saw her coming, and she had never thought (at least until reading this story) to look around and see if one of those smiling fellows had spun about and was coming up behind her with a cudgel. Was that what had happened to those two missing girls? Or, as some people said, had they simply been wandering on one of the beaches, or even swimming, and been swept away? The sky was beautiful here in Monterey at night, at least if the fog hadn't rolled in. So many stars, and such a bright moon. The fellow who told the Poe story said nothing about the sky in Paris.

She read through the part about the murders—the victims were a mother and a daughter, not shot but cut, and the daughter's remains pushed up the flue of the fireplace. She followed his explanation about the nail and about the escape and got used to the gore, just because his explanation made her more and more curious. What struck her the most about Dupin was that he could look at all sorts of injury and destruction and still keep thinking in what you might call a cold and logical way. When she got to the last bit, where Dupin revealed that the killer was an Ourang-Outang, some sort of ape that Eliza had never heard of but that was well described, she was impressed mostly by the idea that a train of logic could lead to something utterly unexpected. She almost believed the tale, and rather liked Mr. Poe, as she hadn't before. And, yes, the first thing Eliza did when she went to get her morning meal was to look up the flue of the fireplace at her rooming house. Nothing except black dust, and too narrow for any remains except maybe a cat's. Later that day, she did happen to see Olive in the open area, and she said, "Olive! Have you read Mr. Poe?" Olive put her hands over her face, then opened her mouth as if she was screaming. They both laughed, but softly, and then, as soon as Mrs. Parks came out of her room, they each went into theirs.

That day, she had an afternoon client, one of the sailors, but not, she saw when he entered her room, that fellow from England. Turned out to be a fellow from Ireland, didn't remind her in the least of Liam, but she was especially kind to him all the same, touched him wherever he wished, ruffled his hair, and let him do his business twice, and, maybe because he was young, that was no effort for him. He left her a tip, too (of course, he had already paid Mrs. Parks)—two bits on her side table. She did ask why he came during the day, and he said that his ship was due to leave well before dawn the next day, and he was afraid he might fall asleep if he didn't watch out. He had done that before, out of Belfast. Had to borrow a horse and gallop down the west bank, then swim to his ship, which was leaving the harbor. Eliza asked him what he'd done with the horse, and he said that he'd ridden without a saddle and just a rope about its neck. He let it go, knowing that it would run back to his friend. Eliza loved this tale, but didn't believe a word of it. She told it to Jean the next day, and they laughed.

She said to Jean, "Don't you wonder what questions that DuPINN fellow would ask about the girls who disappeared?"

Jean said, "DuPANN," then, "I hadn't thought about that. It is an interesting story, but, as I recall, they can make people say what they saw or heard. How would someone in Monterey do that? The first thing anyone would say, at least any fellow, is 'You want a poke in the eye?'"

Eliza said, "Why don't we have constables, as they do in the tale? We had constables in Kalamazoo."

Jean said, "Do you want that? How long would it take for them to decide that our business is their business, and we have to be put in jail, or at least, out of business? Or they could bribe us out of business. The county has a sheriff and a few enforcers. They never look our way. And the vigilantes, too. They are interested in money and feuds. There is so much going on in this state, yes, especially up north, or over in gold country, but even here it's popping compared to Kenosha. Maybe it's different in some place like St. Louis, that's been around for a while, but out here, it's all the sheriff can do to look good and hope for the best."

Then Jean handed her another publication, also a paper from Philadelphia. Jean said, "This is my favorite story, but don't read it if you have any sort of fever or catarrh." Then she laughed. Jean was the healthiest female that Eliza had ever met, so, just after supper, when she was whiling away the time before her customer, she was surprised to see that the story was entitled "The Premature Burial." The first part of that one, about a woman who had seemed dead for several days and then been put in a tomb, only to be discovered three years later, out of her coffin and collapsed on the floor of the tomb, made Eliza give thanks that Peter had been shot through the head. She had seen the wound—the bullet had entered through his throat, passed up through the roof of his mouth, then exited through his cranium, as the doctor called it. The folks who owned the saloon found the very bullet in the ceiling above one of the front windows. And there had been plenty of blood, because as it entered through his throat it tore away an important blood vessel. At the time, Eliza had not wanted to hear the details, but the fact was that doctors were aware that being buried alive was something that many folks thought about. The next bit resonated even more. It was about a girl, also in France, who was married off to a man who mistreated her. It was not said that her husband beat her into unconsciousness, but that was how Eliza pictured it, and then, on the night when she was buried, the fellow who loved her and whom she loved—Eliza imagined Liam Callaghan—dug her up to get one of her curls, and she woke up. They ran off, later lived in secret, as, you might say, Eliza was living in secret. The stories went on, all of them, Eliza thought, believable. Then the narrator got around to telling his own story.

Her customer showed up, and she put aside the periodical. He was a frequent fellow, who told her that he liked her the best, and was otherwise friendly. The only unusual thing that he wanted was for her to let down her hair so that he could run his hand through it while he was doing his business. He'd told her one time that he had known a girl, in Michigan (Battle Creek), who was from an Indian tribe, who had hair to the backs of her knees. He never said that he had loved her, or courted her, or anything like that, but there were many fellows that Eliza had known who were intent on one thing, often something that no one else cared about.

After he had finished his business, he sat quietly on the bed (he was a little old, and needed to recover) while Eliza went to the basin and washed herself inside and out. He picked up the periodical, said, "Goodness me! I read that story when I was in school and never got over it. And then there was a man, an old man, who lived in our town. He died, they buried him, they dug up his coffin two years later, because his wife loved him and wanted to be put with him, and he had turned himself over onto his stomach! Was that ever a shock. Thank heaven, the wife never knew about that!" Eliza didn't ask how they had known for sure. He went on, "It was said around Battle Creek, by some people, that they had always known something was amiss, because his ghost had been seen here and there, in the trees above the house where the wife lived, or lingering over the site of the grave. I suppose that you never know what to believe."

After he left, she couldn't help herself—Eliza thought, not of the fact that Battle Creek was rather close to Kalamazoo and she had never heard that story, but of that time at the Harwoods', when she woke up and things were so unbelievably quiet. That *had* spooked her, and if she had believed in ghosts, she might have seen one.

It turned out that Jean did believe in ghosts. There was a house not far from the plaza at the center of town that had been built twenty years ago—an adobe with one large room and then another above it. After Jean described it, Eliza realized that she had walked past it a number of times, and even admired it. At any rate, Jean swore that she saw a ghost sitting on a bench under a tree beside that house, a man dressed like a Catholic monk, holding a stick. She had walked past him, raised her hand, and smiled, and right then he seemed to stand up, but he didn't actually stand up, he rose up, that dark gown that monks wear stretching and stretching as he went up through the branches of the tree and disappeared. He didn't make any haunting noises or even look at her. It was as if she had frightened him, not the other way around. Eliza said, "I'm not surprised that a monk might be frightened by a trollop." This was a story that she would not have believed if anyone else had told it, but she was happy to give Jean the benefit of the doubt. For a few weeks, as the autumn progressed, they stopped talking about Poe and ghosts and went back to speaking of their customers and the other girls at their establishments and whatever else came up.

Late September and early October was a lovely season in Monterey, not autumn or, what they said in Kalamazoo, "Indian summer," but, rather, warmer, dryer weather with less fog than the summer or the spring. Everyone said that the rains would begin soon, but no one knew just when—it was different every year. Jean had a kindly, well-to-do client, Mrs. Marvin, whom Eliza had met on the street when she was walking with Jean. One day, since the weather was so lovely, Mrs. Marvin offered to take them in her buggy for a ride around the peninsula, just so they might get out of town and see where they were. Going for a ride was her favorite leisure activity, and, she said, she never got over how varied the landscape was. She knew that the girls, as she called them, had no horses of their own and no access to any sort of a carriage, so she thought they might enjoy themselves a great deal. And then she brought along a basket of provisions.

Eliza was impressed by the pair of horses, two bright bays with matching blazes and long tails, and also by the fact that Mrs. Marvin was driving them herself—she was kind to them, and they were kind to her. Mrs. Marvin had tied them up when she came into Jean's establishment to find the girls, and Eliza noticed that when she came out, the two geldings looked toward her with their ears pricked; she went straight to them and handed each one a lump of sugar. As they were driving, Mrs. Marvin sometimes waved the whip in a lackadaisical way, but she never struck either of them. Eliza asked if the two were related, and Mrs. Marvin said they were—the one on the right was a year older than the one on the left, both by the same stallion and out of the same mare.

It was a very pleasant drive. The bright bay pair didn't mind wind—and there was plenty of that—nor were they startled by animals rustling in the bushes, as Eliza was, a couple of times. About halfway through their ride, a bobcat, young, with long legs, emerged from behind a tree and stared at them. The horses looked his way and trotted on. At another point, the two horses were trotting so quickly that both Jean and Eliza grabbed the sides of the buggy. Mrs. Marvin glanced at them and said, "I guess that they are too strong for a buggy as light as this one, but I can't take one off and leave the other behind. The one who is left behind whinnies and bangs the corral he's in, and if I leave him alone, he might even jump out of it and follow us."

First, they went past the docks and headed up along the bay. Eliza was on the left side, and enjoyed looking out at the curving, pale beaches with the waves of the bay simply lapping, not crashing. The water was blue as blue, since the sun shone from behind the hills. The dunes were interesting, too; Eliza had never seen a dune, though she had heard of them. There were four ships visible in the bay, one apparently heading toward the docks, two heading away from the docks, and one moored, for some reason, perhaps a quarter of a mile out in the water—the sails of that one were down, and Eliza could make out some figures standing on the bow, looking toward the docks.

The horses kept trotting. They turned inland. The sun was still bright; the horses were still enjoying themselves. Eliza felt herself calm down. The land was flat now, more arid—all the grass was brown. There were trees, like towers, sprinkled here and there, but it was evident from the number of cattle who were roaming about, seemingly free, that this was a good place for ranching, and Eliza had heard that plenty of fellows from the East had come here thinking they were going to the gold fields and ending up growing this and that. They came to a slightly greener area, where the ranches looked well established. What was enjoyable about it was the mountains in the distance and the few houses they saw—not shacks. Mrs. Marvin said that the cattle were branded, that the land was divided into large parcels that had been handed out by the Spanish to their supporters, and though the Americans did want to get hold of them, they hadn't figured out a way so far.

After about two hours, she brought the horses down to a halt not far from a little grove of trees and she took out a small tub of water, gave the horses something to drink, and put buckets of oats on the ground in front of them. They ate, didn't have to be tied. Mrs. Marvin ate, too, sharing with Eliza and Jean some beans she had baked with pork, some bread, and pieces of an apple cake. She also produced a large flask of beer she had made herself, from hops she had grown. It was bitter, but Eliza was thirsty, indeed, and she drank some, envying the horses their buckets of water just a bit.

It was late afternoon when they started home, by a different route, and Eliza felt sleepy. The landscape was again flat, though there were lovely mountains covered with oak trees in the distance. She was just wondering if she might fall asleep (she was used to the trotting now) when Jean said, "What's that?" Eliza sat up, a bit startled. They were crossing a narrow bridge over a narrow river—hardly a river, at this time of year. Mrs. Marvin brought the horses to a halt and backed them up, and Jean jumped out of the buggy.

Eliza got out and looked down into the shadows flickering over the stones and the mud. Lying there, half in the water and half on the bank, was a crumpled-up figure, a girl or a woman. Mrs. Marvin hoisted herself out of the buggy, too, walked over with the lines in her hand, and said, "Oh, my heavens!"

3

JEAN RAN TO the end of the bridge, scrambled down the bank, which wasn't steep. Eliza followed right behind her. When they got there, though, neither one of them touched the remains, not even the gown, which was soaked with water, draped over the girl, hiding the girl's body but showing her shape. Eliza looked to the left, then to the right. Mrs. Marvin called out, "The headwaters are down south. The mouth is on the bay. She must have floated down the river." Eliza thought this was unlikely, with the river so shallow, but she only said, "How far away are the headwaters?"

"Oh, goodness," said Mrs. Marvin. "Days away."

Eliza put her hands behind her back and bent down to look at the girl's face. Her skin was dry, wrinkled, and red, and her hand, too, the one that was visible (the other one was underneath her), looked desiccated and sort of black rather than bloated. The mouth was slightly open; the lips were wrinkled and dry. The eyes were half closed. Eliza would have thought that if a body was in water for a long time it would be bloated, but this one was not. Thinking of DuPANN, she realized how little she knew about any of this, how no system of logic could lead her anywhere. She shivered.

Jean said, "I don't see a bullet hole." She leaned forward, as if to turn the girl over, but Eliza put her hand on Jean's elbow and said, "If this has been a murder, I think we have to leave things the way they are."

"But who is going to look at it, or do anything about it?"

From up on the bridge, Mrs. Marvin said, "No one. Possibly no one at all, but certainly not us. Leave it there. We can't take it with us, as we haven't the room. It's getting dark. I will tell a man my husband knows who might be able to do something. We know just where it is. I can tell him. It's not going to go far in this weather."

Jean said, "Do you think it's the American girl or the Spanish girl?"

Eliza thought you would be able to tell by the color of the hair, or the length, since the Spanish girls seemed to be able to grow theirs longer. But the girl's hair was mostly underneath her. What was sprayed out over the sand was dark, but, given how long it appeared she had been in the river, that could be dirt, or rot, or something. Eliza knew nothing about hair except how to comb it, how to roll it into a bun, how to push it out of her face. She stared. But she had a thought, and so, when Jean went back up the bank, she grabbed a few strands, pulled them out, put them in a small pocket on the side of her gown. Now one of the horses, who had been standing on the far side of the bridge, looked over the edge, which was built of stone, and shied. Mrs. Marvin turned away, and said, "Come, girls, come! Less and More do not like this! I fear that they will run off."

Less and More. It turned out that Less was Lester, the older one, and More was Morley, the younger one. And they did trot away at a good clip once everyone was back in the buggy.

But, of course, Eliza realized when she was walking home late that night, after her customer left, the girl did not have to be either of the ones everyone knew about. She supposed that the difference between Monterey and Paris was that Paris was a city where, if you did something horrible, someone was bound to hear or see something, but there was so much empty space around Monterey that if you did something horrible to someone, or, at least, to someone who was not prominent, it was much more likely that no one would hear or see a thing. She looked around. It was so late that even the saloons were shut up, and the streets were (or looked) nearly empty. There was a shadow that, for a moment, she mistook for a man, and then she realized that she should be scared, or unnerved, but, for once, she wasn't. She didn't understand why, but she was grateful.

Mrs. Marvin was true to her word. Her husband knew the sheriff, whose name was Roach, and three days later, Jean told Eliza that they had found the body—not under the bridge, but a little farther downstream, where the river curled toward the mountains. Since Mrs. Marvin hadn't gone down below the bridge to see the remains, Jean and Eliza had to go to the place where they were keeping it and have a look. Mrs. Marvin, with Less and More, already had Jean in the carriage when she picked Eliza up at her boarding house. Jean was excited. Eliza was full of dread.

The place where they kept the body, the "morgue," was not far from the docks, and Eliza could understand why—fishing accidents and shipwrecks were not infrequent, and they needed a place to collect the corpses before sending them to their funerals or their graveyards. It was a rather modest building, all adobe, without many windows; Eliza had always thought it was a factory, though she'd never heard any noise coming out of it. It was also only one story, or so it appeared, but all the bodies were down below, in a cooler area. Eliza thought she and Jean would go down together, but the man who let them in, Mr. Lowe, said they couldn't do that, nor could they say anything to one another about what they saw. In order to assure this, he stood Eliza in one corner and Jean in another, and a fellow, a client Eliza had seen at Mrs. Parks's place, stood in the middle of the room, sometimes glancing at her, but not smiling, and not scowling, either.

Jean went first. She was down there long enough for the sun, blazing against the tiny window near Eliza, to vanish behind the branches of one of the oaks. When she came back up, she didn't even look at

Eliza—the man who escorted her wouldn't let her, and Eliza understood from DuPANN why. They each had to say truly what they saw. The man came over and walked Eliza down the steps. They were steep and narrow, and there was no banister. They were stone, and not evenly cut. Eliza watched her feet and imagined herself ending up in this storehouse, merely from toppling over and knocking her head on the wall. There was light, though—they'd made sure of that. The remains were laid out on a table, and the light was sunshine coming through a large window set flat in the roof.

In only three days, the body had gotten darker and more pickled. It also looked as though some fish or rats had eaten their fill, because parts were gone around the left shoulder and down the left arm, two of the fingers. Most of the gown was gone—perhaps it had rotted away—showing that one of the girl's bosoms was gone, too. It was hard to look at it, hard to smell it, but the fellow said, "What do you see that is the same as what you saw the other day?"

Eliza said, "It's the same size. The face looks like the other face, but not exactly like a face, if you know what I mean."

He said, "I know what you mean."

She kept staring, got used to what she was looking at, thought of DuPANN again. Without realizing it, she reached toward the girl, but the fellow grabbed her hand. He said, "Don't touch."

But Eliza wanted to touch her, just to pet her forehead or something, to say that everything was going to be all right. Even though she couldn't see her, Eliza could picture her, a girl in her own business, putting up with something new and maybe unexpected every day, pushing her fears away until, one day, all of her fears were realized, and even though she had imagined many terrible things, what she had imagined didn't prepare her for what was actually happening. Eliza closed her eyes.

The hair in the river had been dark, and this girl's hair was dark, too. Eliza leaned forward, carefully, and looked at the girl's eyes. One of her eyeballs was missing, but the other one was an odd color, more green than blue. She glanced at the fellow. He looked impervious, and Eliza couldn't tell how he felt about this corpse. Maybe, she thought, he had seen so many that he didn't care anything about it. After they left, she thought, that was what she would talk to Jean about—not the girl, but the fellow. She stared at the remains again. She couldn't help herself: she ran her hand down her hip, feeling her own living flesh. It gave her the shivers.

Now he spun toward her and said in a stern voice, "Is there any way you might recognize this chit as someone you would have known before she died?" and Eliza understood perfectly that what Jean had said was true—all of this could become an excuse to drive Mrs. Parks out of business and put all the girls into jail. Or into this room. She summoned as much calm as she could and said, "No, I do not recognize her." Then they stood for a period of time, and at last he sent her up the steep steps, though he stayed behind. The man who had watched her and Jean was standing at the top. He told them to say nothing of this to the citizens of Monterey, and sent them out the door.

They walked toward the lighthouse. It took quite a long time for Jean to say anything. Finally, she said, "That wasn't her."

Eliza said, "I thought it was."

"Her nose was a different shape, longer and thinner."

Eliza said, "I didn't notice that."

They were passing someone on Lighthouse. Jean remained silent until he was out of earshot, then said, "And her earlobes were pierced. Did you notice that?"

Eliza shook her head.

"There's another brothel somewhere, but I don't know where. When the girls come to work there, the owner takes them and has their ears pierced; then he gives them different earrings so he can keep track of them."

"Why doesn't he just give them names?"

"He does, but, according to him, he's terrible at recalling names.

I think he does it for a different reason. Some of the girls wear pearl earrings, some opals, some amethysts. They say he keeps a diamond pair in a safe, but no one gets to wear them except with certain clients. I think they show what they are worth by their earrings."

"I'm going to ask Mrs. Parks about that."

"She knows him. They all know each other."

They turned up Pacific. Eliza said, "I still don't understand how she was killed. I didn't see a bullet hole."

"Strangled," said Jean. "I thought I saw some marks around her neck. Or stabbed in the back. Oh, I don't know."

"He could have stabbed her, then held her down with his hand over her mouth or something like that."

Jean said, "I don't like to think of it, but that makes sense." After they had made their way up the hill, she said, "I saw her ghost."

Eliza stopped and stared at her friend.

"I knew you wouldn't believe me, but I did. There was a shadow, and I looked up. She was staring through that window on the roof. Just staring. She didn't look frightened, she looked serious and determined. I whispered—"

Eliza said, "Everything is going to be all right."

Jean said, "Exactly that. Did you see her?"

"I didn't see her ghost. I saw . . ." And then Eliza thought, "Myself," but she said nothing.

Jean looked upward. "She rose into the sky and floated away. She was wearing white muslin."

At this, Eliza chuckled, and Jean said, "Well, she was!"

The only thing Eliza said was "How come your ghosts aren't scary?"

Jean said, "Ghosts don't have to be scary. I think that ghosts are more likely to be scared themselves than scary."

At Franklin, they had to part. Jean took Eliza's hand. She said, "We have to go back there."

Eliza knew that she meant the bridge, or the river. She said, "That's a long way!"

"We have some money. We can hire some ponies for a day. Can you ride?"

"More or less."

Jean smiled. She said, "I don't think we can borrow those two. But I love to ride. We're going back to that river, and we are not going to be afraid to look around."

As she walked to her place, Eliza tried to recall as many details as she could about the girl under the bridge. Eventually, she decided that it was the same girl, even though, as a rule, Jean was more observant than she was. But their disagreement was a reminder, wasn't it, that neither of them knew what they were doing.

4

M RS. PARKS DID KNOW that brothel. It was down the coast, more in the countryside. You could only get to it in a carriage or on horseback, and it was for wealthy clients, especially those from out of town—say, even as far as San Francisco—who needed, or wished, to be especially secretive. The owner did not, as far as Mrs. Parks knew, employ local girls who needed the money, but brought girls in from the East, places like Cincinnati or New Orleans, or even Boston, whose parents, Mrs. Parks said with a frown, likely didn't know where their daughters had gotten to. She glanced toward the door, which creaked as it opened. Olive came in, dressed in a pale gown, something of a cross between yellow and green. She looked happy, and waved to her and Mrs. Parks. Mrs. Parks nodded politely, but then put her hand on Eliza's knee—Eliza knew what that meant—"Keep this to yourself!" Olive went to her chamber. Mrs. Parks nodded toward Eliza's. As she stood up, Eliza thought of those letters her mother had sent. But Eliza didn't tell Mrs. Parks what she and Jean had done or seen. In some ways, it was too frightening to relate. She thought she would tell her eventually.

Her client that night was a boy who had been sent off as a sailor on a whaling ship. He was from Maine, and this was his first trip.

Already, at fourteen, he had been down the Atlantic, around "the Cape," and up the Pacific, but, according to the two young men who brought him in, he had never even touched a woman, except to give his mother a kiss on the cheek when he left Brunswick. He had five brothers, no sisters. The older sailors went with two of the girls they remembered from a previous trip—in '50, it was—and Eliza took care of the boy. Yes, he had never touched a woman, or a girl, and he was awkward. After some scrambling about, she sat down with him on the floor, cross-legged, and took his hands in hers. She held them, warmed them up, then placed them on her thighs. She looked him in the eye, then ran her hands down his face, over his shoulders, softly, warmly. She rubbed the back of his neck, then loosened his shoulders. She asked him what he did on the ship, and he said that he climbed the masts, stood as lookout, rolled and unrolled the sails. He said, "I'm quick! I can get up there the fastest!"

Eliza said, "Isn't it dangerous?"

The boy shrugged, then said, "Not if you know what you are doing."

Eliza continued to warm him up, get closer. His prick lasted and lasted, and by the time he did the task, she was rather enjoying herself. By the time they finished, the other two sailors were already out in the main area, pacing about, and her next client had come, left again to go get a drink, and told Mrs. Parks he would be back. When he did come back, giving Eliza enough time to sort herself out so that she looked neat, and was twiddling her thumbs, it was certain that he had had more than one drink. Carlos, sitting in the corner, raised his left eyebrow as he always did when he wasn't sure whether to kick the guy out or not. Mrs. Parks was nowhere to be seen—sometimes, this late at night, she went to bed, relying on Carlos to keep her informed.

Eliza tipped her head, then shrugged slightly. The fellow was someone she'd serviced twice before, though he'd not been tipsy those times; he tended to be diffident. But she wasn't a fool. She had seen many drunks in her day, so she knew that alcohol brought things out in them. Sometimes a perfectly kind fellow would drink and then start yelling, hitting other people, stumbling around with his hand on his pistol. Other times, a fellow who always looked off-putting would hoist a few and turn out to be a talker, who would tell you everything about himself and his family and his dog, so busy talking that he wouldn't get his business done. And then there was that—you never knew with a drunk whether he *could* get his business done.

Carlos lifted his right eyebrow, which meant that Eliza should keep the door to her chamber cracked, and Eliza nodded. She went to the fellow and he followed her to the chamber. He had his eyes on her; he did not notice that she left the door slightly ajar. As soon as they got into the room, he blew out the two tapers that were lit and then, as he stepped toward her, he stumbled on the edge of the rug and fell to his knees. First, he said some curse words, and not only "Damnation!," the one Eliza's father always used. Then he grabbed the bedpost and hoisted himself to his feet. Eliza stayed back. Her eyes had adjusted to the darkness, and she didn't see an angry look on his face, but she knew to be cautious. He stood for a moment, then went to the bed, sat down, and started to weep. Eliza stayed still, let him cry it out and take a few breaths, then went over and sat beside him. She knew his name, but she didn't use it. She said, "Friend, may I help you?"

"I'm damned."

He spoke in such a low voice that she didn't quite hear him. She put her hand on his leg, but he shook it off and said, "I'm damned! I'm damned! I can't help myself! I'm going to burn in hell!"

Where had she heard this before? Back in Kalamazoo, of course. Eliza's heart started pounding. Normally, she made herself stop thinking of anything that reminded her of her parents or her parents' church, but in this dark room, after the stresses of the day (and, some-how, even working with or, indeed, luring on that sailor boy seemed taxing), she couldn't stop thinking of being damned.

Eliza said, "Do you mean because you have come to me?"

The fellow nodded.

Eliza said, "Mrs. Parks will give you your funds back." She didn't know if this was true, but she thought it was the safest thing to say. "You can leave."

"I don't want to leave. That's why I'm damned."

Eliza thought, "Me, too."

The fellow said, "Look at me!"

Eliza did.

The fellow said, "There is nothing about me that any lady would be drawn to! I have no property, not even a horse. I carry loads of fish on and off ships day after day, and I stink to high heaven."

"I don't think—"

"I share a room with another fellow. I can't even pay for a room of my own. This is how I get satisfaction once in a while, but it is a sin!"

"You could go to your pastor and confess your sins, or even kneel before your congregation—"

"Back in Philadelphia? I daren't go into a Popish church, and that's all they have here."

"Just go in to have a look at the Savior—"

"No! What I do is proof that I'm already damned! There's nothing I can do about it. I don't know why I am alive. I don't know."

Eliza had heard this before, too. In fact, it was only when she'd gotten to Monterey and survived the death of that fellow, her husband, that she had had enough pleasures to feel that she had a reason to be alive—the trees, the lapping waves, the calls of the seabirds, the kindness of Mrs. Parks, her enjoyment of Jean. It seemed as though, if you were a Covenanter, your only task was to show the world that you were chosen, even though you knew deep in your heart that the odds were against you. But the way you would show that you were chosen was never to enjoy a single worldly thing. She put a hand on his leg, but he slapped it away, saying, "Don't tempt me! You are the reason for my sinning!" He raised his arm, which caused Eliza to jump slightly, but then he smacked himself on the head, and let his arm drop. Eliza sat quietly. She did not say anything that would identify her as a fellow Covenanter, though she did look upward and she did think, "No, God himself is the source of your sin, because he already made up his mind about you." She saw Carlos peek in the door, and he must have seen her, too, because she shook her head and he did not come in; then, of course, she doubted her choice.

She moved a little bit away from the fellow, knowing that, when some people were drunk, any sudden thing could make them get violent. But he didn't get violent—he leaned forward, spewed his guts on the floor, and then fell back, apparently passed out. She stood up quietly, wondering how much he might have had to drink. It was known about Monterey that the saloons often watered down the drink. But maybe he was just one of those fellows who couldn't take it.

She went to the door. Carlos was standing outside with a taper in his hand. She said, "He's passed out. I think you might let him sleep rather than drag him into the street." Carlos nodded, and Eliza made her way outside and over to her place. She'd thought the day's events would keep her up, but they didn't—she went right to sleep and awakened just as the sun peeped through the window. The first thing she thought of was that fellow, and the second thing was Jean. She wanted Jean to see him, to tell her if he seemed like one of those men who might have done in a girl and then gotten rid of the body. It was easy enough to imagine someone like that, out of control, seeing his own sin in the face of a girl, and also easy to imagine the girl doing the wrong thing, and the fellow taking his revenge. She jumped out of bed, pulled on a gown, and ran out of her chamber. When she got to Jean's place, there Jean was, sitting on the front step, eating a biscuit. She leapt to her feet. She was dressed in her pants-and-shirt outfit, with boots and a sombrero. Eliza grabbed her hand and pulled her down the street, toward Mrs. Parks's place. She said, "You have to see this fellow and tell me what you think!"

When they turned the corner, two doors down from Mrs. Parks's, he had just stepped off the last step. He paused, shook his head, pressed his temple with his hand, and sighed. Then he walked toward them. He was disheveled; there was spew on his shirt. He was taking some deep breaths, but he did smile a bit when he passed them— straight at Eliza, as if he knew her, or remembered her. They kept walking. Eliza glanced around, saw him turn the corner. She leaned toward Jean, began telling her about the previous evening. She had just gotten to the part where he had rejected her idea of confession when she heard his footsteps behind her and felt a tingle down her spine. She paused; she thought maybe she should have run, but she couldn't help pausing. He stepped in front of them. Eliza knew that Jean had a stick with her—she often did. He looked at Jean and said, "Pardon me, sir." Then at Eliza. He bent his head down and said, "Miss. Have you seen me lately?"

Ah. He had gotten so drunk that he didn't remember a thing.

Eliza said, hesitantly, "I saw you not long ago. . . ."

"I remember that. But, well, I woke up in that establishment where I've seen you, and I don't know how I got there."

Eliza glanced at Jean. Jean said, in a hearty voice, "Boy, you must have blacked out."

The fellow put his hand to his temple again and pressed it.

Jean said, roughly, "You done that before?"

The fellow said, "One time. At Yule. I thought I would never do that again. I can barely turn my head."

Eliza said, "Might we walk with you?" She glanced at Jean.

The fellow said, "Please do. I'm Jacob."

Jean said, "I'm John." The fellow didn't look as though he doubted her. Jean went over to his left side; Eliza stayed on his right. She put her hand through his arm, and they walked slowly down the street. The street wasn't muddy, but it was rough and dotted with horse droppings. She, sometimes with Jean's help, guided him away from the messy parts, and one time caught him when he stumbled. Jean said, "You need a bite to eat."

The fellow put his hand in his pocket and brought out a few bits.

They walked him to an eating house, one of the inexpensive ones, and took him inside. He looked around, then started and said, "What day is it?"

Eliza said, "Sunday."

He relaxed, and Eliza took from that that he had a day off from his fish-loading work, which was no doubt why he had chosen the night before to come to Mrs. Parks's establishment. They got him seated with some fried eggs and herrings, and then departed. Eliza looked back one time, as she went out the door. He had his elbow on the table, his head resting in his hand, but he was poking at his eggs.

As soon as they were out on the street again—Alvarado, it was—Jean took her by the arm and started talking. "How do we know he's only blacked out one time? I've seen fellows who do it more than they know."

Eliza said, "He's one of those men who has two different beings—when he came to me before, he was mild and even a bit hesitant. I knew he was strong because of the work he does, but I never had a moment's unrest, because he spoke softly and was gentle when he went about his business. I wish I knew what saloon he went to. I would ask the saloon keeper what he drank and how, or even if, he paid for it."

"Everything's closed tonight, but we could ask around tomorrow night. I don't have many clients on Mondays."

"Nor do I," said Eliza.

"We'll go to Mrs. Parks's and then walk around in big circles, starting with the closest saloon. But even if we find that one, and come to know what he had, we should go down toward the docks and look there. One time isn't enough to account for . . ."

They looked at each other, thinking of the dead girl they had seen only the day before.

Then Jean, though kindly, questioned Eliza. She had never met a Covenanter before. Her family did go to church, but it was an abolitionist church that talked more about getting rid of slavery and harboring escaped slaves than Satan and hell or God and heaven—as far as her parents' fellow parishioners were concerned, hell was right there down south in Alabama, and spreading out from Birmingham, ever seeking to drive everyone in these United States into damnation— that, in fact, was what her father called the South, the "Damnation."

Once again, Eliza gave thanks, to herself, for being in California.

$\rightarrowtail$ **5** $\leftarrowtail$

EVEN THOUGH SUNDAY was Eliza's day off, too, she went to Mrs. Parks's. As it was a pleasant day, Mrs. Parks was sitting on the veranda, though this time alone, evidently going over the books. When she saw Eliza, she beckoned her up the steps, and when Eliza got to her, she patted her hand and shook her head, then said, "Carlos helped me clean up the mess. There was plenty of it, but it had dried, thank heaven! Didn't take us long. I am pleased that he didn't hurt you, my dear. I will exclude him from the establishment in the future."

Eliza knew better than to object; in fact, the only reason she might have objected was because she sympathized with the fellow's anxieties, especially now, on a Sunday, when Eliza had no intention of finding a church.

Mrs. Parks said, "You should make use of your free evening and get a good night's rest." Then she handed her a fifty-cent coin, enough for some tasty beef stew, and went back to her books. There had been a moment when Eliza had thought of relating her experience, but Mrs. Parks was a woman of such pleasant mien and positive temperament that she doubted the woman even knew any Covenanters. Someone had said that Mrs. Parks was from Baltimore, but that was all she knew.

She went back to her place and read a book (*not* Mr. Poe), while she waited for Jean. Jean showed up in a gown, neatly turned out, with her face washed. The first thing she said was "You know that grand casa, Casa Munras?"

Eliza shook her head.

"It's up the road, a bit outside of the town. I felt I needed a walk, and went in that direction, and I not only heard the fellow's ghost tromping about, but I saw him on the roof!"

Eliza said, "What fellow?"

"Munras! He owned that whole piece of land, some three thousand acres, I've been told. Well, he was a painter of murals. But he died two years ago. The Casa is shut down for now, but folks hear his ghost all the time. He's a busy one. I walked about, hoping to see it, and I did!" She seemed excited. Now they walked down Pacific toward the docks, then over to High Street, back to Jefferson, up the hill to Dutra, then down Madison to Pacific and back to where they had started. Eleven saloons, some small, some large, not exactly open for business, as it was a Sunday, but some with windows open, a fellow or two inside, and the door unlocked. Down the hill, near the Mission, laws were stricter about what you might do on Sunday. In Monterey, since the ships came and went rather randomly, and the seamen might display their frustration if their wants went unattended, more things were possible if those who wanted them sought them in a quiet manner.

The closest saloon to Mrs. Parks's place, a small one, was at the corner of Munras and Pearl. The door was slightly ajar, and an older woman was inside, sweeping the floor. Eliza and Jean stood outside the door until the woman noticed them, and then she made a tiny gesture with her finger, and they entered, putting the door as it had been after they came inside. There were back windows facing away from the street, a few tables and chairs. The woman stopped sweeping, put her hand on her hip. She said, "Want somethin'?"

She sounded to Eliza as if she had come from down south, maybe Texas.

Jean said, "I have a friend coming into town. He works on a whaling ship. I know he's going to be wanting a good time, and I'm looking for the best spot. I'm new in town."

The woman said, "Since it's the Sabbath, I'm gonna tell ya the truth. This ain't it."

Both girls couldn't help laughing.

The woman went back to sweeping.

Eliza said, "Any thoughts? He hasn't got much in the way of funds."

"Round the corner there's a brothel." She didn't stare at them, or speak in a significant way, as if she knew that Eliza worked there.

Eliza said, "That's not what he's looking for. To tell the truth, he's from Tennessee."

"Whiskey, then."

Eliza nodded.

"It ain't here. This place is run by Mr. Mayer. He makes himself beer. That's what he serves. Your friend should go down the street a bit. You'll see an alley across the way. You go in that back door."

Jean said, "Nothing on Sunday, though."

"I ain't sayin'. Don' know. You got to find out for yourself."

They thanked her, but she didn't respond or even look at them as they pulled the door open and let themselves out. It was about noon. The sky was clear, but the street was still almost empty.

Jean said, "What did you smell on his breath, anything?"

"I didn't have to smell his breath, and I certainly didn't kiss him. That he was pretty much done for was all over him."

They turned into the alley; it was short, and led to a set of steps that went downward. The spot they were looking for was not quite underground, but almost. And the door was unlocked. Jean turned the handle and walked in. The room was empty, but a man came hurrying out from the back. Jean tossed her head, put on a fearful manner, and said, "My heavens! Where am I? My friend from church said she lived here!"

The man said, "No one lives here."

Jean said, "You sell any provisions or anything? We're new around town, and we are looking for a bite."

The man glanced at Eliza. She didn't think he'd been to Mrs. Parks's establishment, but she guessed that he had seen her somewhere, out and about. He said, "All kinds of places like that. Just get out of here and keep looking around."

"Whiskey? You got whiskey?"

The man said, "Not on a Sunday. Git!"

Jean said, "I would suggest that if you want customers, you should learn to be more polite." The man scowled. They left.

When they were out in the street again, Jean said, "My guess is, that's the place. It's close enough so that he could have gotten very drunk but still made it back to you." Eliza didn't disagree, but what she appreciated most about Jean was her bravery. Maybe it was the ghosts that did it—if you weren't afraid of ghosts, then why would you be afraid of anything?

It was Eliza who said, "Let's walk over to the grand casa."

By now, it was early afternoon. Strands of fog were beginning to float in from the bay, fluttering here and there, gathering together. Jean looked up and said, "I'm sure it's sunny there."

They made a point of strolling. On Pearl Street, they stopped at a spot Jean had been to before and ate bowls of lentil soup. When they came out, the fog was like the bill of a hat. They walked up Pearl and then up Munras, out from under the bill. They came to the edge of town, kept walking. The road was muddier but not narrower—it was evident that the town, or someone in it, intended to push into the countryside. In fact, their walk didn't take any time at all. They walked around the adobe casa and also in front of two other buildings not far away, both of them wood, with verandas, like most buildings in the town, but Eliza heard nothing, and neither did Jean. She seemed disappointed and said, "There's a graveyard half a mile down the street. I love walking about in there." Eliza never went there—that was where Peter was buried. But she followed Jean.

They made their way under the trees. To distract herself, Eliza said, "Did you have ghosts in Kenosha?"

"Of course we did! My cousin Eli said there were several in the lighthouse that looked over the lake. I didn't believe him, though."

"Why not?"

"Because I hadn't read Mr. Poe! We'd be sitting in the parlor of my uncle's house, and Eli would say, 'Saw that ghost last night'—their place wasn't far from the lighthouse. And I would say, 'Well, what was it like?' and Eli would shrug and say, 'Oh, y'know.' I would say, 'You mean white, like it was wearing a sheet?' And he would say, 'Nah.' But he didn't have the gift of gab. Mr. Poe got me to see them for myself. I'd bet my life that Mr. Poe pretended he was just writing a story, but in fact he really saw them. Too bad his ghost isn't around here. I'd love to talk to him."

Eliza, sincerely hoping that there would be no ghost of Peter lurking about the graveyard, said, "I can't believe I never asked you how you got to California. Everyone has a story."

"You do, too."

"I never told you?"

"No, but Mrs. Marvin heard about your husband getting shot in that saloon."

"Did she hear about the fact that in the end I was glad of it?"

"She didn't say anything about that." Jean stopped and turned toward her. She said, "Were you?"

"I was. I barely knew him when my parents handed me off to him. I was . . ." She paused, thought of Liam, then said, "They were afraid I would marry an Irishman." She didn't say anything about sin. "I don't know that I would have, since the Irishman hadn't made any advances other than sweet smiles and one touch of the hand. But the one who got shot, he never thought twice about doing his business whenever he wanted and pushing me around. He knew who was the servant, and it was me."

"How did he get shot?"

"I wasn't there, and no one ever said, but my guess is that he lost his temper, and the other fellow was quicker on the draw. The fellow who ran the saloon found my husband's Colt revolver on the floor after it all, but I wouldn't take it back."

Jean stared at her for a long moment, and Eliza thought maybe Jean was deciding that she was heartless and not worth knowing, but then Jean put her arms around her. She said, "What part of the graveyard is he buried in?"

Eliza said, "Over on the far side. Not hard to avoid."

They started walking again. Jean said, "My pa was eyeing some-one for me to marry, too, but he didn't get very far. Cousin Eli's brother, Jake, was two years older than Eli, and he offered himself to a girl from a big family who had a farm outside of town—eight girls in a row, and all of them beautiful, which was a good thing, because the father was aching to be rid of them. Jake's betrothed was named Emma. She was fourth in line, and I think her dowry was two cows and their calves. Uncle Elmer had plenty of funds from his business, shipping goods across the lake to Michigan." She lifted her eyebrow at Eliza. "So—he funded the wedding, and it was quite a celebration, and I was standing there in the front row of the church, and I knew at that very moment that Jake meant nothing to me compared to Emma—she was so bright and lovely, and all I wanted to do was take her in my arms."

Eliza said, "How old were you?"

"I'd just turned sixteen."

"Did you tell them?"

"My ma could see it in my face. And anyway, her sister, Aunt Fannie, lived with a woman in Madison, so she understood it. I guess she and Pa argued about it for a year, and then decided to send me to Aunt Fannie, but the whole time they were arguing, I was doing this and that around Kenosha—taking care of children, picking apples, helping in a shop. They sent me off to Aunt Fannie, and when I got there, I showed her my funds and told her I wanted to go to California, and she just doubled my funds and found a family who were headed here, set me up with them. She knows what I'm doing here, and says that it is a service to all women."

Eliza said, "How does she support herself in Madison?"

"She and Aunt Edith are both teachers. They do well enough to have a small place of their own."

"Are the folks who brought you still here?"

"They thought Monterey was too Spanish, so they moved up to San Jose, but this was the place that I loved. San Jose is cold and dry—or, at least, colder and dryer than here."

They passed a tall adobe wall that, Eliza knew, protected the grounds of another mission, or chapel, or something. She had heard some people call it a cathedral and others call it a chapel, but she had never walked into it. They continued down a small hill, came to the graveyard. Jean said, "This one belongs to the church." She cocked her head toward the building they had just passed.

Eliza said, "Is it a cathedral or a chapel?"

Jean said, "They call it the Royal Chapel, whatever that means. Mrs. Marvin says it used to be called the Chapel of San José. And it was bigger than it is now. When the Americans took it over from the Spanish, a lot of the stones were taken away by the Ohlone to build their own places, I suppose. The city graveyard is up the hill a bit." They walked on, a little nervous about trespassing on the grounds of the chapel or the cathedral, or whatever it was.

The city graveyard was green, and you could see the bay off in the distance, just some blue, the flat line where the sea met the sky, always odd, but riveting to look at. The gravestones were modest, though not all of them were as modest as Peter's, which was just a little square of granite with his name etched into it. The ones in the church graveyard were larger and more elaborate, for whole families, the way they were back in Kalamazoo. The city graveyard was more a park than anything else. Eliza glanced across the expanse, toward Peter's spot, and said, "Any ghosts?"

Jean didn't say anything. She did look around, and she did walk from stone to stone. Sometimes she stopped, looked one direction and then another. She seemed to sense something, but since she wasn't talking, Eliza wandered here and there and did her best to appreciate the place. Perhaps because it was just up from the bay, there were all sorts of trees—oaks and pines, but others, too, lighter and more open, which she could not name. They made their way to the far end, came to Pearl Street. The walk back into town was easy—along the edge of the bay, flat, less than a mile, for sure—but Eliza could see that Jean was not happy. At the corner of Adams, in a bit of a messy area where Eliza didn't think she'd been before, she stopped and said, "Tell me."

Jean went two more steps and turned around. She said, "No ghosts. But there was, I don't know . . . something. I kept my eye out, and I looked here and there. The place seemed quiet, but it made me very uneasy. It was as though there was someone behind a tree, peeking at us, or, maybe, up in a tree. But even when I pretended to be looking one way but was actually looking another way, I didn't see anyone. It rattled me. I've never felt like that before."

Eliza could see that Jean was more disturbed than she was, even though her very own husband had been nearby. She remembered the time she and Jean had walked up Carmel Hill for two hours. Lots of trees and ravines, a good breeze that made the tree limbs creak and the leaves rustle, the sound of men shouting, from time to time, and of a horse whinnying, and hoofbeats. Eliza had been both exhausted and a little nervous—no one to see if someone might jump out of the trees and grab them (in Monterey, at least, someone was likely to see, if not to care). That day, Jean had just tramped along, taking plenty of deep breaths and smiling.

Or the fellow that morning, in such a temper that he seemed ready to push them out of the whiskey place, and Jean standing up to him without a second thought.

Jean closed her eyes.

It was mid-afternoon now, bright and warm. It seemed to Eliza that their walks should have taken longer. More people were out on the streets, but it was still Sunday. Wives would be busy preparing a good Sunday dinner; husbands would be lounging about, drinking a bit of something and smoking those cigars they'd been saving all week. Children would be fidgeting, resenting their Sunday outfits, so itchy and confining, especially the boots. Wasn't it the case with your fancy shoes that you had to keep wearing them until your feet simply burst out of them? Even in Kalamazoo, cold as could be, Eliza had preferred going barefoot to wearing those boots.

They came to the corner of the street where Jean lived, and Jean sighed, took Eliza's hand, squeezed it, let it go, and then turned away and headed toward her own place. Eliza ran to her, said, "Tomorrow we're going to find that saloon." Jean nodded, walked on.

Eliza watched her for a minute, went to the corner. Then, as if she couldn't help herself, she hurried back to Casa Munras, then to the cemetery. She didn't know if she was being stupid or brave—or perhaps she was just being inquisitive, because there was daylight, and she knew she would be busy during the coming week, so she had to do it. Along the way, she picked up a stick—not quite a club, but made of oak, and thick enough to give a good bruise if she had to smack someone. She walked into the cemetery.

Of course, it was different even an hour later: longer shadows, darker grass. She didn't wander this time; she was methodical. She walked the paths, looked around every tree and into the grass beside the graves. As it was Sunday, others had walked here, paused there, perhaps put their hands to their chests and prayed for their relatives. If she had thought that the evidence of whoever it was who frightened Jean would pop out at her, she was wrong. But as she walked around, she noticed two interesting sets of footprints.

One was at the far end of the graveyard, where you could see the bay. Eliza carefully set her foot next to one of the two prints. Her shoe was slightly smaller than that imprint; the print could be a woman's, but the shoe that person was wearing was wider and heavier, more the one hand, she had imagined it very clearly, the two men, one slightly injured, the other strong and full of himself. On the other hand, she thought, how was she to know if they had even been in the graveyard at the same time? Yes, their footprints were both more distinct than any other footprints she had seen (including her own; she did walk a few steps and then look down at them, to see if she had made any impressions, and she also looked for anything from earlier in the day, along the paths she and Jean had followed, for a print that was similar to hers). By the time she got to the Bear, Eliza decided that the only conclusion she might draw was that the men had been there at a similar time of day, probably in the morning, when the soil was damper, and that, wherever they had walked about, those spots where their prints remained were spots where no one else happened to walk in the course of the day. How this fit in with Jean's anxieties, or, perhaps, sensitivities, Eliza had no idea.

Her supper was good—cost three bits, but she was hungry from all the walking and she had always liked some roasted duck (or that's what they called it; in Monterey, perhaps it was a roasted gull or a booby—just thinking of that gave Eliza a smile).

like a workman's boot, with little dots in the front area, like hob-nails. Mrs. Parks didn't allow those in her establishment, because they damaged the floorboards—Eliza had seen them sitting neatly beside the front entrance. So a short fellow, perhaps. But the two impressions weren't alike. The left one was straight and solidly in the mud. The right one was twisted inward and slightly deeper on the outside, as if the fellow had a limp of some sort. Eliza thought at once of Mrs. Harwood, and looked for evidence of a cane or a crutch, but didn't see any. She stared out over the graveyard with care; it was getting later.

The second pair of prints was in a muddy area next to a tree. She assumed they would be the same as the first set, but they weren't. They were also work boots, given the shape of the soles, but whoever was wearing them stood evenly, with his feet slightly apart, and no hobnails poked into the mud. Just looking at the boots, Eliza could imagine a strong fellow, standing with his hands in his pockets and a hat pushed back on his head, chewing tobacco and making up his mind what he was going to do with his pay—a brothel or a saloon, or maybe both.

She looked at those prints, then turned, and looked toward where the other two were; a slight rise and a tree blocked that view. She walked back to the other two and turned toward the entrance of the graveyard. The spot where she had seen the second set was less blocked, because of the angle of the tree. So if, like DuPANN, Eliza had a theory, it was that the fellow with the limp had been watching the other fellow, and, let's say, Jean had sensed that while she herself had not.

Eliza walked down Pearl Street again and got a bit of spray off the shoreline, since the wind had picked up and the waves were crashing more loudly. In Kalamazoo, Eliza's mother would have said, "Ach! North wind! Now, that never brings anything good!" But here, the north wind was really a west wind, and one never knew what it might bring. As she walked, Eliza reconsidered what she had imagined. On

⟿ **6** ⟾

THE NEXT MORNING, Eliza got up early, before Mrs. Clayton,
even. She was hoping to see Jean sitting on the steps outside, but
she didn't, and then, when she heard Mrs. Clayton beginning to stoke
the firepit, she left, walked about, keeping her eye out for Jean. She
didn't see her. She passed the house where Jean lived—very quiet—
then the establishment on Pearl Street where she worked—quiet
there, also (but all the brothels were quiet this time of day). She and
Jean had two tasks that seemed, on a Monday morning, to be pressing on Eliza—to somehow get a couple of horses and ride to that spot
where they'd seen the girl's remains, and to figure out where the boy
had bought his whiskey.

But the weather was chilly and wet, and neither quest was at all
appealing. She knew Mrs. Parks's establishment would be warm and
friendly, and that was what she looked forward to. As for customers,
with bad weather, no one could say. If the ships couldn't get out, then
some number of sailors would come, but the regular customers, who
preferred to walk to the establishment (or the saloons), would stay
home. Jean had told her at some point that bad weather kept her
customers at home, seeing to the leaks or the fire or the blowing trees.
And, even as Eliza was thinking this, the wind picked up.

She could go back to the Bear and have some corncakes or pork belly for her morning meal, but in fact she wasn't at all hungry. She went back to her boarding house, rustled around for a whalebone parasol she had bought her first winter in Monterey. It was unwieldy but useful, and not as large as many others were.

Since she was from Kalamazoo, Eliza didn't think she could be impressed by a storm—rain, snow, thunder, lightning, a tornado sighting or two (not by her, but by people around town). In Monterey, she hadn't even heard thunder, and lightning seemed to strike out in the bay more than in town. The sailors sometimes spoke of "hurricanes" or "cyclones," which people in Kalamazoo never talked about. According to the sailors, those storms (which sounded like extra-large rainy tornadoes to Eliza) started out in the eastern part of the Atlantic Ocean, down by the coast of Africa, and then went west to some islands or the Gulf of Mexico or South Carolina. The one everyone talked about had happened not long before Eliza met Liam Callaghan—it was called "the New England Hurricane," and came in the fall, when the leaves had already turned. Everyone said that the storm slithered right up the East Coast, from one of the Carolinas to Boston, an act of God, according to Eliza's mother, until, at any rate, it got to Boston and did damage there. Eliza's mother respected Boston and its history—some of her relatives lived there—and so, when folks were killed in the storm and a church steeple came down, her mother fell silent about God and just shook her head.

One time, Eliza had been doing business with a sailor when the wind came up and rattled the shutters in the room. She had started, and maybe let out a little gasp, thinking of that hurricane. The sailor had finished his business and then, while he was wiping himself off, blowing his nose, and washing his hands in the basin of water that Mrs. Parks provided in all of her rooms, he told Eliza that north of the equator hurricanes only went from east to west, so there were no hurricanes on this coast. Then she had him explain what the equator was, and after he laughed a bit, and Eliza scowled, he told her that he was laughing because before he got to be a sailor he didn't know what the equator was, either—he thought it was a heavy, long animal with huge jaws, and that turned out to be an alligator! He explained the equator to her (he had crossed it four times), and then talked for a couple of minutes about ports he had been to that were near the equator—he especially liked one called Manta, on the west coast of South America, but what he said about it didn't make her want to go there.

Eliza had believed him, though—no hurricanes in Monterey. After she had been outside with her parasol, walking down Scott Street for a bit, she wondered if he was correct, and also if that sailor was out on some ship along the coast, holding the gunnels with two hands and rethinking his profession. The trees were waving and cracking, the wind was screaming around the buildings, and the rain was coming down the way it did in Michigan. The parasol was of no use—when it was open, it pulled away so that she had to hold it with both hands. She wrestled it closed, and then simply put up with the rain soaking her. And then, oddly enough, the wind suddenly settled, and there was only rain. One of the things she had liked about Monterey was that, because of the dry weather, the streets were usually flat and hard—smashed down by the constant traffic of people walking and horses pulling carriages and wagons. Even when she was looking around earlier for Jean, there hadn't been much of a problem—most of the rainwater slid down the streets toward the bay. But now it had soaked in; the mud was getting thicker and more slippery. She had to watch her step and the hem of her gown, which she tried to hold up as best she could. And then she got used to that, too. The fact was that creeping around (she couldn't call it walking, or even strolling, because of the mud) was perhaps more fascinating than usual. Almost everyone was shut up inside with a taper or two, and she could see those flickering through the windows. Sometimes, as she peeked in, she would see a woman bending over her needlework, or a man sleeping, or a child running across the room. One boy she saw stumbled, fell, hit his head upon the table that the taper was sitting on, sat up, started crying—Eliza, remembering doing the same thing, almost cried out in surprise, but she stayed quiet, kept watching. His mother stood him up, said something rather angrily, then went away, came back, took the boy in her lap, and held a wet rag to his head. A few people were reading papers, one or two reading books; Eliza couldn't tell what they were. No one looked toward her as if sensing that someone was spying—perhaps the noise of the rain meant that no one heard her walk by, pause. She was reminded of the times her mother had told her to keep her eyes down, not to stare. But, she now thought, if her mother had never stared, how was it that she and her friends could gossip as much as they did about their neighbors and their fellow parishioners?

After a while, she did get hungry after all, but she was so muddy and bedraggled that she didn't dare walk into any eating establishment. She turned to go back to her boarding house, paused, looked down at her boots. They might as well have been made of mud. She was staring at them and wondering what she was going to do about that when she saw something odd off in the distance.

She wasn't far from the wharf, a little up from the Presidio. There was a pleasant building by the corner of the street. A man and a woman had come down the steps, and then the woman paused and the man pushed her toward the spot where the road they were on turned away from the water. The woman resisted again, and the man smacked her across the face. She dipped her head, started walking where he directed her. Eliza waited a moment, then followed the two of them as best she could through the mud, stepping to one side of the puddles and trying not to sink in deep enough so that her boot might be pulled off. By the time she got to the corner, the man and the woman had disappeared. She stood in the shadow of the building on the corner and looked everywhere she could—up the hill and down the hill, even back where she had come from. Just at the very moment when she thought the best thing to do was to give up and go change her clothes for her day's employment, she heard a woman's scream flutter in the air, perhaps amplified by the wet weather. It seemed to be coming from up the hill, and Eliza could not help stumbling through the mud toward it. No sounds followed it—no more screams, no sound of a pistol shot, no moans or cries, not even any harsh demands of the sort that her own husband had liked to make before pushing her (yes, he had done that). Nor did anyone come out onto their verandas to see what might be happening; the houses were shut up in their adobe silence, and she was alone on the street. Eliza did her best to stumble a little farther up the hill, but it seemed to be of no use. At Cooper Street, she turned and made her way back to her boarding house. The rain eased off, and by the time she had undressed herself, put on the only other decent gown she had, fixed her hair, and scraped her boots, there was sun everywhere.

When she got to Mrs. Parks's establishment, she was a little early, and nothing was going on. Mrs. Parks said, "Ah, Eliza! There you are. My goodness, your boots!"

Eliza took them off, and Mrs. Parks carefully wrapped them in some paper. Then she said, "Well, you have been out and about! I can't imagine why! Would you care for some tea?"

They sat together in the front room. Carlos had not yet arrived, and neither had any customers; Olive was back in her room, doing some needlework, and Amelia hadn't yet shown up. Eliza told Mrs. Parks about her walk, idly, as if nothing had happened; then she said, "Oh my, well, I did see one interesting thing," and she recounted the incident as casually but also as carefully as she could. When she was done, Mrs. Parks said nothing, merely took a sip of her tea. Eliza said, "I didn't know what to think."

Mrs. Parks said, "What is there to think? Men are like that. Why do you think I employ Carlos? You've had to put up with similar things yourself. Everyone knows that this is a dangerous business, but, between you and me, being a woman is a dangerous business, and don't let anyone tell you otherwise. Oh, those men would talk about how they fight Indians and wrestle cattle and climb the masts and look for justice, and indeed they do, but they do it for themselves, if you ask me. And what they want of women, they want for themselves, too." She glanced at Eliza, to see if, perhaps, Eliza agreed with her. And perhaps Eliza did, but it seemed as though getting herself to the point of saying something of the sort was rather like climbing that muddy street—tricky, slippery, and with some risks.

Mrs. Parks glanced at her and said, "I wonder if I know him. What did he look like?"

Eliza closed her eyes, thought for a moment. "He had one of those mustaches, you know, that turn up at the ends, but it wasn't turning up, what with all the rain. He was wearing a bowler hat." She thought again, then said, "Not tall, I would say, strong, but not agile like a sailor would be." Then she saw it, the nose—long and pointed with a prominent tip, and she saw another thing, too—his Adam's apple, though how she saw that from a distance she could not have said. She described those things, said, "He looked about forty, a little worn."

Mrs. Parks shook her head, said, "No, I don't know him," but, judging by the look on her face, Eliza suspected that she did, even though he was not anyone Eliza had ever seen as a customer.

Thinking that she was perhaps being a little sassy, Eliza said, "But if men are like that, as you said, then why do you have Carlos? He's a man."

"I did think of a few other strategies, including making my pistol evident when I allow the customers in, but this seemed like the best option. Carlos would never hurt a female—child or woman. You don't know this, but his older brother killed their mother, strangled her right in front of Carlos when he was about fifteen. Carlos tried to grab him and stop him, but the brother was bigger and quicker." Mrs. Parks sighed, then said, "Down in Carmel it was, not far from the Mission."

Eliza was more than surprised, she was startled. She said, "I've never seen a Spanish man even be impolite to a woman."

Mrs. Parks said, "Men are men."

After Olive came out of her room, bringing her finished piece of needlework with her—a fire screen depicting some birds flying over trees that were recognizable Monterey oaks—Eliza, Olive, and Mrs. Parks had a bite to eat, and then whiled away the time until Carlos and eventually two customers showed up. Eliza complimented Olive on the fire screen, and Mrs. Parks nodded. She said, "Olive, you have quite a talent there." Eliza wanted to ask how Olive had learned such a thing, but she knew Mrs. Parks would disapprove. She hoped she would remember to ask sometime in the future.

Olive got the younger man, Eliza the older man. They went into her room. The fellow looked about thirty, somewhat down at heel. She stood near the bed. He went straight to it, sat down, and put his face in his hands. Eliza's heart started pounding, thinking this might be another sinner ready to take his sins out on her, but then he looked up, smiled, said, "I am sorry, dear. It's been a very long day, and I thought this would perk me up, but I'm not sure I have it in me."

Eliza remained silent, though smiling, hoping that he would go on. He did remove his jacket. Then he said, "You know how, when you go toward the Mission, there's a spot where there are lots of ravines?"

Eliza said, "And pines? I love that area, if only for the fragrance."

"Yes. There. Well, I have a small ranch there, and we got so much rain that when I woke up this morning I discovered that three head of my cattle had slid down the hill into one of the ravines. Two of them broke legs and the third was healthy, but it was hell on earth to get that one out of the ravine. The others we had to shoot in the head, and then try to pull their carcasses up, because we can't let the beef go to waste, and there are plenty of wolves and foxes and cougars who would be on it in a second."

He fell silent, sighed again.

Eliza put her hand lightly on his shoulder.

"And my cabin is leaking. That's mainly why I came. A pleasant night in a warm, dry place. I knew I couldn't afford it with what happened today, but I didn't know if I would make it without some respite."

Eliza remembered the sailors she had serviced, some by just letting them sleep. She said, "Are you hungry, then? I could bring you some sandwiches from the kitchen. We had a good meal. . . ."

"Ah," the fellow said, "you are a kind hussy, aren't you?"

Eliza took her hand off his shoulder. She thought of doing for him what she had done with some of the overworked sailors—rubbing him here and there, especially across the shoulders, where his muscles might be tight. And she did look at the door of her chamber to make sure it was cracked. But he knew what he wanted. The fact that he could not get it he blamed on her rather than himself, his own exhaustion. No matter what she tried to do—engage him in conversation, or stroke him here and there, or parade around the room unclothed—his prick failed to respond, and after some period of time, he was complaining—"Well, girl, if you weren't so pasty-looking," "A girl in your profession ought to have some ass, anyway," "Why are you looking at me like that? What a face!," "I knew I shoulda grabbed the other girl when I had the chance." Finally, after not touching her at all, he was the one that threw an object at the door—his own muddy boot—and Carlos appeared, saw the angry look on his face, told him to get himself dressed, and escorted him out the front entrance.

Then Carlos came back, after Eliza had her drawers and her camisole on, and told her to stay until morning, as he didn't have any idea whether the fellow might lurk about outside. Eliza said, "He came a ways, probably on his horse."

"He'd've put him up at the place on Pacific, then. They close that place all night. Can't get your horse till dawn."

Eliza stayed where she was, rolled up in the coverlid on the bed, the taper still flickering.

It was well past dawn when she awoke. One thing you never saw in Monterey was a sunrise: by the time the sun was peeping over the mountains and the trees, it might be mid-morning. When she woke up, it was as if she was waking from the dead—no dreams, no tossing and turning, not even any fears. The sun was pouring through the window, which looked out into a small courtyard with fruit trees that Mrs. Parks liked to nurture. Her taper had burned out, and there was tallow hardened on the table beside her bed. Eliza pushed her way out of the coverlid, shook her hair out of her face, took some deep breaths. The first thing she thought was that her day yesterday had been very strange, and the second thing she thought was something else about the fellow who had pushed his woman and then hit her—he had a limp. As he walked, when he put down his right foot, he hurried and dipped a little bit with each step. How many steps had she seen? Four, maybe five. She jumped up. She knew she had to get to that corner and look for footprints. She knew so thoroughly that she had to get there that she wasn't even hungry.

It was late enough in the day that a fair number of people were out, holding their bags tight and slipping in the mud. Some were in carriages, and the horses were careful, too, but even that wasn't a guarantee—she saw a chestnut climbing Van Buren Street slip to his knees, patiently hoist himself back onto his feet, and then cautiously move forward again. And he wasn't the only horse with mud on his cannons. When she got to the spot where she had seen the man push the woman, she stopped and tucked herself against the building, just as she had done the day before, and then she stared down the street toward the steps, the narrow walk, the corner, until she could picture the event as clearly as she could remember it. Luckily, no one was around. She went out into the mud, so that she could go around rather than stepping through the narrow walk where the footprints might be (DuPANN would have been proud of her), then did her inspection. And there was plenty of mud, but even a few hours of sunshine had hardened it up a little.

What she had not reckoned with was that the prints she saw in the graveyard were put there by a man who was standing still. The good thing was that prints were still here. Evidently, it had been late enough on a rainy day so that no one had walked over them, and close enough to the end of the rain so that they weren't washed away. She could make out five, as well as three of the woman's prints. As Eliza might have expected, a man with a limp stepped more quickly on the side that hurt, and more firmly on the side that didn't, but the quick step, because of imbalance, was sharp enough. Eliza set her foot next to the limp-step, and her foot was slightly smaller; the limping foot did turn inward, and its outer edge was more sharply printed than the inner edge. Eliza was fairly sure that the man she had seen was the same man who had been in the graveyard. Then she inspected the woman's prints—they were small, two left, one right. The heels of the woman's boots sank in fairly deeply, and the toes were pointed. The first two prints showed an even step, then, a bit down the hill, the toe sank in, the heel was barely visible, and a few feet in front of the print, another possible image of the toe—this was where he smacked, knocked her forward. Eliza bit her lip, thinking of what she might do to the fellow if he ever showed himself at Mrs. Parks's establishment.

She went around the corner, up the next street, still looking for prints, but the walkway hadn't gotten as much rain, as there was a narrow gutter just beside it and, given how wet that was, she could see that it had siphoned off a lot of the water. She kept walking. A man went by on his horse; the horse was stepping carefully, and the man was allowing him to do it his way. She looked at the buildings, one large, one more like a cabin. The large one had a nicely worked door, probably oak. She paused to admire it and then looked down. Lying in the mud just beside the wooden planks of the veranda was a small, wet, stained white leather glove. Eliza bent down to pick it up. Half under it was something else, which she picked up, too. She lifted it toward the sky, stared at it. It was a bonnet string. She slipped them into her shopping bag.

She stepped back, looked more carefully at the building. It was newer than many of the other buildings in town, built of wood, not adobe, but in the same style, with decent-sized windows. On each side of the veranda, someone had planted rosebushes, perhaps brought from the East. They were fairly tall and thick, with a few buds and a few spent blossoms. Eliza went to give those a sniff, and it was a good thing she did, because the handsome door creaked and then opened, and a woman stepped out—not the young woman she had seen, but an older one. She was scowling. She said, "You here for a reason, girl? If not, go away."

Eliza said, "The only reason is, I saw the roses. I miss those. I wanted a whiff. I apologize."

The woman snorted, said, "Well, those are a pain in the neck, let me tell you." Then she waved her hand, and Eliza obeyed, stepped off the veranda, and continued up the street, holding her bag a little away from her skirt, as if to say, "We all have shopping to do." The woman went back into the building.

There was something about the woman that unnerved her, though. At first she thought it might be a resemblance to her mother—not in looks but in demeanor, in the way she scowled, in the way her voice popped out of her, promising a whipping and then a prayer. Eliza had hated whippings (mild though they were compared to ones that other children were suffering), but the prayer was worse, when her mother made Eliza kneel beside her on the hard flooring and then detailed all of Eliza's sins (talking back, not coming when she was called, not dipping her head when they happened to see the pastor in the street and her mother paused to chat with him, not closing her eyes when they said grace at the table). Maybe these memories had been waiting inside her since that fellow had reminded her, the other night, that she was damned. But Eliza also remembered that she had never believed what her mother was saying, never believed that an "all-knowing God" would care about such matters, because, for one thing, she said that God was male, and the only male she really knew, her father, was much more kindly than her mother.

As she walked up the street, side-stepping the muck, she thought that her "investigation" might get her into trouble, that she might find out something that was a danger to her. She shivered and remembered her mother saying, "Curiosity killed the cat." When her mother first said this, Eliza, at five, had thought she meant the stray marmalade that she sometimes saw in the alley behind their house, and she'd gone out into her mother's garden and cried, but then the marmalade came sliding out from behind a tree and looked at her. Even so, her mother said it enough that Eliza was surprised that when she had decided, with Jean, to "investigate," it hadn't occurred to her. She shivered again, and sped up.

$\rightarrow\!\!=\!\!\circ$ 7 $\circ\!\!=\!\!\leftarrow$

W HEN SHE GOT TO her boarding house, there was Jean, looking
absolutely normal (for Jean—she was wearing men's clothing),
sitting on the step. Eliza kissed her on the forehead and said, "I wish
you might give me a pair of pants and a jacket. This gown is a muddy
burden."

Jean said, "You've done a lovely job. The mud is knee-high."

Eliza said, "Take a look at my boots!"

They both laughed.

Eliza took off her boots, handed Jean her bag, went into the boarding house to change, but came right back out. She said, "I only have
two other gowns. I don't want to test Mrs. Parks's patience by showing up in the messy one, and I can't do any washing until the weather
clears for good, so this will be my outside gown."

Jean nodded. She stood up, gave Eliza her bag, and picked up her
own, and they walked toward Mrs. Parks's establishment. Without
even talking about it, Eliza knew they were going to make another
visit to the semi-underground spot that sold whiskey, though she
wasn't sure why—it was early in the day. What she really wanted to
do was take Jean aside, tell her about the man with the limp and the
pointed nose, see if she had ever seen anyone like that around town,

but Jean seemed happy to be out and about, somehow fresh in her mood and not edgy, as she had been the last time.

Just before they got near the whiskey place, she said, "Do you have any idea what made you edgy in the graveyard?"

"Honestly, I do not. It wasn't the ghosts. They were, you might say, feeling right at home."

"How many did you see?"

"Five or six."

"What did they look like?"

Jean put her hand on Eliza's arm, lifted her eyebrow. Eliza fell silent. They stopped to step aside for others, and then Jean looked the building up and down. Eliza decided that the best way to go about things was to let Jean do as she pleased, so she stood quietly, not looking at the building, but looking at the men and women walking by. She did not think that the woman she had seen the day before was as distinctive as the man, and she did not think that she would recognize her, but she remembered that the woman was small, with a narrow waist. No one like that walked by, but at this time of day, most of the folks out and about were men. She thought of the scream, how piercing it was, and hoped that it had done something—not, perhaps, chased the man away, but sparked some sort of intervention, the kind Carlos provided. Jean stepped forward, looked down the stairs in front of the whiskey establishment, and said, "All right. Too early. I suppose we'll have to return later."

Eliza said, "I have a thought. You know that fellow up on the corner there, Mr. Cooper?"

Jean said, "Everyone does."

"I think we should go peek into his place. He keeps lots of horses. Racing horses, they say, but maybe there are others."

Jean said, "I wasn't thinking of him, but why not? His place is right in the center of things. Does he, um . . . Is he one of your customers?"

"Never seen him," said Eliza.

They walked up the street. Jean seemed willing to take her time.

After a moment, she glanced at Eliza and said, "I looked in your bag."

Eliza said, "I expected that you would."

"Where did you find those items?"

"Down toward the wharf a ways. Do you know that rather new wooden house where they got some rosebushes to grow?"

"Yes, indeed. You have to sneak in, but the red ones smell delightful. I saw a . . ."

And then Eliza told Jean about the footprints, the man, the woman, and the scream.

Jean said, "She screamed?"

"They were around the corner. I don't know that she was the one who screamed, as I didn't see it. But putting two and two together . . ."

Jean said, "Let's walk by there!"

She seemed excited. Eliza wondered if she was planning on seeing a ghost. Eliza said, "Let's have a look at the horses first, see if Mr. Cooper—or anyone else, for that matter—comes out."

They went past the Cooper place, which was large, and Eliza heard the sounds of horses behind the wall Cooper had built— a whinny or two, some hoofbeats, a fellow saying, "Git off me, you nag!" which made both Eliza and Jean smile. They could smell it, too—the fragrance of fresh horse droppings. Jean said, "They say he has a lovely garden."

They walked around the place, jumped the gulch that ran behind it. The property was well taken care of, but not *perfectly* taken care of, and they did find a split in the wall that Jean said was caused by an earthquake and Eliza said was caused by the bank of the gulch subsiding. It was shaded by trees, so they could pause, peek in. Eliza could see six horses eating their hay, two bays, two chestnuts, a gray, and one she had heard of but never seen, which the Spanish people called a "palomino." The horse was almost pure gold. The mane was neatly combed, and the tail, also well cared for, dropped nearly to the ground; it was swishing gently back and forth as the horse ate its hay.

The horses were loose in the yard, but seemed to be getting along. Jean said, "None of those in Kenosha!" It was evident that all six of the horses were prized possessions, and this was not the place for two young women to hire mounts for their trip to the river. But they stood and watched—it was restful to do so, and the man inside, scowling, evidently the one who had reprimanded the "nag," didn't see them. When they walked away, back up Pearl Street in the direction of the graveyard, Eliza decided that the time had come to discuss what was in her bag. The first thing she said was "You haven't seen a ghost today, have you?"

Jean said, "I wish I had, and I wish they would talk to me about what happened to them, but they just float around, and then, when you stare at them, they disappear." She seemed not to be joking.

Eliza said, "I do think that glove most likely belonged to the woman, since it's very small, and nice leather. I've been looking around all morning, and I haven't seen anyone quite as small as she was. She was dressed like a woman, and had a woman's figure, but was hardly bigger than a child."

Jean nodded, then said, "Did you look at the string?"

"No. That housekeeper was shooing me away. I didn't want her to know that I'd picked up anything."

"I looked at it while you were in your place. I ran my fingers over it."

Eliza said, "I thought it was interesting that it wasn't a ribbon, but I suppose that was because of the weather."

"It wasn't a ribbon because it isn't a bonnet string. It's a piece of twine."

"It seems too smooth and neatly made for that."

"Well, then, let's say it's for pulling a shade up and down, something like that, something you would use in a well-furnished manse."

Eliza stopped, stepped to one side of the road, pulled it out of her bag, saw that Jean was most likely correct—the shades would be heavy ones, made of something thick, like cotton, covered with something smooth, like silk. The two of them exchanged a glance.

Eliza said, "What did you feel when you ran your fingers along it?"

Jean said, "Dirt."

"I found it in the dirt, underneath the glove, and the glove is dirty."

Jean said, "You ask me, I think it would be perfect for strangling someone, and I think our job is to find the body."

Eliza thought so, too, but right then, thinking of curiosity killing the cat, she felt her heart begin to pound. She glanced at Jean, who seemed so calm and ready that she didn't divulge her fear. Instead, as they walked toward High Street, Eliza said, "Have you seen Mrs. Marvin?"

Jean nodded. She said, "I saw her driving Less and More down Jefferson a few days ago."

"Did she say anything about the sheriff, or what happened after we . . ."

"Identified the—?"

Eliza nodded.

"She only said that her husband prodded the fellow. Noticed him in the plaza and actually went to see him in the pouring rain, but it's as if her husband's request just dropped into a hole, far as she can tell. But you never know what's going on behind the curtain."

Eliza said, in something of a whisper, "I guess it's up to us, for now." Then they both nodded, and Eliza's heart pounded even harder.

Jean said, "Around here, all around California, it looks like, females are rare enough, so you'd think the ones in charge would work on it."

Eliza heard herself say, "Unless they themselves did it." She said it casually, but then the two of them shared a startled glance, and Eliza suddenly took Jean's hand. She said, "This is a dangerous business."

Jean looked her right in the eye and said, "What isn't?" They stared at each other for a long moment, and then, all of a sudden, Eliza got hold of herself, felt herself calm down. She nodded, and they started walking.

———

THE QUESTION WAS where to look. As Eliza had learned from the bad weather, there were gullies and rivulets everywhere. If a killer was wealthy enough to have a cart or a carriage, he could take the remains up into the mountains and throw them out. Eliza said, "When my husband was shot, no one bothered to hide a thing. I never found out who pulled out his pistol first, and it could have been Peter, because he had quite a temper. But the fellow who shot him got away. I guess the vigilantes didn't see the point of looking for him, since Peter was from Michigan and he kept me pretty much locked in our boarding house, which turned out to be fine with me, though I hated it at the time. Meant I could keep my head down, change my name, earn some funds—"

"Mrs. Parks knew who you were."

"But she never said how, and I doubt she would tell me if I asked her."

Jean said, "I'm guessing she knows more about these girls than she's letting on."

Eliza gave a little shrug and said, "Can we rent a couple of horses? There's somewhere I want to go."

Jean looked at her as if she had gone crazy—not because this was a bad idea, but because she had never imagined, Eliza thought, that Eliza would choose to do such a thing. Jean grinned, grabbed her hand, took her to a place on Franklin where a fellow had five horses. Jean took one she had taken before, a decent-looking dark bay, and Eliza got the elderly one (almost entirely white, even around the eye-lashes), who, once she was hoisted into the sidesaddle, followed the dark bay in a dogged but pleasant fashion. They walked through the mud up Pacific Street into the woods. What Eliza wanted to look at was how the glens and the ravines were laid out, how the water flowed, where the deepest spots were. She wanted to get herself to think as the murderer might think, a fellow not interested in show-ing off his anger or his sense of insult, but, rather, a fellow who had a theory and a plan, who wanted to stay in the background and do more girls in. She was eager, and she knew it was Jean's presence that calmed her fears.

As they got higher, the road got more uneven—wet in some places, dry in others. The horses were adept at following the path. They rode deeper into the forest, and then Jean and Eliza both noticed a trail that went to the left, up into the mountains, and, without saying a word, they turned up that trail. At first it went along the base of the mountains; then, abruptly, a sharp turn took them upward.

Afterward, Eliza thought that, even if she hadn't been looking for anything, she would have taken great pleasure in this ride. The trail was well trodden and rather wide. At one point, Jean reined her horse back and said, "I guarantee you that the Indians live up here, and that there are more of them about than anyone tells us." Eliza looked around, and not only at the gullies and the trees. She had to admit to herself that she was pleased to see nothing—no skeleton half hidden in a grove of oaks, no Spanish moss dripping from a tree limb and pointing to a severed head or even a thick hank of hair. Birds, leaves, and puddles were all they saw. Jean's horse looked here and there, pricking his ears; Eliza's horse plodded along. She told herself that was because he was very experienced, and knew what to pay attention to.

Not long after the fork, there was an open spot where they could see directly out over the bay, and Eliza saw what they had come for—a view of Monterey in the distance, then the water, blue, flat, brilliant with sunshine, then mountains, also blue, on the other side of the water, and above that, sky, a few thin clouds scuttling past. They dismounted, let the horses wander a bit, snuffling for leaves and weeds. Jean handed Eliza a piece of dried beef of the sort that sailors were used to, and also half of a biscuit. They ate silently, staring at the view. The spectacle was enlightening, but Eliza didn't quite know how.

They mounted again. The path wove back and forth between the cliffs and the ravines. It forked in one spot. They went to the right, thinking perhaps it was less steep, but the horses were panting soon enough, even though they were only walking. At one sharp turn, Eliza thought they might stop and go back, but she saw Jean drop her reins to give the horse the choice, and the horse chose to keep climbing. Jean glanced back at Eliza and lifted her eyebrows. Just then, Eliza glanced up the precipice they were treading in the shadow of, and she saw a sharp-nosed gray face look down at her— a fox. And then another—perhaps its mate. Both of the foxes looked curious—the first one actually stepped closer to the edge and bent its head toward them. The horses didn't notice. When they had gone a little farther, Eliza looked back and saw the foxes from behind, their tails thick, twitching from one side to the other as they disappeared into the trees. Just then, Jean said, "There." Jean's mount was already looking, and now Eliza's gray did, too—off to the left, on a small ridge between two ravines, three deer, evidently males. The larger one had two prongs; the smaller two each had tiny horns that looked more like sausages poking out of their heads. The horses didn't care. They looked away, headed up the trail. The forest narrowed, then opened up, narrowed, then opened up. She felt hope jostle with fear as she gazed at the larger perspective. Perhaps, in spite of the ravines and the forest, the killer wouldn't be able to hide as long as he thought he would (that was, forever), and perhaps he was nearby, right this minute watching them.

When they went back down, the lower parts of the forest were in shadows because of the sinking sun, but the tops of the trees were brilliantly green and fluttering, even sparkling, in the breeze. Eliza looked up toward the sky. It was the most beautiful sight she had ever seen, and she wondered, since Kalamazoo also had plenty of hills and forests, why she had never looked up in this way before—it was as if her eyes had always been on her feet. And perhaps they had, since her mother had always encouraged modesty, self-effacement, living in a state of prayer. It was only after she came to Monterey that she had learned to explore.

The ride down had its moments. It was almost dark; there was rustling among the trees; a bit of the path broke away into a ravine as the bay horse stepped on it. He didn't actually stumble, but he did start a bit, and shift his weight. However, the horses were hungry for their fodder, and they seemed to know the way home. They walked a little faster. Toward the bottom of the trail, Eliza's gray caught up to Jean's bay, but the trail was wide enough so that they could walk together. Then Jean asked what Eliza knew she would: "Did you see the ghosts?"

"No. Where were they?"

"Among the trees. Lots of them."

"Could you tell who they were?"

"Either Rumsen or Ohlone."

"Indians?"

Jean nodded.

And why not? thought Eliza, since the Indians would have lived here forever. Somehow, the thought made her sad, but it also re-assured her—Jean's ghosts were always reassuring.

They walked along.

And then, after they had returned the horses to the stable, and it was late enough that Eliza had to go straight to Mrs. Parks's estab-lishment without changing her gown, Mrs. Parks looked her up and down, handed her four dollars, told her the name of a seamstress on Tyler, and said that Eliza should indulge herself—she suggested mus-lin, some pleasant dark color—a silvery blue, perhaps.

$\leftarrow\!\!\Longrightarrow$ **8** $\Longleftarrow\!\!\rightarrow$

FTER THAT TRIP, Eliza's days fell into a rhythm that it was hard to get out of. As she had noticed the previous winter, days went around and around between brilliant sunshine, heavy rain, dense fog, windy cold, and gloomy cloud cover. How to decide at the beginning of the day what to take along? Eliza hated the whalebone parasol, and so usually opted for wrapping herself in her longest shawl and then hoping she might dry it out for the next day. But all of this was better than snow, and she knew not to complain, even to herself. Some days, she even got out and about for something of a walk. On one of the pleasanter days, she actually ran into Olive on Scott Street. They smiled a greeting, and then walked along, side by side, for maybe ten minutes. The only information they shared was what they each had had for breakfast—hotcakes, boiled eggs for Eliza, of course, and herrings and muffins for Olive. Olive said, "I never had herrings before. I love them! Much better than whatever it was that my pa caught back home!" It was only after Olive turned up Van Buren that Eliza remembered how curious she had been about that fire screen Olive had embroidered. Meanwhile, she watched for both the petite (as Mrs. Parks would say) girl and the fellow with the sharp nose and the limp, but she didn't see either of them.

Before Christmas, some ten days or so, just when Eliza's new gown was completed and she wore it for the first time, business picked up. Mrs. Parks said, "You must know, my dear, many of the men about town are giving themselves the Yuletide treat they've been saving for." That Saturday, a week before Yule, Eliza even had three customers—a sailor whose ship couldn't get out of the bay, a boy whose father was a prominent cattle rancher, and a rather resentful fellow who, it happened, had been turned away from the posh place down the peninsula where the girls wore jeweled earrings. He had been so fired up that he'd ridden all the way into town and come to Mrs. Parks's place, although it was almost dawn. He told Mrs. Parks that once he wanted it he couldn't go without, and she said, "Behave yourself and I will see what I can do about getting the other place to take you in after the New Year."

He was dressed to the nines, as Eliza's mother would have said. She herself was hardly dressed at all when he was brought to her room—Carlos pushed the door open enough to let him in, but not enough to see Eliza. She was a little surprised and put out, but then he set his top hat on the chair, slapped a dollar coin on the desk by the bed, and, beside that, a tiny pouch of gold dust. He said, "Look inside if you don't trust me," and she did. It did not sparkle, was very like dirt. She thought she would ask Jean, but even if it was only dirt, the dollar was enough. The fellow was tired, but he produced his prick even before he had his pants off—he was so eager that he stumbled across the floor, and Eliza had to reach out to steady him. They fell onto the bed, and he was done with his business in a few seconds. He rolled over onto his back, took a deep sigh, and said, "Believe me, I have plenty of funds. What would you take for another?"

Eliza hoisted herself up on her elbow, looked him in the face, began undoing his shiny black bow tie (silk for sure). He gave the sort of smile that showed that smiling was second nature to him, and Eliza suspected that he was the kind of fellow who was tempestuous, not ill-tempered, who hopped between anger and amusement and kindness and, probably, fear, without much self-possession. She said, "Depends on how old you are." Now he really did smile, and then said, "Twenty-three."

"You're young enough, then, for an extra helping," and so they went about it more slowly, and he had no trouble with the prick. After the second time, they both fell into a doze, and it wasn't until Carlos opened the door to see if everything was all right that Eliza opened her eyes.

The fellow woke up as she did, and looked out the window. Then he sat up, snuffled, yawned, cracked his neck, first left, then right. He said, "Time for breakfast," reached for his trousers, turned to Eliza, and said, "Want to come along?"—for all the world as if she was not a prostitute, but just a young woman.

Eliza looked at her new gown, which was hanging over the chair. The seamstress—Miss Lowrey, it was—had done a stylish job, the way some seamstresses did, as if they had a good eye and couldn't help making the tucks just right. She said, "I would enjoy that. Thank you."

He even helped her do up the buttons on the back of the gown. She put her coin and the packet of dirt into her bag.

Mrs. Parks was in the parlor as they walked out. One eyebrow lifted, but she did smile, and Eliza saw that she had no objection to this outing. The fellow was dressed as he had been the night before, but without the tie, which he had stuffed into a pocket. The sun was up, and the sky was blue. Eliza said, "Do you have any idea what time it is?"

"I'd say half past nine."

Out on the street, the few passersby glanced at him, and Eliza noticed that most of the men seemed to look down on the fellow (even though he was taller than many of them), while each of the three women smiled in his direction, as if he was adding some respectability to the neighborhood. Eliza had her hand through his elbow, resting on his forearm. At one point, he sneezed, and she handed him her clean kerchief, which he took with a dip of the head. All in all, it was as if they were masquerading as a respectable couple. Eliza might have said she preferred being out and about on her own, but the masquerade was amusing.

Given his mode of dressing and his feeling that he had a right to go to the brothel down south, Eliza was surprised when they went to the Bear. She had never seen him there, but, then, she usually ate early in the day. They sat near a window; he ordered hotcakes and fried potatoes for himself, and she ordered her usual. He had not been talkative on the way, but he had done his best to make sure she avoided puddles and the one drunken fellow who staggered toward them. He was good-natured about the fellow—he said, "Must have finished up his Christmas punch a little too soon," then chuckled.

When they were eating, he looked at her and said, "By the way, I'm Lucas. Are you really Eliza?"

"I am."

"I'm going to guess where you came here from." He closed his eyes, and she saw that he had long lashes. He opened them and said, "Toledo."

Eliza said, "Not quite, but not far. How did you guess?"

He smiled. "I didn't. That's where I came from. Toledo to St. Louis, down to the Gulf, then by sailing ship to Tampico, then a very slow ride on a very sway-backed mule across Mexico to Mazatlán—not much of a port, I must say—then by sailing ship up to here. My uncle has a rancho on the other side of the bay. He raises cattle for the gold diggers. You can't believe how the price of the beef has gone up. He was struggling a couple of years ago, but now he's built himself quite a manse, I must say."

Eliza said, "What do you do for him?"

"Nothing so far, as I'm not much good on a horse, but I can add and subtract, so I keep the books."

He was pleasant, until another customer backed into his seat and bumped him. She saw a storm of anger blow across his visage. It was gone by the time he turned to look at the fellow, who possibly didn't realize anything, because he was looking at another man, who was coming through the door. The man who had bumped Lucas pulled out his pistol. Eliza saw that the man who had come through the door already had his drawn, and slid from her chair underneath the table. Lucas was braver than she was. He fell out of his chair and pulled the man who had bumped him down beside him. The shots from the man by the door went past the fellow and through the wall. The shots from the man on the ground went into the ceiling. Now two customers leapt on the man by the door, and one of them smacked him in the face. Eliza crawled away, over toward a rather dark corner, and hoped for the best. As a rule, this kind of fracas happened in saloons, at night. She saw Lucas look around, notice her, look back. Then he stood up, calm as could be, put his hand in his pocket. No telling what was in there, and evidently the others had run out of bullets. There was a pause, and then he pulled out a pipe. The man who had fired first pulled away from the fellow who was pushing him against the wall and ran at Lucas, and, supple as could be, Lucas stepped out of the way. The man fell down, hit his face on the leg of the table. Lucas pulled out a match, struck it on the wall, and lit his pipe. Then he came over to Eliza, helped her up, and escorted her out of the establishment, leaving two hotcakes and half of his fried potatoes on his plate. Fortunately, Eliza had eaten all of her meal. She held tight to his arm, panting. He didn't look frightened until they were almost to High Street; then he suddenly shuddered and said, "Damn me!"

Eliza said, "Are you sure you're only twenty-three?" When that failed to elicit a smile, she said, "That's how my husband died. Bar fight. A year ago, now. Someone shot him."

Lucas said, "How old were you when you were wed?"

"Eighteen."

"That's how old my wife was, too. Back in Toledo. I was twenty." He glanced at her. "She died a month after she told me she was with child. No one knew why. She had sudden stabbing pains in her belly, and then she fell down, and blood began to pour out of her. She died the next morning."

Eliza couldn't help herself; she said, "You sound as if you grieved."

"I did. I was most fond of her. I thought that if I hadn't pressed her to wed at her age, she would have lived. Did you—?"

"Not for a moment. He was a bully and a fraud."

They walked on. She glanced at him, saw nothing in his visage except pleasure in the walk, until suddenly he stopped, and there was the fear. He shook his head and said, "Do you believe in ghosts?"

Instead of saying no, Eliza said, "I don't know."

"She came to me a week after she died, and then a month after that. She leaned toward me and put her hand on my cheek, then disappeared. She was there, and then she was gone."

"Did you ever hear noises around the house?"

"No. I wished I had. I even went to a medium when I was passing through St. Louis. There was one in Toledo that people talked about, but I didn't want to go to anyone who knew about me or Edna, so I went to this woman who lived near where the ferry landed in St. Louis, on the north side. She told me that Edna had said her goodbyes." Now Eliza saw him tear up, and she wondered what she should do. They were down by the docks; she sincerely hoped that the bay did not remind him of the Mississippi. And then a whale breached, something Eliza hadn't seen before, though Jean had. The front end, dark, wet, came straight up out of the water, the fin stretched away from the body, and then the whale rolled to one side and disappeared, only to reappear, roll again, and go into the water backward.

Lucas stood with his hands in his pockets, watching, and the tears turned to a smile. Eliza began to wonder how this episode was going to end. It was not something she was used to; as a rule, her customers came and went, and no matter how well she seemed to get along with whoever it was, they both (of course with exception of that English sailor—Ralph, his name was—in the summer) went their own ways afterward. But in addition to that, Eliza couldn't think of any man

she had known before who had been so—what was the word?—
agreeable toward women. But that wasn't it, given his irritability the
night before. Maybe the word was "thoughtless," or "free." Compared to him, every man she had ever known seemed to have been
housed in a fortress of demeanor and self-consciousness, a house that
was often guarded by weapons. But it was getting late. She said, "I
expect you need to get on with things. But might I ask for one favor?"

The whale had gone. Lucas looked at her in a serious way, just a
flicker of dread in his face.

She said, "Might I go to the stables where you left your horse, and
have a look? They strike me as the most beautiful of animals."

He laughed, and then, of all things, kissed her on the cheek. Ten
minutes later, they were at the stables. She'd been hoping that his
horse might be one of those palominos. It wasn't, but it was a handsome dun with a narrow blaze and pleasant eyes. What Eliza thought
was the best thing about the animal was that he nickered when he
saw Lucas. Lucas looked at him fondly, too. He said, "That boy! He
is very patient with me. He even moves to the side if I start to slide off.
Perhaps he will turn me into a decent horseman."

Eliza walked to her boarding house by herself.

JEAN APPEARED around noon. Eliza was sitting on the veranda of
her boarding house, eating some dried apples. Jean sat down, and
Eliza handed her one of the slices, then told Jean of her adventure.
Jean was more skeptical than Eliza. After hearing all about it, she
said, "Well, let's hope it remains a good memory, and doesn't lead
to anything." Eliza didn't respond immediately, because she didn't
know what she hoped for, but then she said, "He does believe in
ghosts," and repeated what Lucas had said about the wife and the
two visitations. Jean said, "She visited him! That's so what I long for!
I see them, but they don't seem to see me. It's like I'm looking through
a peephole that they don't know exists. It's very frustrating!"

Eliza said, "But what do you want from them?"

"Well, for one thing, information! Have they seen the girls? How many girls are there, in truth? Why can't the girls come to us and tell us what happened? There don't seem to be any rules, or if there are, how can we learn them?"

Eliza said, "Have you ever been to a medium?"

"No! You'd think that here, of all places, there would be one."

"Why is that?"

"All kinds of people here—Indians, Spanish, us, sailors, and gold seekers from all over. And ghosts galore!"

Eliza said, "A medium helps you talk to ghosts, is that right?"

"Yes! There was one in the town where my aunt lives—you know, Madison? You didn't have any in Kalamazoo, did you?"

"I have no idea. Anyway, my parents would have thought someone like that was working for Satan himself." Then Eliza said, "I wish we had more time to look around, or go for another ride. I loved the one we took, but we should have gone to that bridge where we saw the girl." She shook her head. "Now our business is booming."

Jean said, "Not mine. I sit around, twiddling my thumbs and wishing I was a seamstress. I could ride to the bridge on my own." They shared a glance, and Eliza said, "Please, don't. We'll do it when the weather improves."

Jean nodded, then said, "All my customers are busy preparing for the Yule, such as they can. Even Mrs. Marvin hasn't come around in the last two weeks, which is unusual for her. I asked Mrs. Jacobs, who owns our place, but she said it's all to do with the season."

Eliza felt a hint of alarm for Mrs. Marvin. She said, "We should go to Mrs. Marvin's place, just to give her some Yuletide greetings. She's such a kindly soul."

Jean said, "Let's do!"

Eliza said, "Where does she live?"

"Not far from here, in fact. A little ways up Jefferson."

The walk was not taxing, though it was uphill. Eliza looked at all the houses and the trees; she was about to mention her fondness for the pines up in the mountains when Jean said, "Do you understand how pretty you are?"

Eliza laughed. "Pretty?"

"Fair. Pulchritudinous."

They both laughed at that one; then Eliza said, "Actually not. No, I'm telling the truth. We had no mirror in our house when I was growing up. My mother didn't want to encourage vanity, because vanity is a sin. If we went out, she would assess my appearance and fix my hair it if needed it." The only person who had ever said she was pretty had been Liam Callaghan, who had approached her on the street, whispered, "Aye, you air a pretty thing, airn't ya?"

"Your mother never complimented you?"

"Only if I behaved properly."

Jean tossed her head. They walked in silence for a little bit longer, and Eliza looked down at her hands. Were they pretty? How strange to think of them at all! She glanced over at Jean's hands, which were strong, with long fingers. Right then, when Jean straightened her bonnet, her fingers opened up in an expressive way, as if she were greeting someone. Eliza's own hands stayed together, clasped, closed, secretive. She realized that that was how she was, secretive, even to herself. Without wanting to, she thought that, if she were to look within, she would find sin.

WHEN THEY GOT to the house, Eliza saw that Mrs. Marvin lived directly across from the Harwood place. It was more modest than the Harwoods', adobe with a tile roof. There was something of a garden, but not a lot of rustling trees. A wide, flat path ran along the left side. Just then, she heard two loud whinnies, one sharp and piercing, the other a little lower in tone. Two different whinnies, Less and More. She grabbed Jean's hand, and they made their way, not quite tiptoeing, around to the back. She saw that Less and More were not in a barn, but in two small corrals. They were pacing back and forth. When they saw Eliza and Jean, they whinnied together. Jean ran over to the barrel in Less's corral and called out, "No water!" She touched the inside of the barrel, and called, "Pretty dry!" And there was no hay, either. Eliza shivered. If this was what DuPANN called "the things which will lead me to the answer," then those things were very bad. Eliza felt herself freeze up for a moment; then she turned around. Mrs. Marvin's house did not have many windows in the back, only two small ones to the right side of a door. When Eliza went over and looked into them, she saw that the curtains were drawn. She reached for the doorknob, and then Jean was right next to her. Jean put her hand on Eliza's, said, "Don't touch anything." Eliza felt curiosity and fear seesaw in her chest.

The door opened.

9

THE CURTAINS WERE drawn in every room—the interior of the house was so dark that, for a few moments, Eliza couldn't see a thing. She and Jean stood absolutely still, waiting. No one showed up, no one shouted, though one of the horses whinnied again. Jean spun around and went out the door, no doubt to find a well from which to draw them some water, but Eliza was not happy about being left alone in the silent house.

When her sight had adjusted, she put her hands behind her waist and crept here and there. Yes, the house was modest from the outside, but the interior was almost luxurious. The seats of the chairs and the sofa were satin, and the backs of the chairs, the desk, and the cabinet were intricately carved of something rich and red—rosewood, Eliza thought. There were two side tables, and on them both were nice trinkets—a carved box, a vase of drooping roses, a leather-bound book. The rug looked as if it was from far away—Persia, Eliza suspected. The floor creaked a bit as she stepped around, but still no sounds, no one coming in, and why wasn't the door latched? Because, she thought, it could only be latched from the inside, and just as she had this thought, she saw a foot, bare, no boot, sticking out from the entryway to the pantry, which was between the parlor she was in and a back kitchen. She stared at the foot, heard the door open, waiting for Jean without looking around (she knew Jean's step perfectly well). Jean came in saying, "Well, that wasn't easy. I'm surprised their well isn't more topped up, given the season, but I must say, Less and—" Then, "Oh, heavens!"

She was braver than Eliza. She stepped past her to the pantry, pulled Eliza by the hand.

It was indeed Mrs. Marvin. She was sprawled against the shelves, and some of the provisions had spread across her body—cornmeal, dried peas, small potatoes. She was wearing her nightdress; her mouth was open, the blood that had poured out of it dry and dark. Mrs. Marvin had been hit on the head repeatedly, until the right side of her skull was bashed in. Perhaps the weapon was right there beside her, a rolling pin.

They stood there for a moment. Eliza was feeling the shock like a tingle in her body, and she could see that Jean was, too. Eliza said, "We have to look for signs."

"About who did it? Yes, but then we have to remember what we saw."

"No way to write it down." Eliza glanced around. She didn't see ink or a quill.

Jean took a few deep breaths, then said, "We repeat it until we can remember it."

Eliza said, "Empty, dry water barrel."

Jean said, "She hasn't been out to the horses in a day, maybe two."

"Door unlatched."

"Killer couldn't latch the door from outside."

"Small windows."

"Had to go out by the door."

"Nightdress."

"It's late afternoon right now," Jean said. "She was killed early this morning, before she went to the horses; late last night, after she went to the horses; or yesterday morning, before she went to the horses."

"Dry barrel in moist weather."

"Yesterday morning or before."

"Rolling pin."

"He didn't expect to kill her, grabbed the nearest weapon."

"Husband?"

Jean looked at Eliza, swallowed, then said, "I thought there was one. She sometimes referred to a 'Matthew.'"

"Matthew Marvin." Eliza put her hand on the wall, as she felt a little weak in the knees.

"He might be dead, too. We need to look around."

They turned away from the body. Eliza said, "The blood on her face isn't fresh. It's almost black."

"Another sign that this took place yesterday or before that."

Eliza nodded, then said, "Would the body smell after a day?"

Jean said, "I have no idea. It's not hot."

As they made their way carefully through the parlor, Jean said, "No sign that anything was stolen."

There was a door to the left, slightly open. Without touching it, Eliza pushed it with her toe. The hinge squealed as the door moved. The bed was messy, the coverlid thrown back on one side, still neatly draped on the other. No boots, no trousers, no hat. She said, "No evidence of a husband."

Jean said, "She talked about her husband. She said he had influence, and would get someone to look into the killings, and he did. That's why we went to that place and looked at the girl."

Eliza said, "I do remember that. I feel like every new thing is driving all the old things out."

They eased out the front door. Jean was still flushed, and Eliza's heart was still pounding. The neighborhood was quiet. The Harwood house was unlit, surrounded by trees; it looked uninhabited. Eliza said, "Did you give the horses some hay?"

"Lots, but spread around, so they can't eat it too fast. And I filled the barrels."

When it came time to part, they paused on the corner of Jefferson and Pacific, stared at each other. Simultaneously, they both said, "Remember."

When Eliza got to the brothel, it was a little early. Mrs. Parks was doing books in the parlor. Eliza went and sat down beside her, waited as she added up her column of figures, then looked at her with a smile.

Eliza said, "Do you know a woman named Mrs. Marvin? Or her husband, Mr. Marvin?"

Mrs. Parks said, "My dear, you might know him. He comes around fairly often. He always asks for Mary, even when she is off somewhere. If she's gone, he doesn't . . ."

Mary was the one Eliza didn't know very well. She had a different schedule—most of her customers came during the day, Eliza thought. Since she was the only girl who worked those hours, the place would be very quiet. Evidently, Carlos didn't have to come for those customers, because they were not as drunk or as rowdy.

Mrs. Parks said, "I will say that Mr. Marvin seems like a kindly man, and he always pays up. That's about all I know of him."

Eliza took a deep breath, and told Mrs. Parks about what she had seen in the Marvin house.

Mrs. Parks said, "Oh, heavens! Oh, heavens! Where is it, again?"

Eliza said, "Across from Mr. Harwood's place, up Jefferson."

"And you were there because?"

"My friend Jean works for Mrs. Jacobs. Mrs. Marvin was one of her customers."

"Ah, yes," said Mrs. Parks. "I had heard something about that."

Now seemed the right time to tell Mrs. Parks about her so-called investigations with Jean, but Eliza refrained, though she was not sure why. Perhaps there was something about the killing of Mrs. Marvin that made her distrust everyone, even Mrs. Parks. She looked at her hand on the table, saw that it was trembling, put it in her lap.

"Oh dear," said Mrs. Parks. "What a shame for you to see that.

You may do as you please today, Eliza—anything to help you get hold of yourself."

Eliza had no idea what that might be.

Mrs. Parks put her books away, threw on a shawl and her bonnet, and scurried out of the room. Eliza looked around. She was now alone, which she did not like. Better to be out on the street, no matter what was going on, than by herself, thinking of Mrs. Marvin and her foot. She went over to the corner where Carlos would sit, picked up one of the cudgels that were stored there, slipped it into her bag, and went out the door. It was cloudy, but the clouds were beginning to thin, and the air was getting a bit brighter.

She walked here and there, though nowhere near Jefferson Street. Mostly, she crept up and down Alvarado, almost to the docks but not quite, then almost to Pearl but not quite. There were plenty of people around now, as the church services were over. Normally, she would glance or gaze at them, but almost everything anyone did—stumbling, looking at her, coming out of a door, running past—startled her. There were only a couple of drunks, staggering rather than yelling; they looked like sailors. And, as always, she was greeted with smiles, if she was greeted at all, even by the two drunken sailors. She took a lot of deep breaths, but she didn't dare close her eyes. What she hadn't expected, in her curiosity about the girls who were killed, was how dramatic and fearsome seeing the place and the aftermath of a crime was. All the deaths she had witnessed—her cousin who died of typhoid fever, a boy in her neighborhood in Kalamazoo who drowned in the river—had been, in some sense, peaceful. She remembered the death of her grandfather rather often. When she was six, her mother had been in the kitchen, making a bite to eat for her grandfather, who had been living with them for about half a year. Her mother had handed Eliza a warm cup of cocoa to take to him. She'd pushed the door open with her shoulder, carrying the cup in both hands. His chin was in the air, and his hand hung over the side of the bed. His eyes were wide open. She stood there for a long moment, then heard the creak of the door, turned around, saw her mother's face change from kindly to shocked to sad as she stared at her father. Eliza cried out, and it was Papa who came, took the cup of cocoa out of her hand, and led her from the room. Her mother went into the parlor, collapsed on the floor, and recited prayers. The boy who drowned had called out, then gone down without a sound. The fellows who ran for a boat and paddled out to him worked hard to get there, but were surrounded by sky and trees and calm water. Everyone was shocked, everyone grieved, but no one felt this rattling panic that she was feeling now. Some even said that, if you had to go, if God called you, then drowning was the best way—better, said her relatives, than typhoid fever.

She tried to keep walking, but once in a while she leaned against the side of one of the buildings, because the experience had exhausted her. She wondered if Jean was having similar feelings. She passed the Bear. It was too late for her midday meal, and in fact she wasn't hungry. She wandered toward the docks, then back toward Pearl. Only the blue line of the bay in the distance calmed her a little.

Late in the day, she realized what she was doing—she was keeping her ears open for any mention of the killing, of Mrs. Marvin or Mr. Marvin. At last, sometime after dark, outside one of the saloons, she heard two fellows talking about it. They didn't mention the name, but she knew what they were talking about. The taller one, who had full whiskers and a grand mustache, and so was evidently prosperous, said, "Old lady. No one ever said a bad word about her."

The other one, leaner and more scruffy, a pipe in his hand, said, "Had those two nice horses. Wonder if those will get sold."

"That's all you ever care about."

"That's all I knew about 'er. Can't care about every dame."

"Took the husband in. They say he did it."

"Seen that before. Where'd they catch 'im?"

"They didn't. He was coming into Roach's office to report the crime, and they threw him behind bars right there. Said she was beat to death with a rolling pin—who would do that besides the man of the house?"

Eliza walked away. For some reason, she felt as if she was freezing to death. She glanced back after a few steps, but neither of them was looking at her. She was reasonably certain that the men had not noticed her eavesdropping.

She spent the night in her boarding house, waking, sleeping, waking, sleeping. What roused her in the morning was pouring rain, belting the window of her room and the tiles on the roof. She turned over onto her back, closed her eyes. She dreaded going out and had no idea what to wear. The gown she had worn the day before was her warmest and most bedraggled—she'd purchased it in Kalamazoo before she came to California. But donning it again filled her with horror—there was no telling what might have gotten on the hem in Mrs. Marvin's house. In fact, the dread was familiar—she had felt the same thing when she woke up and knew that she had to spend the day doing Peter's bidding, and putting up with his temper. Then she wondered if Matthew Marvin was the same sort of fellow—kinder and more respectful to strangers than he was to his wife. Eliza sighed.

The rain continued, but there was enough light to read. Eliza felt for her book underneath some papers and other items. It had been so long since she read it that she didn't even remember its title—oh, yes, *The Wide, Wide World*, written by a woman. The volume was not very large: another reason she had brought it with her. Simply for the sake of distraction, she opened the cover, went to the first page. She didn't remember a thing about it, but then, right away, there was a bit that made her smile. "Rain was falling, and made the street and everything in it look dull and gloomy." She read on. The book was meant to be sad, and as Eliza continued, she remembered some of the sympathy she had felt for the girl and her mother—Ellen, the girl's name was, and perhaps Eliza had felt touched by its similarity to her own. Reading the book made her understand how her life had departed from the innocence she had once known, from the hopes she had once had, simple though they were—Liam Callaghan and herself, together, with some sort of decent income and a small house to live in, a child or two (or ten—you never knew how that was going to turn out, especially if you truly loved the fellow). The years passing from winter to summer and back to winter in a regular, if taxing, way (yes, beautiful flowers in the spring, beautiful leaves in the fall, but drought and snow always waiting in the distance—or tornadoes and blizzards, thunderstorms and floods, for that matter). She read on a bit, but it was painful to be reminded of such things and to wonder about the person she was now, the ways in which curiosity—yes, that was it, her own and Peter's—had transformed her. She closed the book, set it on the side table.

And, indeed, she was hungry. She got up, and as soon as she began donning her clothing (the only decent gown was the new one, but she could wrap herself in her biggest shawl, which was dry), she felt herself coming back. Perhaps this had always been true, too—dread faded away as she proceeded, step by step, toward the very thing she dreaded.

Outside, she smiled again when, as in that book, she "plashed" through the puddles and the muck. Her first thought about Mrs. Marvin, as she walked along, was whether the rolling pin had actually been her weapon against the husband's attack, if it was lying there because it fell out of her hand. But what else might the husband have used? She and Jean had forgotten to look at the kettles. Eliza put her hand in her bag and stroked the cudgel she had taken from Mrs. Parks's establishment.

10

RUPERT, HER FAVORITE SERVER, met her at the door of the Bear. He looked her over carefully, then stepped aside and said, "I saw you pass yesterday. I almost ran after you to give you some bread, because you looked so down in the mouth. Do you feel better?"

Eliza said, not quite lying, "I feel fine. How about you? That was quite a ruckus yesterday."

"That fellow! What a temper he's got." He glanced over at the wall. Eliza looked, too—the bullet holes were still evident, and, indeed, how could they be gotten rid of? Eliza had no idea.

Then, across the room, she saw Lucas looking at her, smiling. He touched the seat beside his, and she went and sat down. He seemed utterly calm and untouched by the fracas, something that Eliza herself had forgotten in the rush of later events. She thought of that phrase, "deathly quiet." Perhaps what she had seen at Mrs. Marvin's was more horrifying than the shooting she only now was recalling because of the quiet. Eliza shivered. She said, "Perhaps I didn't tell you how much I admired your presence of mind yesterday."

And it was hard to believe that it was only one day ago that she had done just this thing, sat at this table beside Lucas while he ordered her her breakfast as if nothing would happen, as if that day, a day she would always remember, was destined to be as normal and forgettable as any other day. He smiled again, in the way he had of not being able to help himself, shrugged off her compliment, then said, "I went looking for you last night."

Eliza said, "I suppose you saw that Mrs. Parks's place isn't open for business on Sunday." She glanced at the rain on the small window. She said, "I was talking to a friend of mine about you yesterday. She was very envious of your ghostly experiences."

Lucas lowered his eyebrows, tossed his head.

Eliza said, "She sees ghosts all the time, but they never talk to her, or, she says, acknowledge her. The first one she told me about was the ghost of a monk who was dressed in black, who was sitting beside a tree over by the plaza. She greeted him, and just then he rose up and disappeared. Once, we walked past the Casa Munras, and she said she saw one prancing about on the roof."

Lucas laughed.

"At any rate, she lives for some ghostly acknowledgment of her interest."

"Does she, um, work at your place?"

"No. She works at another place, though. Mrs. Jacobs's place." Eliza watched Lucas's face, but no recognition passed over it. He said, "I don't know that one. At any rate, I wish it would clear up. I don't even mind a fog bank, compared to this. But I would like to get on my horse and go home, I must say." Then he looked at her, and said, "You liked my horse. Do you ride?"

Eliza said, "Not as I wish to. My friend Jean, she rides astride, and she often wears trousers and a big hat. If a man stares at her, she snaps at him in a deep voice."

"She sounds amusing."

"Indeed, she is my best friend, and not like any friend I've ever had." At last, Rupert brought some provisions—hotcakes for Eliza; muffins, ham, and fried potatoes for Lucas. Eliza said, "They forgot your sardines." They both laughed. Eliza had never tried sardines, and neither, apparently, had Lucas.

Lucas said, "Thank goodness. I asked for pork belly, but they're out of that."

Eliza was more ravenous than she had expected to be, and all four of her hotcakes disappeared in a hurry. When she looked up at Lucas again, he was watching her, but he didn't say anything, only went back to finishing his muffin. Eliza couldn't help herself; she said, "Do you know the Marvins?"

Lucas shook his head. He said, "I knew a fellow named Marvin back in Toledo—Marvin Kruger. His father had a lumber mill. They would bring the logs by boat over the lake from the East or up north. It was a good business." He spoke idly. Eliza said, "I knew someone who had a lumber mill." She didn't say it was her father. She thought of Liam Callaghan, then said, "Many, if not most of the fellows in Kalamazoo worked in a lumber mill." She took a deep breath, perhaps her first deep breath in twenty-four hours. And what was there to worry about? Mr. Marvin was in jail. Mrs. Parks had gone to the sheriff, and no doubt taken Mrs. Jacobs with her. But still. She shook her head. Lucas saw her. He said, "You seem disturbed. Perhaps I should be, too, as I had no idea yesterday whether I was going to be shot or not, and when I thought about the incident later in the evening, I reckoned that I might have been more cautious and come over to the corner where you were. I must say that I didn't even look for another way out. They cook up the food somewhere. We might have gone there."

Eliza put her hand out and touched his, lightly.

He went on, "When I get back to the ranch, if I relate all of this to my uncle, he will jump all over me about taking a little care, as he always does. He is a cautious man, and his overseer was not. Perhaps you don't know the area very well, since you don't ride, but there are so many treacherous paths and steep hillsides."

Eliza said, "I have seen several of those."

"A year ago, before I came, in the wet season—and I'm sure you know how the rivulets just run down the sides of the mountains, hundreds of little rivers—at any rate, a pair of the cattle got down into a ravine, and Joe went after them with a rope. But he was going too fast, and his horse ended up tumbling over and sliding down into the trees. Broke its leg, and Joe broke his arm. And then, when the weather dried up, the cattle just climbed the hill and went back to the herd. They were a little thin, but that was all. My uncle was fit to be tied, and Joe was lucky to retain his job, but my uncle isn't the sort of fellow who sends someone in a splint out on his own, however much he rages on. At any rate, perhaps the tale of my savoir faire won't get back to him. Across the bay, they aren't so interested in the goings-on in Monterey as they are on this side of the bay. No one was killed, so I suppose everyone will forget it. Except me, of course."

And me as well, thought Eliza. She hoped that she would never forget the amused and self-confident look on Lucas's face as he stared down the ruffians and lit his pipe. If that was this "savoir faire," it was an excellent quality. Perhaps, she thought, that was what DuPANN had.

She glanced over at Rupert, expecting him to toss his head toward the door, but instead he came over to them, now the only customers left in the room, and said, "You may stay as long as you please, and, because of yesterday, you may also have your meal on the house. I will say, for myself, that that fracas almost made me want to go back to Little Dixie, until I remembered all of the fracases I've seen there." He smiled.

Lucas said, "You don't talk like a Southerner."

Rupert said, "Little Dixie is in Missouri." He rolled his eyes and walked away.

Eliza relaxed in her seat. She said, "What was the most interesting incident of your journey to Monterey?"

Lucas said, "There was one, but you have to go first."

Eliza preferred to think of Kalamazoo and Monterey as two separate worlds. If she were to recall the trip, then the path back to Michigan would be open, and she didn't want that. But, looking at Lucas, she had to remember something. She took a deep breath, and here it came, a flood of memories, but also a bit of appreciation.

She began: "I will say for Peter that, although I had no idea what we were doing, as I didn't even suspect how large this nation was, he had some sense, and he spent whatever money he could come up with on a decent wagon and a pair of strong horses. The wagon had large wheels and a pale cover that was sufficient for keeping out both the sun and the rain, though there wasn't much of that once we got into the Plains. The best thing he did was join up with a group of other wagons, and then leave in late April. There were five in the group to begin with—one family was quite taken with the vista and the greenery in Iowa, and decided to find a spot there. They say that now the trip takes six months over land, but, perhaps because of the time of year or the wheels or the horses, it took Peter and me more like five. And we got here in September, also a pleasant time of year. We were bored to tears the whole way. I suppose the most intimidating bits were starting up the mountains. It wasn't as hot as I had expected it would be, but when we got to a creek or a river, we liked to walk about in it with our feet bare and dip our hands up to the elbows. No one died, not even of any sickness among the children. Mrs. Cannon was with child, and I really didn't understand much about that, so I was afraid she would give birth somewhere in the mountains, but she knew what she was doing, and they were already settled in their adobe on Monroe Street when the baby came. They've gone now—up to San Jose, I believe. We didn't understand how rare our boring journey was until we chatted with others, who lost their families or their livestock on the way. We were lucky." Eliza thought for a moment, then said, "And I was too young to know it."

It was also true, though she said nothing about it, that, even in the wagon, at night, after a long day, Peter had pressed her to accommodate him, no matter that their fellow travelers might hear them. How young she had been, indeed, to be embarrassed about such a thing! She went on: "The wagon and the horses were in good shape when we arrived, and valuable! Peter sold them to fund the next six months of our time here while he decided what to do with himself." Which turned out to be the next two months for the both of them, and then four months for her alone.

Lucas said, "I do believe that journey would have been beyond me. If you travel by boat, all you need to do, most of the time, is stare at the sailors doing their business and wonder how they got so agile."

Eliza nodded, thinking of those boys she serviced from time to time.

"I suppose that the only time I had some sort of a struggle was when we crossed Mexico," Lucas said. Then he looked at her, a tiny flash in his eye, and said, "Are you an abolitionist?"

Eliza knew this was a dangerous question, even in Michigan. It was also dangerous to pause before answering, because then the person asking you would know that you wavered in your opinion. She looked at him, said, "I'm from Michigan. My parents are Covenanters."

"There were English Covenanters involved in the slave trade."

From this response, Eliza knew she could give an honest answer. She said, "I think that slavery should be gotten rid of."

Lucas said nothing in response, just went on with his story. "I should say that my ride across Mexico was a physical struggle, but my trip down the Mississippi from St. Louis was worse. I told you about going to that medium not far from the river. Then I took a little walk about the town, and I saw a slave auction by the courthouse. I dared not watch, but I couldn't stop myself. All trussed up, with their faces down, staring at the ground, men with whips standing nearby." Now his face was flushed and scowling. "I wished I had a pistol. I knew if I shot anyone they would have taken me down in an instant, but I didn't care."

Eliza said, "You would have been a saint." She thought of his ghost, hovering over the auction market for the next hundred years.

Lucas said, "I fear not. I suspect I would have been considered a fool and forgotten. But then it was worse, going down the river, catching glimpses of the fields, and the men working themselves to death, a fellow with a whip never far behind. And not just men, strong girls, too. And plenty of chitchat on the boat about how well off they were, to have such kindly masters. And it was still worse in New Orleans. Huge market, the knowledge that, unlike in St. Louis, not a single Negro that you saw was free, and this prosperity all around you was produced by slaves. I must say that, when I left there, I was in no mood to ever return to that country. I'm glad the path back there is so long and arduous!" Lucas clenched his fists. Eliza, whose feelings about slavery had been proper but a little remote (like all of her feelings, as she now understood), since the only slaves she had ever seen were escaped ones, felt herself wind up, as if she was connecting with his feelings willy-nilly. She thought, but didn't say, "Is this love?"

The windows were brighter, and the rain had tapered off. Lucas did his customary thing, which was to change his mood. He said, "We need a walk. We need to find a whale in the bay to remind us that we aren't back there."

Eliza's shawl had gotten quite wet when she was coming to the Bear, but she had spread it over the back of an empty seat. She felt it; the wool had sucked up much of the dampness. She wrapped it around herself. She saw that Lucas had a thick jacket, also wool, the sort that would normally be too thick for Monterey, but usable this time of year. And it was lined with blue silk. He slipped his arms into the sleeves and offered her his elbow, and they walked out into the street, Lucas tipping his hat to Rupert in thanks for giving them a free meal. Before they stepped into the mud, Eliza paused to tie her bonnet. As she did so, she remembered that string, or piece of twine, she had found on that veranda. That place was where she should go, she thought. She didn't know if she could get Lucas to walk past that place, but she could try. In the meantime, the sky continued to brighten. And it was also true that Lucas's presence, no matter how much he laughed at himself, was calming.

There were a few ships tied up at the docks, and as the rain tapered off, men began carrying barrels and trunks down the gangplanks—slowly, of course, because the planks would be slippery, as were the docks. She walked with Lucas past the ships to where they could see the waters of the bay, still choppy and cresting, but also blue rather than gray. No whales, no porpoises (something Eliza had yet to see, though Jean had seen them). Plenty of birds, though, flying over the water and peering down, then diving. Pelicans, said Lucas. They were gray. Even as they were watching, Eliza saw three of them, one large, two not quite as large, pulling silvery fish out of the water and flying upward. Then another one, evidently old, staggered up the sand, stared at the others, and waited. Lucas pulled something out of his pocket—a bit of bread it looked like—and tossed it. It landed in front of the elderly pelican. The pelican picked it up and ate it, then looked toward Lucas as if acknowledging his kindness. Lucas laughed. Eliza decided that she had never seen such a man before. She glanced at him. He looked happy, as if the mere sight of the bay relaxed him, as it did her.

They watched the pelican for a few more minutes, as well as some gulls and guillemots, which looked like black pigeons. The surface of the water calmed even more. Eliza decided that her strategy would be to stroll along the docks, then ramble up the hill as if she was wandering about, and perhaps Lucas would follow her, as a dog follows its owner, sometimes going off but eventually coming back. It worked well enough, and the benefit was that the walk up from the water was easy, full of many pauses. Lucas bent down, looked at weeds and flowers, looked up at the trees, the leaves, but also the peculiar ways that the oaks twisted themselves, bent their limbs as if they had elbows. Other trees (cypress, Jean said) grew any which way. Ones on outcroppings looked like they were blowing in the wind even when there wasn't any wind. Others, more protected, seemed to be made of a bundle of narrow trunks that grew straight up, then spread into branches. Sometimes Lucas looked toward the sun, as if to gauge what time it was, but he didn't seem to care much about it. At last, they turned the corner and headed up the street where the house was. Eliza could see the roses, and the veranda, in the distance. The roses seemed to be flourishing. The house seemed to be still and maybe empty.

Lucas said, "I thought it would be muddier and more slippery. These hills are certainly steeper than the ones we had in Toledo."

Eliza said, "A good reason to have an agreeable horse."

Lucas said, "May he live forever."

They got closer and closer. Eliza cast her eye toward Lucas. She said, "Those are lovely roses."

He said, "My uncle brought some rosebushes from the East. They aren't doing as well as these. I suppose these get more light." Now he looked at the rest of the veranda, and then at the building.

Eliza said, "Lovely place."

Lucas said, "I do think these houses are less gloomy than those tall stone ones we have in the East. Even if the windows are small, you know the sunlight is out there. I can't say that's true in Toledo."

Eliza said, "So the weather in Toledo is much like—"

And then the door opened, and the man stepped out, the one with the pointed nose and the Adam's apple and the limp. He pulled the door shut behind himself, preoccupied with pulling on his black leather gloves. He was wearing a silk top hat. He limped toward the steps, and had just gone carefully down the first one when Lucas said, "Zeke! How are you?"

The man started, looked up, squinted, nearly stumbled down the second step; but then he pulled himself together, stared at Lucas for a moment, and said, "Ah, Lucas! What in heaven's name are you doing in this neighborhood?"

Lucas said, "Looking for whales."

The man lifted his arm and pointed down the hill, then said, in a good-humored voice, "Whales live in the ocean, boy! I suppose you never learned that back in Ohio. And who is this?"

Eliza was relieved that she had never seen this fellow in her establishment, that he didn't recognize her, but she was curious to see what Lucas might say.

He said, "This is Miss Ripple. She is from the Far North, as we are."

"Indeed," said Zeke. "Shall we have a contest? I know you grew up in Toledo; you know I grew up in Syracuse. Miss Ripple?"

"Kalamazoo."

"Ah, well, I beat you by just under a degree."

Eliza said, "What does that mean?"

"Do you know what latitude is?"

"No."

"Think of lines that go straight around the globe, beginning at the equator."

"I know what that is." Eliza thought of that sailor she had talked to a few weeks before.

"The North Pole would be at ninety degrees."

Lucas said, "Don't be a bore, Zeke." He handed Zeke two bits. "Here are your winnings, boy."

Then they both laughed, because Zeke was clearly ten years older than Lucas, or more. Zeke said, "Not my winnings, my compensation for a sour youth in Syracuse."

They continued up the hill, Zeke limping sometimes more than others, perhaps because the ground was uneven. Eliza didn't know what to think. Then she did know what to think. She feigned panting, not obviously, put her hand on Lucas's arm.

Zeke said, "Steep."

Eliza said, "I do prefer to stroll about the public cemetery. Do you know where that is?"

Lucas said, "I do not."

Zeke said, "Pleasant spot indeed. We interred a friend of mine there."

Eliza knew that if Jean were with them she would know what question to ask, but Eliza couldn't think of one. She felt her theories begin to slip away. The best bet, she thought, was to appear friendly and a little foolish, so, every time Zeke glanced at her, she smiled (modestly), pushed a curl behind her ear, and opened her mouth a little bit. She held up her skirt with the hand that wasn't on Lucas's arm. Zeke gave her a few pleasant looks, and she hoped that, someday, he would give her an opportunity to speak with him. She would say, she thought, that she had walked near his place once, and heard a ghost scream—had he ever heard that? She must have gotten an amused look on her face when she thought of it, because he smiled back at her.

When he had parted from them, Eliza said, " 'Zeke' is an odd name. I didn't even know a Zeke in my parents' church in Kalamazoo."

Lucas said, "Ezekiel Cornish." He laughed. "Or so he says. Lots of folks change their names when they get to California."

Eliza said, "I know."

11

Eliza was late getting to Mrs. Parks's, mostly because she had asked Lucas for another look at his horse, and then waved good-bye after he decided that the weather was good enough, and the mud was dry enough, that he could make his way back to his uncle's. He said, "The horse knows the way."

Eliza said, "I've heard that! Please, remind me!"

Lucas chanted, "Over the river and through the wood, to Grand-father's house we go; the horse knows the way to carry the sleigh through the white and drifted snow."

Then he mounted, leaned down, and squeezed her hand, and the horse did, indeed, know the way. Eliza watched its lovely dun haunches amble off.

She wanted to ask if Mrs. Parks knew anyone named Zeke, but she didn't have the time. Her customer was already in the chamber. Carlos had handed him a draft of beer and said that Eliza was "round back" (which meant in the outhouse). When she went into the chamber, she saw it was one of the sailors she had seen before, though she couldn't remember his name. She smiled, then ostentatiously washed her hands twice and her face once. The customer lay back on the bed, and Eliza began to remove her apparel piece by piece, leaving her bonnet until last, which seemed to amuse the customer, especially when she touched her head and pretended to be surprised that her bonnet was still there. As she did this, she remembered something about him—he was the one who liked hair—and so she sat down on the bed and let him take out the pins and settle her locks around her shoulders, then stroke it. It did the trick, and he had finished his business within a few minutes. Afterward, she allowed him to continue to stroke her hair (it was very pleasant), and he appreciated it even though stroking her hair didn't resurrect his prick for a second go. He accepted this, finished his beer, asked how she was getting along. Now she remembered that he was chatty, which she didn't mind. She told him about the elderly pelican.

The next day, she and Mrs. Parks went to a ceremony honoring the death of Mrs. Marvin. It was not held at a church—rather, at a private home on Pacific Street with a pleasant garden. Eliza had thought there would be a multitude of mourners, but there were perhaps twenty, including Jean, whom she and Mrs. Parks stood next to. Perhaps Mrs. Jacobs was there, but Eliza didn't know her. None of the other girls from Mrs. Parks's establishment were there. Eliza hadn't told Olive about Mrs. Marvin—she'd seen her only in passing since that day. The service was not religious; one man in a dark outfit did invoke the Lord, but he was the only one. Most of the mourners were women, and there were plenty of tears, but nothing was said about Mr. Marvin, about the nature of Mrs. Marvin's death, about what might happen to Less and More. The house was still shut up, but whether the sheriff was busying himself there, no one knew. Eliza did hear Mrs. Parks mutter something about "least said, soonest mended," but she did not agree with that. It appeared that Eliza and Jean were the only ones who were looking into the death: the city office that had summoned them to look at the body of that girl in the morgue hadn't come to either of them, though of course they knew where to find both of them, and there was no gossip about whether Mr. Marvin had confessed or not. All in all, Eliza and Jean agreed when they spoke for a moment afterward that Mrs. Marvin herself would have been extremely dissatisfied with the service.

Eliza tried not to hope that Lucas would show up again. He lived far away, he couldn't ride a horse very well, it was almost Christmas, there was plenty of rain—she gave him many excuses, and then she realized that her cascading thoughts were endangering herself. In the middle of a session on December 23 (they did no business on Christmas Eve Day or on Christmas Day) with an older man, one whom she didn't know but Mrs. Parks was familiar with, one who very kindly smoothed lavender oil all over himself before he appeared at the brothel, she couldn't remember if she had inserted her pessary, and became so distracted by the question (yes, Mrs. Parks would give her a dose of nutmeg if the worst happened, but, then, a dose of nutmeg could be dangerous, though just how dangerous no one knew) that the man finally pulled out without finishing and said, "I see that I have lost your attention."

Eliza made an effort to reinvigorate him, but failed to do so (he must have been fifty, at least). As soon as she stood up, she felt the pessary, so she had inserted it. She picked up the dollar coin that her previous customer had left for her as a tip, and put it in the fellow's palm as he was leaving, gently closing his fingers around it, then kissed him on the cheek, dearly hoping that he would say nothing to Mrs. Parks. She then vowed to stop thinking about the deaths of the girls, and even about Lucas.

Christmas came, and she did the best she could to read her book or wish whomever she saw on the street well. The weather was pleasant, and so the gift she and Jean gave themselves was to go back to the place where they had rented the pale gray horse and the dark bay, and rent them again. They let the horses stroll around the town—as far up as the Casa Munras, then into Iris Canyon. It was only in that very private area, when Eliza sped her gray horse up so that she and Jean were side by side, that she said anything about the thoughts that were preoccupying both of them. What she said was "I would have thought—"

Jean glanced at her, said, "I thought so, too. We were all prepared for what they might ask us. I can still go through that list of the things we saw as if it were written down. I saw that fellow a few days ago, when I was walking down Del Monte—the one who accompanied me in the morgue—and I looked straight at him. He looked back at me, but his face turned to stone, as if to say that Mrs. Marvin was none of my business." She sighed. "But think of it. When we saw that girl in the morgue, it was so long ago—the beginning of October— and as far as I have heard, there have been no killings since then, at least of our girls." She glanced at Eliza, "Of course, what those fellows do in the saloons, when they pull out their pistols and lose their minds, those aren't the same. I don't care about those!"

"Nor do I," said Eliza.

The town was quiet, except for the ringing of church bells, which the horses didn't mind. Eliza kept her eye out for this Zeke fellow, with no luck.

And then, two days later, she went so far as to walk down to that house where she had seen him and the young woman turn the corner. She hoped she might succeed in luring him into some friendly conversation. She did not see him there, but later in the evening, as she was making her way to Mrs. Parks's, she passed him on the street without noticing him (she was stepping carefully around puddles), and he tapped her lightly on the arm and said, "Ah, miss! I recognize you!"

Once again, he looked open and friendly. He was not handsome, but he was one of those, like Lucas, to whom a smile comes automatically, seeming to brighten his face as if a light suddenly shone upon it. Eliza said, "Sir! I recognize you, as well. Given your friendly countenance, I'm sure everyone does!"

He laughed. "They do, indeed, and the fellows who work for me recognize that they can touch me for anything they want, and are likely to get it." He laughed again.

Eliza said, "What is your business, then?"

"Building. Milling. Mostly oak, some pine." He looked around, pointed to a pleasant house with a large veranda that faced a garden rather than the street. He said, "That is our most recent construction."

Eliza saw her opening. "Perhaps you don't remember this, but I did see you a while ago, as you rounded the corner of Van Buren. You were with a young lady." She didn't say that he had pushed the young woman he was with, or that he had slapped her, but she did say, "I believe I heard her scream after the two of you were out of my sight." She did not stare openly at this Zeke fellow, but she glanced at him as she spoke. Not a single look of shame crossed his visage. First he looked thoughtful; then he opened his mouth and said, "Oh Lord! Of course I remember that well! She screamed because she felt something under her skirt, and then, when she stamped her foot and shook her skirt, a tarantula fell out! I nearly screamed myself! It was enormous! You know, those females live for thirty years! It was dark brown. It dropped out, righted itself, and then just sashayed up the street. Too big to step on, I will say."

Eliza laughed. There was something about the way he related this story that made Eliza believe him, and as she did, the manner in which he had pushed and slapped the young lady dissolved in her memory from a cruel sort of behavior to a playful one, the way a boy might push and slap his sister. And, indeed, every woman in the world had been pushed and slapped, including Eliza herself—angrily, by Peter; playfully, by her cousin Michael back in Kalamazoo, when she'd snatched a cookie from his hand. What were they, ten? She had pushed him and slapped him right back, then broken the cookie in two, handed him the larger half, and tickled him while he ate it.

They came within sight of Mrs. Parks's establishment. She wondered how he would respond to her climbing the steps, but all he did was wave, as if he knew nothing about what went on there. She wondered if he might show up one day and be amazed at what she did for a living.

Her customer that night was another sailor, slight but not young. He was neatly dressed; his cravat had no sweaty brown stains, and his trousers carried no mud around the lower edge. When he took off his sailor hat, it left no moisture or oils on her table. He was quiet to begin with—he greeted her, but didn't say a thing. Evidently, all he wanted to do was touch her, top to bottom, front and back, including the soles of her feet—but several of her customers were like that. Once he had finished his business, he lay back on the bed, heaved a deep sigh, and reached for the cherrywood pipe he had set on the table beside the bed, struck a match on the wall, and lit up. He said, "You know how long it's been since I even gazed at a lady? Forty-two days. I'm not saying that I mind going to Tahiti, and the trip back wasn't as bumpy as I feared, but . . ."

Eliza said, "Where is Tahiti? I've never heard of that spot."

The fellow said, "Well, you might say it's in the middle of the ocean, or you might say it's in the middle of nowhere. Our ship is a schooner. We brought back forty thousand oranges and a good quantity of limes, too. Let's see, it's about halfway between here and Australia. We were supposed to dock at San Francisco, but for once it was more turbulent there than in this bay. Smooth as silk here, for some reason." He inhaled from his pipe again, then said, "This time last year, I worked on a clipper. We were at sea a hundred and thirteen days, out from New York, down around Cape Horn. One day, the winds were so high we sailed two hundred and ninety miles. I thought sure we'd tip over, but we had such a cargo—let's see, butter, cases of glassware and soap, not to mention loads of shovels, vises, shoes and boots, pipes"—he held up the one he was smoking—"tobacco, fifty-three plates of boiler iron, two wagons, a keg of shot and balls, horseshoes, tons of coal, and some wine. Oh, yes, thirty-eight anvils! Those must have steadied us, but maybe they slowed us down. Long trip."

Eliza said, "Where is Cape Horn?"

"Well you might ask! Down at the tip of South America, and what a spot! It's as if the winds and the oceans are having a battle there. A ship is as likely to go down as to stay afloat. There are plenty of islands to ram into. They say the Antarctic is reaching out its little finger toward the Cape, but I never got further south and saw that." He shook his head. Eliza didn't say anything, and the man said, "I've been at sea twenty years now, and going around Cape Horn was the only time I ever thought that I might have done better to stay back in Grand Rapids and plant potatoes."

Eliza laughed. She said, "I grew up in Kalamazoo."

The fellow said, "You can sympathize, then."

Eliza said, "Indeed. But compared to almost everyone I've met since arriving here, we had a very easy journey across the Plains, and over the mountains, as well."

The man said, "Not many fellows from Grand Rapids end up on the ocean. If they like to sail, they are content with the lakes. But I was ornery, and so that's how it's been. I haven't seen my wife in two years."

Eliza said, "Where is she?"

"Boston."

Eliza wondered whether the sailor had ever been to Olive, but she didn't ask. The conversation ended—Eliza always knew better than to ask her customers about their wives, and none of them ever offered more information than this fellow had, unless their wives had died and they missed them. After he left, she slept in that room, as it was late and she didn't want to walk back to her place.

12

WHEN HER EYES OPENED in the morning, she saw that the fellow had left his pipe behind, on the table beside the bed, and the first thing she remembered about the interesting things he had told her was how many days he would be at sea—forty if he was lucky, a hundred and ten if he wasn't. It was now almost ninety days since she and Jean had seen that girl in the morgue. If the killer was a sailor, then he could certainly be at sea, perhaps coming back to Monterey any day now. After she dressed herself, she took the pipe to the front area, put it on Mrs. Parks's desk, and walked out the door. It was December 29. The house her parents lived in back in Kalamazoo would be up to its eaves in snow, but here the sun was sparkling over the bay and the air was pleasant. Eliza didn't quite know what a clipper looked like, but as she strolled along the edge of the bay, she did see two very large ships with three tall masts and evidently large hulls rocking in the water. She knew she would not see that sailor again tonight; the captains of the ships would be aching to make use of this good weather and get themselves and their ships out of the bay as soon as they could.

She walked for a ways along the shore, went out to the end of one of the points, as they were called. Normally, she didn't do this, because of the wind and her fear of scrambling among the rocks, but today she felt comfortable. She saw both birds and fish—the water was so quiet and clear that, from the highest spot on the point, she could see groups of fish, no doubt cod, swimming along, and did she see an octopus? Something shimmering with long appendages, but perhaps it was an illusion. She stared and stared, wishing Jean was with her, since Jean knew the names of many fishes and other sea creatures. She walked on. By the time she was ready for her first meal of the day, her belly was almost aching with hunger.

That evening, she had a new customer. He was waiting in the front room when she walked in the door, sitting quietly beside the window. He was wearing a top hat, had plenty of hair on his face, looked slender and, because of the way he leaned to one side with his ankle nonchalantly on his knee, graceful. Carlos looked toward him and lifted his finger, and the fellow followed Eliza into her room. She set her bag on the table. When she began disrobing, he did, too— after she took off her left boot, he took off his right boot, and so on. Finally, she was down to her chemise and her bonnet, and he was down to his shirt, his drawers, and his top hat, which shaded his face. Eliza went first, taking off her bonnet and unveiling herself. The fellow paused, and then paused a little longer, and then what did he do but toss his top hat onto the bed and strip off his whiskers. There he was, now a she—Jean! Eliza burst out laughing, and Jean did, too, and then they fell onto the bed and muffled their giggles with the pillows. Jean turned toward her, said in a low voice, "I know my business is going to pick up in a few days, once my customers are done with all of their holiday work, and anyway, today I saw a ghost!"

Eliza felt her eyebrows pop upward. She exclaimed, softly, "Where?"

"Point Alones! It was a ghost of you, and I saw you rise up into the sky and dissipate like the dew."

Eliza said, "You may indeed have seen me, as I did creep out onto the rocks."

"I didn't think that was possible!"

They both laughed again.

Jean said, "I would have crept out there with you, but I was carrying a load of salted fish back to my place, and I knew I stank to high heaven, so when I got back, as I had to bathe myself top to bottom anyway, I thought I would go through my togs and see what I haven't put on in a while. This is what I chose. Then, before I came here, I spent an hour walking along Alvarado, tipping my head and touching my hat to every woman I saw. It was amusing. And look what I brought!"

Eliza had noticed Jean's bag, but she hadn't recognized it. Jean jumped up, went over to where she had set it, pulled out some muffins and two oranges. They sat on the edge of the bed and ate their provisions while Eliza told Jean about the sailor from Tahiti. Jean said, "That's the only thing I regret about my proclivities. I would love to hear my customers rattle on about Tahiti and cattle and breaking horses and climbing a mast or two, but they don't. If they say anything, it is about their offspring or laundry or what they wish they might do if they weren't so burdened by their duties." Eliza glanced at Jean and sighed, then said, "Or how many of their babies didn't make it past infancy. Always the darling, it was, who died."

At the thought of this, Eliza lay back on the bedstead and held out her arms. Jean cuddled against her, and they sighed several times. Eliza suspected they were both thinking the same thing—how lucky they were to have been spared childbirth, child death.

Now the room was cool. Eliza pulled up the coverlid, and they slept, all night, neatly locked together. At one point, Eliza woke up, listened to Jean breathing, and thought how familiar that rhythm was, as familiar as if Jean were the sister she'd never had.

In the morning, as they dressed, Eliza related her theory that the killer might have been a sailor who left, and might someday return.

Jean said, "How do we get information about whether there are killings like ours up in San Francisco, or even New York or Tahiti? Ships go everywhere these days."

Eliza had no idea. She said, "Chances are, in those places, they care as little for girls in our line of work as they do here."

"Or less," said Jean. "What are there, about ten men for every seven women around here? When I dressed as a woman in Kenosha or Madison, which was always, I was overlooked or sneered at, or even pushed around." She tossed her head, said, "And I was, as you can imagine, one of those who pushed back. Here, at least, the ones who aren't stumbling drunk give you a smile or a tip of the hat. When I am togged up as a fellow, no telling what another fellow might do. That's why I carry my pistol."

And, indeed, Eliza could see a bulge in the pocket of Jean's trousers. As a female here in Monterey, even after those killings, after Peter's killing, Eliza had walked about as she wished, only sometimes feeling edgy; perhaps she was a fool. They left the establishment. Jean was hungry, but Eliza was not, so they parted at the door of the Bear, and Eliza went back to her boarding house. When she entered, Mrs. Clayton gave her a smile. She said, "My dear, please, do me a favor. I have tried out a new way of making biscuits. These are termed 'scones' in Scotland, I believe. At any rate, I need you to judge their quality."

Eliza followed Mrs. Clayton into the cooking area, and ate one biscuit and one scone. She said, "Ma'am, they are different, but they are both delicious. I can't choose!"

Mrs. Clayton said, "I do believe that is the best possible response!"

It was only when she got to her room that she thought of Jean's remark about seeing her ghost. In order to be a ghost, you had to be dead. Jean was so matter-of-fact about that, Eliza thought, that Jean either didn't worry about being dead or, perhaps, thought death was just another adventure. Had Eliza's mother ever spoken about ghosts? Not that she could remember, but another idea crept into her mind, and that was that ghosts were the dead people who had not been chosen, who wandered about because God had not given them the opportunity to go to heaven. And then she thought, No wonder they never speak, no wonder they flit away. Eliza shook these thoughts out of her head, then sorted through the few possessions that she kept in her room. She sat on her bed and picked up her book. Between laughing with Zeke and spending the night with Jean and her own courage and fear, which ebbed and flowed like the waves at Point Alones, she felt like she didn't know a thing anymore, not, as some of her customers would say, a d——ned thing.

Because it was so late in the year, the sun went down long before she was due at Mrs. Parks's establishment. Often, she strolled about on the way, but the sunny day had turned into a very cloudy evening, so gloomy that Eliza was tempted to take a taper with her, as if that would stay lit in the slightest breeze. She put off leaving, but she hated to be tardy, so, at last, she huddled into her warmest shawl and headed out. There were a few fellows here and there, but most of them looked down in the mouth, and chilled, too, hiding a cigar in one of their hands to keep it from getting too moist. Two horses that passed her had their heads down, their ears flopped. Whatever the pleasures of the Yuletide season were, Eliza thought, they had now vanished.

She passed the place owned by the Cooper fellow, thought of how she had enjoyed peeking through the fence at his horses, and then, as she rounded the corner and looked back, hoping to hear a whinny, she herself saw a ghost. It was white but not white—more like one of the sea creatures she had seen from the point—shiny and translucent—standing on the second-story balcony. Eliza glanced around, hoping there might be someone who would tell her she was wrong (or right), but she was alone. After a moment, she shook her head and decided that it was not a ghost but, rather, a lady in some sort of silk gown—silk, especially gray silk, sometimes looked eerie—but then the being turned and ran, or floated, along the balcony, and then leapt over the railing onto the roof of the building right beside it, floated up the roof and into the air. Eliza shook her head, closed her eyes and opened them. The street was deathly quiet, and Eliza thought that if she were not wearing her bonnet her hair would be standing up on end. Given what she had been thinking earlier, she never wanted to see such a thing again. She did not run to Mrs. Parks's, but she walked quickly, and when Carlos opened the door, having heard her footsteps, she threw her arms around him and laid her head upon his chest. Her heart was pounding; she could feel it against his chest. Carlos put his arm around her and guided her into the front area, then went and got her a cup of tea. Mrs. Parks was nowhere to be seen.

Her customer was a bit late. Unusually for California, he was a heavy fellow, more like older men she had seen in Michigan, who had plenty of money and servants, whose acres were worked by poorly paid, gaunt fellows. For a moment, Eliza didn't know why she was thinking this—the man didn't look unpleasant—but then she remembered a friend of her parents', who visited sometimes for supper. He ate everything on the table and complained about the rain or the dry weather or one of his workers' breaking an arm during the threshing, and why couldn't he keep at it—he still had the other arm! Even Eliza's parents, who were strong believers in hard work and servile compliance as the path to heaven, would cough, exchange a glance, send Eliza out of the room for some made-up reason. She changed the subject by saying, "Ah, sir! Such a gloomy night out there! I'm a bit surprised that you braved the darkness!"

The customer laughed and said, "I did not brave it—my horse did. I huddled on the seat of my trap with my hat pulled down and my bandanna over my nose. I will say for him that he doesn't mind the weather. He has a roomy shack in his paddock, but even in the rain, he's always out in the grass."

Eliza said, "Did you come by way of the Cooper place?"

"I did. I know Cooper. The place looks dark. They must be off somewhere." He said nothing about a ghost.

By now, he had stripped down to his shirt, which covered his belly, and he was sitting expectantly on the bed, which sank under his weight. He waved his hand, and Eliza knew what he meant. She began to remove her gown. Though she did not ask his name, she suspected that he was some important fellow around town. Perhaps, later, she would ask Mrs. Parks.

The man leaned toward her, grabbed the hem of her gown, and lifted the skirt. Eliza stood still, facing away from him as he gazed, though what he might be able to see in a room lit only by a single taper she could not imagine. As a rule, the customers waited until she was bare. There were plenty of customers who enjoyed looking at her rump more than they enjoyed looking at her bosoms, but they preferred that she dance around, or sashay here and there. The man dropped her skirt, and she continued undoing the bodice, then slipped her arms out of the sleeves, dropped the gown, and stepped out of it. The man reached out his hand, said, "Let me hold it."

She handed it to him, and he bunched it in his lap, stroking it as he stared at her. Eliza should not have found this either strange or disconcerting—the things men did in the privacy of her chamber were often surprising—but her state of mind was uneasy. He raised his finger and summoned her. She stepped up to him, glanced over at the door of her chamber; it was not cracked. Carlos and Mrs. Parks evidently did not see this fellow as sinister, though whether he was a regular customer, Eliza did not know. Now he put his hands on her shoulders, tossed her gown out of his lap, and pushed her down. She saw that she was to service him orally, which made sense, given his bulk. And, indeed, because of his bulk, his prick was hard to find, even though, as she saw when she found it, it was fully fleshed out. She leaned forward, pressed her forehead against his belly, and did her best. This sort of thing was not quite new to her, but Peter had never desired this, and so she had had no coaching. As she exerted herself, his hands on her shoulders pushed and released in a sort of rhythm. She knew that he was about to complete himself when he pressed so hard that both of her shoulders gave her a flash of pain. Fortunately, she did not bite down in shock. His prick fell out of her mouth and she staggered to her feet and went to her basin, spit the leavings into it, and poured herself a glass of water. When she turned around, the fellow was flat out on the bed, panting. It took him a while to recover, long enough for her to put her gown back on, though not to fasten all the hooks, and then he said, "Miss!" and beckoned her. She approached him. As it turned out, she had to help him roll over, and then help him to his feet, which was no easy task. She walked out of the chamber while he put on his clothing. She did not expect a tip, nor did she want one. She went over into a dark corner of the front area and waited for him to leave.

It was not until the morning, which was sunny but windy, when she was sitting over her morning meal, that it occurred to her that this fellow might be the one, because thinking of him, she sensed even more strongly a kind of resentment or even rage that he held in, this time successfully, but perhaps unsuccessfully in the past. The question was how he got those remains out of town, but, yes, he had a trustworthy horse and a decent carriage. He could have carried them out at the darkest time of the night, after he'd done them in, then driven them into the countryside, tossed them.

She got up from her morning meal, paid for it, and went to find Jean, which wasn't at all difficult, since she was strolling down Pearl Street, in her woman's garb, with her chin slightly raised, as if she were holding a lorgnette and looking down upon everyone else on the street. Eliza went up to her and tipped her head. They both laughed, and headed toward the graveyard, which would certainly be green and sunny. They traded a few commonplaces, and then Eliza said, "I know who it might be."

Jean's head swiveled toward her.

"He came to me last night. Perhaps forty-five or forty-six, evidently prosperous. The top of my head came about to his earlobe, so he's tall enough, but bulky. Tremendous paunch. Couldn't do his business in the usual way because of that. I had to go to my knees and service him that way."

"You've not done that before?"

"I have, but never with anyone who so resented having to do it that way. It was as if he thought his whole difficulty was my fault, and the longer I serviced him, the more irritable he got. When he finally finished his business, he nearly broke my"—Eliza thought "shoulders," but said—"neck."

Jean's eyes popped open. "He put his hands around your neck?"

"In truth, he did not, but he did hurt my shoulders, and it was as if he was longing to throttle me. Maybe that's the way he did those girls in."

"Did the one we saw have marks? I don't remember whether we saw any."

"No one told us what to look for, so perhaps we didn't see what was there." She paused, put her hand on Jean's arm. "It was more than that. He was, he was . . . Yes, he was like a storm system that hangs restlessly over your town, and then some event triggers a twister, and it passes through some neighborhood. Everyone wonders why the twister came to them—whether it was God or the Devil, but only the storm system knows, or doesn't know. Maybe, if you asked the storm system, it would say, These things just happen!"

Jean laughed.

Eliza said, "He was so bulky that I had to roll him over and help him out of the bed. He couldn't even lift his own weight."

"How could he get away with it, then?"

"Get away with what? In the middle of the night, which was when we were doing this, you can get away with just about anything."

"I mean, if he can't hoist himself, how can he hoist a corpse?"

They had come to that spot on Pearl Street where you could see the top of a hill in one direction, trees in the other direction, and, straight ahead, blue sky and a wisp of a cloud floating along. The air was both salty and sweet. Eliza said, "Why wouldn't he just kick it along in front of himself, or drag it by the hair?" But she admitted to herself that Jean had a point. She said, "He did have a gig and a reliable horse. That's how he got them into the countryside."

"What sort of gig?"

"He said it was a trap."

"Is it four-wheeled or two-wheeled? And both of those are open to the sky. I don't see how . . ."

Eliza closed her eyes, said, "The first thing I should have done when I left the place was go down the street to where the customers leave their gigs, but I didn't." She shook her head.

Jean said, "If he is as bulky as you say he is, and rides about in a light trap, we should keep our eye out for him. Those sorts of fellows are rare around here."

"That's what I thought. Too many sailors, too much salted fish to eat, not nearly enough potatoes!"

They both smiled. But Eliza could see that Jean was unconvinced. Yes, the fellow was a mean jackass, and perhaps he aspired to do what Eliza suspected he had done, but was he likely to get away with it? DuPANN prodded her a bit: more investigation was essential. She sighed, then said, "Listen to us! We are thinking that no one knows who killed those girls, that this is a mystery to the sheriff and the vigilantes. But this guy did not tell me his name, and he is evidently prosperous, and neither Mrs. Parks nor Carlos gave me any warning about him. Maybe there are some folks who know he did it, who helped him get away with it, and don't plan to do anything about it."

Jean said, "That could easily be true even if that wasn't the fellow."

Eliza nodded. "Do you find all of this confusing? I feel like so many thoughts are swirling around in my head, over and over, that I *can't* find the logic trail. Sometimes I think it's there but I can't see it, and other times I think it isn't there. That not even the sheriff can put all of this together, so why should we?"

Jean said, "Because we have to. So what if we are beginners and have no idea what we're doing?"

13

THAT EVENING, Mrs. Parks was at her place again. When Eliza came toward her, she lifted her hand and said, "My dear, I've been down with something, maybe the grippe, and perhaps I shouldn't have come out of my quarters, but at any rate, do avoid me, as I don't want to give it to you." She walked toward an open window, and Eliza followed her. As she stood there, she described the fellow and her experience. Mrs. Parks wrinkled her brow and shook her head. She said, "You don't know that one, because I told him he couldn't come here about two years ago. Then he went off somewhere, certainly up to San Francisco, and maybe elsewhere. When he came back to this place before Christmas, he appealed to me in a kindly manner to allow him to return, and I thought for a bit, and decided that you were the likeliest of the girls to be able to handle him. I apologize, my dear."

Eliza said, "What is his name?"

But Mrs. Parks shook her head. Evidence that the fellow had something to hide.

Just after that, Eliza's customer showed up, another sailor. Eliza went to wash her hands and face, then went into her chamber, where the fellow was already sitting on the bed. He was handsome—high cheekbones, attractive eyebrows. When he opened his mouth and spoke, she couldn't understand a word. She said, "Pardon me?"

He laughed, said, "Hoo are thoo cheepin'?"

Eliza shook her head. The fellow laughed again, said, "Whale, A was jis testin' ya. A hale fra Orkney. Ya kna, up an tap a Scotlund." He held out his hand and Eliza stepped toward him. He paused a moment, then began very gently unhooking her bodice. When he was about half done, he stood up, undid his own trousers. He looked as though he was enjoying himself, but suddenly he started and glanced around, first over toward the window, then up toward the ceiling. Eliza glanced toward the window and saw that a branch of one of the cedars outside was tapping against it. Then the building creaked.

The sailor exclaimed, "Da ya sae it, thin?"

Eliza said, "You mean the storm?"

The sailor nodded, did up his trousers again, said, "Mae ship wos ta bae laevin' in the marnin', boot it mae bae the cap'n'll bae want'n to bate the starm ut a the bye. Sarry ta lave ya, miss." He put a coin in her hand and ran out the door. Eliza could hear him running across the front room, and then that door slammed. A moment later, Mrs. Parks appeared.

Eliza said, "He ran for his ship. When did this storm come up? The weather was fine when I was making my way here."

Mrs. Parks said, "I looked out my window maybe a quarter of an hour ago. A tree down the street was shaking, and the one right out my window was still as a rock. That's the weather around here, especially in the winter. Of course, snow is worse, but I admit there is something calming about snow."

For the first time, Eliza realized that Mrs. Parks had a background, too. She said, "I never asked you! Where did you live before you came to California?"

"Albany."

"Where is that?"

"Upstate New York. Oddly enough, it's the capital." She shook her head. "The year I turned ten, we got ten feet of snow—that's how I remember it. I was five feet tall, ten years old, ten feet of snow. It seemed like magic."

Eliza did not ask what year it was that Mrs. Parks had turned ten. She said, "I thought things were bad in Kalamazoo." Then she said, "Someone told me you were from Baltimore."

"My goodness! I wish! My family did live for a year in Bethlehem, on a farm by Beckers Corners. That's south of Albany, a couple of hours if your horse is old and slow." Mrs. Parks looked at her, dipped her head to one side, and smiled. For once, her smile looked a little sad. She said, "For most of us, things were bad in those places. That's why we made this trip, settled ourselves here." She sighed.

Suddenly, Eliza wondered if she was really *Mrs.* Parks. No one had ever mentioned a Mr. Parks. But she knew she couldn't ask about that. She said, "I, for one, am infinitely glad to be here, no matter what." She knew that Jean was, too, and she hoped that Mrs. Parks was. She held out her hand and opened it. Mrs. Parks bent down and looked at the coin, but didn't take it. Then she looked surprised, and said, "How amusing! It's a five-franc French coin! I believe the French themselves call it an écu. I haven't see one of those in years, and I have no idea what you might spend it on unless you find yourself in Paris, and in that regard, you never know what might happen, my dear! Keep it safe, and tell yourself it's your good-luck coin!" She smiled, turned, walked out, closed the door.

Eliza stared at the coin, then set it on the side table, beside the taper, and continued to look at it as she did up her hooks. Even if Mrs. Parks showed up in the next few minutes with a new customer (unlikely, since the storm was pressing harder on the building, and causing frequent creaks), that customer would want to undress her, or watch her undress herself, and would not care to be reminded of any customers that might have preceded him. Eliza intended to go back to her place, but then the storm got rainier, though not gustier, so she lay down on the bed, her hand on the coin, blew out her taper, and fell asleep.

She did wake up in the middle of the night, almost breathless, then realized her bodice was still hooked, so she unhooked it down to her waist and fell back to sleep. The thing she appreciated about that when she woke up was that it only took her a few minutes to hook herself up again, pull on her boots, and get out the door.

The rain had ceased, but the wind was, indeed, howling around the corners of the buildings, and the trees were bending this way and that. The wind would seem to be coming from one direction—say, west—and then seem to spin around and pour in from the north. Because of the bay, Eliza had found it difficult to understand directions in Monterey. Yes, Jean told her, the Pacific was the Western ocean, but the south end of the bay was J-shaped, and the town was at the bottom of the J. The wind whipped into the bay and then swirled around. At least, she said, they were protected by the mountains from the east winds, which were hot and dry. Eliza wrapped her shawl, held it tight, and made her way to the Bear. When she got there, she had to stand a bit—evidently, plenty of the citizens of Monterey were taking refuge from the storm.

Eliza was glad to be there—the building was adobe, sturdy, no creaking, and, once she was inside with the door shut, no howling. Thinking of Jean, she looked around, and as she did, she recalled her theory about the bulky fellow, but he was not present, either. She unwrapped herself, folded up her shawl, put her hand into her pocket to make sure she had remembered her lucky coin, and also to make sure she had the funds for her hotcakes and maybe a piece of ham or a slice of bacon.

It was then that she saw a fellow gazing at her. He was looking her up and down, quite frankly assessing her. Eliza knew that her demeanor in public did not give away her business. She was as demure as a girl could be. This fellow, she was certain, had been a customer (a forgettable one, to be sure), or had seen her in Mrs. Parks's establishment, perhaps when he was going to another of the girls. She glanced at the men to either side of him. One had scooted slightly away from the fellow, and the other was staring at his cup of coffee. Neither seemed to be his friend. But, given the crowd, and the fact that every seat had to be taken, and that this was the sort of place where friends did not dine together but, rather, prepared themselves for the day's work, there was nothing unusual about that.

The fellow kept scanning her, if anything even more intently. Eliza returned his favor and placed his face inside her memory, detail by detail, bottom to top—neatly trimmed beard and mustache, thin lips, flat cheeks, no visible cheekbones, sharp nose (that was his best feature), prominent ears, thin hair, formerly straw-colored, as her mother would have said, now heading for gray, receding hairline, thin gray eyebrows. As for the eyes, he was the kind of fellow who had squinted so much over the years that his actual eyeballs were hardly visible; his eyelids covered them, so no telling if they were brown or blue. The hat hanging on the back of his chair was brown, with a wide brim. His fingers, as he picked up his biscuit, were long and thick; apart from the intensity of his gaze, that was the most threatening thing about him. The hands of the bulky guy had pushed down on her, but his fingers had been short, not long. He would not have been able to throttle her, but this fellow would be able to do so. She understood that, for most of her life, this thought would never have come into her head, but now, because of her curiosity, it did. Though she wanted to look away, she made herself register one more detail—after one bite of his biscuit, he was dissatisfied, dropped it onto his plate, and smashed it with his fist hard enough that the fellow to the right of him scooted even farther away. She turned her head, vowing to keep her eye out for the fellow, possibly by lurking around Mrs. Parks's establishment before she was due to arrive, to see whether the fellow showed up. Then she had a better idea: Jean would do the lurking, since, even when she was busy, most of her business was earlier in the day than Eliza's business.

When, at last, it came time for Eliza to be seated, she was put at a table facing the door. Rupert brought her a muffin and a slice of ham without being asked. The fellow walked out. He was moderately tall and had big feet, as he had big hands, and there was mud on his boots. His jacket was wool, no patches. Probably not a wealthy fellow, but not impoverished, either. Eliza imagined that he was stuck in Monterey, without the funds to get to San Francisco, no gold dust in his pocket, and much annoyed that he was, say, forty, and had run through all of his options for making a tycoon of himself. And, if he was eating at this place, no wife nearby, and no doubt living in a boarding house.

By the time she had finished her meal, the rain had stopped, but the fog was like a cloud lying over the town. There were many puddles to step around, and not many people on the street, but even so, Eliza was now so filled with curiosity (and a substantial breakfast) that all she wanted to do was reconnoiter. (Who had she heard use that word? Ah—it was Peter. He had said exactly that when they arrived in Monterey and put up at her boarding house.) She took the long way round to her place. She went down toward the wharf. All the ships were out of the bay except one rather large one that was rocking in the surf, so her customer the night before wasn't the only sailor who had had to flee. Then she went toward that fellow Zeke's house, around the corner, up Scott, past Van Buren to Larkin, then up Larkin to Madison, back around Cooper's place, then down Pearl toward the bay. She was pleased that the hills didn't bother her anymore, and her walk was invigorating, but she did not see that fellow, nor did he show up that night. The customers she had for the next two nights were ones she knew well enough, who did not act suspicious. Nevertheless, she was herself more cautious—traded a few glances with Carlos, kept her door slightly ajar so that Carlos might hear whatever was going on, inspected each fellow's pockets and any bag he might have, asked him a little more than usual about how he was feeling and what he was doing.

Her favorite came after the New Year, a boy whose father was educating him. He was nicely dressed, with a thick mop of dark hair that seemed to pop out of his hat when he took it off. He was not shy but not pushy—above all things, he seemed curious. He said that his family had a cattle ranch down south. They had ridden into town— two hours it took, though they had stopped for a rest and a bite to eat about halfway up the hill. The boy only came to Monterey three or four times a year, but he enjoyed the ranch—flat enough for cattle but up against the hills, where he liked riding his horse.

"What color is your horse?" said Eliza, "I hope a palomino."

The boy laughed. "I saw one of those. No, Ripley is a bay, but he's got four white socks and a star that actually looks like a star. Pa's mare is a dappled gray. She's twelve and still dappled. Pa says that never happens, but it did with her. Her name is Lizzie."

Eliza laughed.

Evidently, the boy's father had told him a good deal about his business, because he was eager to try everything—to touch Eliza everywhere, to look at all of her body parts, even at all of her apparel (thank heaven, she had laundered her knickers and her chemise two days before). He held her feet, stared at them, ran his fingers over her toes. It might have been creepy, but the boy was so curious that it was not. It was Eliza who had to direct him toward his business, by toying with his prick and then lying back and opening her legs. For-tunately, he was young, and so his prick didn't die when he became entranced by the mere sight of her crotch. He entered. Eliza made him go slowly. When he finished, he sat on the bed and gazed at her. Finally, he said, "I so want to be a doctor! You, miss, are the first woman I've ever seen. Ma says I am not to look at my sisters, and they wouldn't let me anyway. But how might I treat ladies who are ill if I don't even know what they look like? You go to school for being a doctor, but what I've heard is that all you get to see are cadavers."

Eliza said, "What is a cadaver?"

"A dead person that's been embalmed and stored away. I mean, some of them have been swiped from their graves, you know, from that section of the graveyard where the graves are close together and the markers are small. Rich people don't like that sort of thing to happen to their relatives. But I don't see why not. We eat cows and male calves and sheep and lambs, and even horses. Why shouldn't human corpses be of use?"

Eliza said, thinking of her parents, "What about the Resurrection?"

The boy's eye twinkled, and he said, "Well, you may believe what you wish." Then he said, "Might I come to you again? Maybe during the day? Pa says that some fellows come here during the day. If there was plenty of light, I could watch you move around and bend over and jump and some other things. I so want to see how your bones and muscles rearrange themselves! I look at myself, but I can only see myself from above. It's tremendously annoying!"

Eliza laughed.

The boy said, "Well, it is!"

She gave him a kiss on the cheek and said, "Where would you study medicine in California?"

"Oh, I would have to go back east somewhere. My grandparents are in Chicago. There's that kind of school there. But I have a question that Pa hasn't answered. How can I do this to you without giving you a baby?"

"I think you should ask your mother."

"I have, but she won't say a word about it. My sister slapped me when I asked her."

Eliza explained what a pessary was, and then told him what little she knew about nutmeg and Queen Anne's lace. The boy stared at her, fascinated, then said, "I wonder if a doctor can specialize in treating women?"

Eliza said, "I guess you will find out." Then she said, "Of course you may come back."

It was rather late when the boy left. Eliza glimpsed his father in the front area. She was wide awake and might have gone back to her place, as there was no rain, but instead she straightened up her chamber and went around back, to make use of the outhouse. As she passed the window to Olive's room, she heard a laugh. Olive had two tapers lit—one on either side of the bed, and the fellow sitting on the bed was the heavy one who had frightened Eliza. He seemed to be in a pleasant mood, and, as best she could, Eliza tried to make out Olive's visage—any sense of dread or worry—but Olive looked easy and amused. She said something that made both of them laugh again. Eliza breathed a sigh of relief.

Back in her room, Eliza blew out her taper and sat quietly, looking at the tree and the sky through the small window. It was now 1853, and if anyone had told her two years ago what the next two years were going to show her—Peter, then that trip across the prairie and up the mountains, then the beauty and strangeness of Monterey— she would not have believed them. But then, thinking of that fellow in the Bear, she wondered if she would survive until 1854. There was plenty to be learned in California, and Eliza was ready to learn all sorts of things—the names of birds, the adventures of the people she saw around her and of her customers, the ways that the Spanish folk looked at things, what it felt like to climb the mountains or ride a boat in the bay. But one thing she had learned was how quickly death comes, and for most of those to whom it comes suddenly, whether by drowning in the bay or being shot in a bar, there is nothing they can do about it. What came much more rarely, and was therefore a little scarier, was true friendship, of the sort she had with Jean. The tree rustled in the breeze, and Eliza made her New Year's resolution— that, even though she could be one of those who didn't make it to 1854, she did plan to keep her eyes open and do her best to get there.

14

A WEEK LATER, when Eliza got to Mrs. Parks's establishment, Mrs. Parks saw her through the doorway to her own quarters, got up, came out, and handed Eliza an envelope. It was from her mother, and it was not addressed to her or to Mrs. Parks, but to "Sheriff, Monterey, California." The envelope was creased and dirty. Eliza took it to her own chamber, stared at it for a few minutes, then opened it and read the letter by the light of her taper. It read:

To the Sheriff of Monterey,

There is a girl running around in your town. Her name is Eliza Cargill. She has been there for maybe a year and a few months. Her husband was Peter Cargill. I understand he was shot sometime around Thanksgiving (if they celebrate that in Monterey) a year ago. My husband says to say that we do NOT know if she is running around. For all we know, she could have been shot, too, as your town is a very violent one. However, I am at my wits' end, which is why I am writing you, just to see if our girl is still alive. She is a little over five feet tall, with blue eyes and straw-colored hair, somewhat on

the thin side, with pink cheeks and full lips. I have no sketch
of her, or I would send it. She does have a birthmark. It is on
her right shoulder, and is shaped like a teardrop. If she has
been killed, someone might have noticed that. I don't know
what else to say.

Yours truly,
Mrs. Joseph McCracken
Bulkley Street
Kalamazoo, State of Michigan

When Eliza came out of her room (her customer still had not
arrived, but at this time of year, they often did not, because of the
weather and other difficulties), Mrs. Parks was already there, with a
piece of paper, a quill, and an ink pot. There was no place to write in
Eliza's chamber, so Mrs. Parks showed her into her own, sat herself
over in the corner, and picked up her knitting. Mrs. Parks's room had
five tapers, all of them lit—quite a luxury, but the room did smell a
bit of whale oil.

Eliza wrote:

Dear Mother,

   I have seen the letter you wrote to the sheriff. I have to
say that it fills me with regret that I have not sent you any-
thing for a year, and that that has given you so many worries.
I don't know quite what to do to show my remorse, as I don't
feel that I can make up for the pain I have caused you. How-
ever, I do want you to know that I am indeed alive, and also
well, here in Monterey. Nothing has happened to me, and I
am able to live and eat. Monterey is an extremely pleasant
spot, and I have no intention of leaving here.

She paused for a moment, hearing footsteps in the front area, but
the fellow went into Olive's room. She continued:

One thing I need you to understand is that I have given up the name of "Cargill" in favor of the name "Ripple." The reason I did this is that Peter had no virtues as a husband. Although he behaved well enough in front of you when we were living in Kalamazoo, he was never hesitant about pushing me around or slapping me. You wanted me to have children, but he did not, at least not then. You have always told me that it is the wife's job to act as a helpmeet to her husband, but Peter considered me more of a servant, or even a slave, especially to his desires. As I look back, I would say that I wish I had fled our marriage before he was shot, but I did not, as I did not know what to do with myself. When he was shot, I was relieved, and I continue to be relieved. Now that I am out in the world, at least this world, I see that most men are kinder and more respectful than he was.

You may be shocked at this, but I feel that if we are to be in contact with one another, if only by letter, you need to know the truth. You may continue to write me, and I will continue to write back, but I will only write what is true, not what you wish to hear.

I do hope that this letter finds you and Pa well and that it relieves you of your worries.

At this point, Eliza paused, thinking of her mother saying, more than once, that it was better for a woman to die than to live a sinful, disobedient life. She shook that thought out of her head and went on:

I will sign off now. I hope that you have a pleasant year, not too much snow, followed by a lovely spring. I look forward to hearing from you again.

Love,

Eliza

Yes, she paused over the word "Love." She might have used "Best regards." But now that she had written the letter, now that she had revealed her thoughts with honesty, she thought that there were things that she loved about her mother. Eliza had been whipped, but not hard enough to produce welts. She had never been locked in her room or denied a meal. If she talked back or misbehaved, her mother would pray with her, but she always put Eliza's plate of stew on the table, or even her slice of pie. Her mother's bark had been worse than her bite, and her father knew this, too. And she was very good about contributing to whatever charitable cause that her church put forward. Eliza folded the letter, set the quill on the mat beside the ink pot. Mrs. Parks looked over and set down her knitting. She said, "I do have an envelope." As if she did not trust Eliza to mail the letter herself, she took it, addressed the envelope, and put it into her pocket. She said, "Don't worry about it, my dear. I must go to the post office tomorrow anyway."

Her customer showed up late, a little agitated. Eliza was in the front area, replacing her taper. She did not announce herself—it was Mrs. Parks who did that. The fellow said he had left his horse down the street and run to the establishment. It was not a long way, but he was panting. Mrs. Parks gazed at him, invited him to sit down, brought him a glass of water. He continued panting, put his hand on his chest. He was not a bad-looking fellow, somewhere in his thirties, but he was remarkably thin, even for Monterey.

Eliza saw Mrs. Parks and Carlos exchange a glance. Mrs. Parks said, "Mr. Reilly, perhaps you are suffering from the grippe."

He shook his head, then finally got out some words. "Madam, I don't know what it is. Came on, won't go away." He coughed twice into his sleeve.

Mrs. Parks said, "When did it come on?"

"In the dry season. I thought it was dust, and the rains would get rid of it, but not so far." He coughed again.

Mrs. Parks said, "I apologize, sir, but I dare not expose my girls to whatever it is that you are suffering from."

The man put his face in his hands; Eliza went along the back of the room, through a darker area, to her chamber, and closed the door. Some minutes later, Mrs. Parks knocked, pushed the door open slightly, and said, "The fellow is gone. Looks to me like he's gotten a case of the consumption. I haven't seen him since September, according to my records. He was in good health then."

Eliza hadn't realized that Mrs. Parks kept detailed records, but of course she did.

Mrs. Parks said, "You may leave or stay, as you wish. Before you decide, you should know that I purchased some excellent muffins today."

She smiled. Then she said, "My dear, did your mother always talk about fresh air and how it would cure all your ills?"

Eliza said, "Praying was what she depended upon."

"Well, in my experience, neither of those works. Care, sharp observation, and cleanliness work much of the time, but not always." She sighed.

Eliza sat quietly for a moment, then said, "I wouldn't mind reading that book you were reading the other day. You looked as though you were enjoying it."

"Ah. *The Scarlet Letter.*"

Mrs. Parks smiled, left, came back with the book, and handed it to her. She said, "I am so glad that those days are behind us."

When Eliza arrived the next day, though, Mrs. Parks was in a much more sour mood. She beckoned to Eliza, and when Eliza was standing close to her, she said, "Where is Olive?"

Eliza shook her head and said that she had no idea.

Mrs. Parks took a deep breath, and said, "She's missed her customers for two nights in a row! I wonder what she thinks she is doing!"

Eliza immediately thought of the heavy fellow, and then of those girls. She said, "Has she ever failed to show up before?"

Mrs. Parks shook her head, then said, "But she has seemed restless lately. She is a pleasant girl, but she isn't as reliable as you are, Eliza." She got up and walked into her room, letting the door bang shut.

Eliza was alarmed, and as the night progressed, she got more alarmed. She did her best with her customer (thank heaven, only one), and then, after he left, she waited until Carlos dozed off in his chair, and, as quietly as she could, went to the chamber where Olive did her business and looked around. Everything was neat. In the corner she saw the beginnings of a new embroidery project, possibly another fire screen. Feeling that she didn't dare stay there any longer, she went back to her chamber, leaving the door to Olive's chamber about four inches ajar. When she left the establishment the next morning, Olive's door was still four inches ajar.

After getting as much sleep as she could, she went looking for Jean, but she couldn't find her, so she walked around by herself, first to the market, then up the street that she thought she remembered Olive mentioning. There were two buildings that looked like boarding houses on that street, and a woman came out of one of them. Eliza thought of asking that woman if she knew Olive, but she didn't—she was too afraid that maybe she looked like a whore, and if she even asked about Olive . . . She shook her head. It was a little suspect, even in Monterey, for a young woman to walk around alone: the women who could walk around alone without anyone's noticing were the older ones, the ones who looked like they'd had plenty of children, and whose mops of hair were tied up in buns, with some hats put on any which way.

It was a pleasant day, considering the time of year, but the more she walked around, the more worried she got, thinking that she should have told Olive about her investigations with Jean, and warned her. Then she thought of what Mrs. Parks had said, that gossiping was like opening a door, and she thought that was true, too. The thing about an investigation was that it had to be secretive in order to work, even if the investigators fumbled around and didn't know what they were doing. And thinking this made her think that maybe Mrs. Parks was truly innocent of any involvement in the killing of those girls—her sharp anger was a sign, Eliza thought, that if Olive was one of the victims she didn't know anything about it.

Eliza also looked for the heavy man; she remembered that he drove a trap, so she looked at all of the men driving carriages, but none of them looked like him. One man, in the plaza, looked a little like him from behind, but from the front looked much different—high forehead, sharp cheekbones, mouth that ran from side to side. She exhausted herself walking and went back to her boarding house, where she took a long nap.

The first thing she asked Carlos when she got to Mrs. Parks's place that evening was whether Olive had returned. He shook his head. They both sighed. Mrs. Parks didn't seem to be around. Fortunately, Eliza's customer was one she knew, friendly, always left a dollar coin on her table. He was short and slight; what he seemed to appreciate about Eliza was that she, too, was short. How he made his money he never said, but he seemed to have some—he was well dressed and owned his own place, a small house on Van Buren. He was one of those fellows who seemed to be satisfied with the lives they had made for themselves. He had never said where he'd come from, and Eliza was tempted to ask, but she didn't. She knew she was distracted when she was doing her task, and she could tell that he knew it, too, since he left her only a fifty-cent piece, but at least he left that.

The next day was Saturday. Eliza woke up in despair, fully convinced that Olive had been done in. She decided to go to the Bear and stay there as long as she could, in hopes that Jean would show up, and they could come up with some sort of plan. As she walked there, one thing she wondered was why she should be so frightened thinking of Olive as one of the missing girls—she was much more frightened about Olive, it seemed, than she had been about herself or Jean. But then she thought that, of the three of them, Olive was the one who was unprepared—who didn't know what was going on and was therefore more vulnerable. And then Eliza regretted that she hadn't come up with a way to tell Olive what she knew, and warn her. Her despair turned into shame.

She almost passed the front entrance to the Bear, but the door was open, and the fragrance of bacon and muffins reminded her. She sighed and went in. Rupert took her to her usual table, seated her with her back to the door.

Which was why, as she was picking up her muffin, she didn't see Olive enter, and so she nearly fell out of her chair when Olive took a seat across the table from her, and smiled. Then they both looked around, but no sign of Mrs. Parks (and she never came to the Bear anyway).

Eliza said, "Tell me!"

Olive said, "I left a note, but I guess someone opened a window, and it blew off that table and slipped under a chest. I should have anchored it with something."

"But where?"

"Up north a ways, not far from the shore."

Eliza ate more of her muffin, waiting, and Rupert came over. Olive ordered the herring and some hotcakes. Olive said, "He was upset that I couldn't cook."

"Who?"

"Alfred, his name is. He comes once in a while and always asks for me. I thought I liked him, or, rather, I thought he would do if he would get me out of this business, and maybe he thought I would do, too, and we got along well enough, but when we woke up the morning after he took me there, he just stared at me until I said, 'What?,' and he said, 'Aren't you going to make me something?' and I said, 'I didn't bring any stitching supplies with me,' and he said, 'I mean something to eat—eggs, anything.' And then I told him that I don't know how to cook, never have."

Eliza hid her alarm, and said, "Did he seem angry?"

Olive shook her head. "He did seem disappointed. He asked me if I knew how to milk a cow, but I don't know how to do that, either."

"I thought you said you lived on a farm."

"We picked the fruit, but Papa milked the cows."

Thinking of Lucas, Eliza said, "Up north? You mean by Santa Cruz?"

"Not that far outside of town. There's a spot up there that looks like prairie, but really it's mostly sand, as far as I could tell. Not many trees." Olive shrugged.

"Did you feel . . . did you feel in danger?"

"Not until I got back to Mrs. Parks and she raked me over the coals! I do worry that if I do something wrong again she will fire me, and then what?"

Eliza squeezed Olive's hand and went back to eating. Finally, she made up her mind and said, "You didn't give a thought to those girls?"

"Which ones?"

"The ones who were . . ."

"That's so long ago! If that was still a danger, I'm sure we would be warned by the sheriff or someone. No one talks about those girls anymore."

Eliza didn't know whether she admired Olive's fortitude or feared her ignorance. But she was thrilled to see her again.

ON SUNDAY, a sunny day, Eliza was sitting on the front porch of her boarding house, enjoying the blue sky and the calls of the birds. Jean came walking up the street, in men's togs and a new, wide-brimmed hat. It was black, the brim on either side turned up; the hatband was colorful and looked as though it had been crocheted. When Jean stopped at Eliza's stoop, she leaned her elbow on the railing at the bottom of the steps, crossed her legs, and cocked her head to one side. Then she pretended to remove a cigar from her lips and said, in a deep voice, "Shall we go for a ride, dear girl?"

Eliza said, "Yes, sir!"

Jean lifted her chin and pretended to put the cigar between her lips. Eliza was wearing her day gown. She had been planning on going to the market for some provisions, so she had funds in her pocket and her bonnet in her lap. She gave Jean a few more moments to entertain passersby, and then they walked to the stable where they had rented the horses. On the way, Eliza told Jean about Olive's disappearance and return, doing what she thought Olive would have done—making it into a funny story. Jean listened, but didn't say anything. When they got to the stable, the horses they preferred were already taken, so they looked over the others. Jean chose a chestnut mare, and Eliza chose a paint gelding, bay and white; on the nearside, the white part formed itself into a question mark, and, indeed, the horse's name was Query. It turned out to be an appropriate name, because he liked to go first, he looked here and there, and his ears were constantly flicking, as if to say, "What's that?" But he wasn't spooky, perhaps because he was so observant.

Jean said, "Do you want to go somewhere we haven't been before? Up along the shore? Into the mountains?"

Eliza said, "I think that everywhere in Monterey is a place we haven't been before, even if we have. We should go to that bridge, the spot where we saw that girl. We should have gone there after we found Mrs. Marvin. I remember we talked about it."

Jean nodded, but then said, "You didn't want me to do it on my own, but I seriously contemplated it at one point. I even went looking for a horse, but I couldn't remember how long it took Less and More to get us there, or even how to get there."

"It took most of the day. Do you have any idea how to get there now?"

Jean shook her head. "I don't even have a sense of how far it is. There must be someone we might talk to, now that . . ."

They both sighed.

Jean said, "Okay. We shall let the horses decide, because we need to get to know them. They can do as they please this time, and we will try to figure out how we might get them to the bridge the next time."

Eliza thought she might lighten things up a little, and said, "Maybe they'll go to a saloon. Back in Michigan, I think in Paw Paw, there was an old horse—twenty, they said—who had quite a penchant for drinking whiskey, and his owner let him do it. They say that it started when he colicked, but he liked it. The owner would give him whiskey with apple cider mixed in."

But these horses turned away from the area where the saloons were, and headed up the hill toward the graveyard, past the Casa Munras. Sometimes they would trot and sometimes they would walk, but it was evident that they were pleased to get out. Eliza expected Query to turn right and head up that narrow canyon where she liked to walk, but he kept going until he came to a grassy open area that Eliza hadn't seen before: no ravines, no trickling creeks, but rolling and sunny. They halted. Jean and the mare came up beside her, and Eliza said, "This is a lovely spot! Have you seen it?"

"Indeed, no. Must be someone's rancho. No cattle, though."

Eliza said, "But it is so large! And close enough to town. How would you manage to fence in a place like this? I can't imagine."

They let the horses graze here and there; then they cantered along the edge of the forest to the east. Query had a decent canter, Eliza thought, even for someone riding sidesaddle, as she was.

She was panting a little when they pulled up, and Query was sweating. Then, as Eliza was adjusting her bodice and blowing her nose in her kerchief, Jean said, "What's that?"

She turned the mare, Nutmeg, and went back toward one of the larger oaks—one of the kinds they had in Monterey, which seemed to lay their branches on the ground and spread out their own tiny forests. The leaves of the tree reached almost to the grass, and Eliza saw nothing through them. Jean jumped off Nutmeg, handed the reins to Eliza, and pushed her way in. Eliza's heart began to pound. Maybe five minutes later, Jean reemerged, her hair covered in leaves and her boots muddy. She came over to Eliza, held up her open hand. Across her palm lay a thick lock of hair. Jean said, "I cut it off with my knife."

Eliza said, "The entire body is in there?"

Jean said, "On her side, curled toward the trunk of the tree."

"How long do you think it's been there?"

"I'd say since before Christmas."

Eliza prepared to dismount. Query was looking toward the tree, ears pricked. He snorted. Jean said, "Don't." But Eliza was determined, and even though she stumbled slightly and stepped on the hem of her gown when she dismounted, she found a small opening in the drooping branches and pushed her way in.

Eliza had seen corpses in coffins, had seen that girl in the water, but nothing she had seen was like this. Much of the fabric that made up the gown the girl had been wearing had been eaten, or torn away, or rotted. The spine, the ribs, the shoulder blades were all prominently displayed. The skin was dark and leathery. Eliza crept over to look at the face. No eyes, no teeth, no nose, mouth wide open as if screaming. The hair was dark, but Eliza had no idea whether that would have been its original color. It was the hand that was familiar, the right hand, the one Eliza could see, missing the baby finger. She remembered that, when she first began working for Mrs. Parks, one of the other girls had been missing a baby finger. Eliza had stared at the hand but never asked how the girl lost it. Now she moved closer, stared at the bony neck; whatever evidence there might have been of a choking was gone. She could see nothing along the girl's back, either—no bullet hole, no stab wound. Her head was intact. Eliza pushed the shoulder with her knee. It jiggled, and the arm fell toward the trunk of the tree, and there it was, a line that began a few inches below her armpit, ran along her rib. It was a thin line, not precisely horrific-looking, but, then, sometimes a bullet hole wasn't horrific-looking in and of itself. Eliza was sure it was a stab wound, and suspected that if they rolled the girl on her back there would be more. But she didn't touch the girl, knowing that they had to leave her as intact as they could.

She backed out from under the tree. Jean had taken the horses into the grass, and was holding them, letting them graze. Eliza walked over to her. She said, "I think I saw a stab wound. On her right side. I don't quite see how that would kill her, but maybe there are more. I didn't touch the body."

Jean handed her Query's reins, then said, "It isn't the stabbing that kills. It's when the blade is pulled out, and the bleeding starts. She might not have been dead when the fellow ran off, just too weak to move."

Eliza said, "If they were stabbed, we can stop wondering about the twine." Then, after a long moment, she went on, "I do know who she was. When I first started at Mrs. Parks's place, her chamber was on the other end of the veranda." She said nothing about the finger.

"When was the last time you saw her?"

"I think the summer, but Mrs. Parks keeps a record of everything. I'll ask her."

Jean said, "You do that. I'll go to that fellow who showed us the girls in the morgue."

They didn't say much on their walk back into town. When they got to the stable where the horses were kept, Jean went back to swaggering and deepening her voice. She even smacked the fellow who was minding the horses on the shoulder and then handed him four bits and said, "Give these broncs some extra provisions today. They were good!"

The fellow said, "Yup. Got 'em from one of them guys from back east somewhere. Bought himself a rancho, spent too much money on it, went away with his tail between his legs. Knew something about breaking nags, though. Told me these were running wild. He went out and roped 'em when he first got here, in the winter, when the grass hadn't started growing yet, and they were pretty much eating the bark off the trees. They didn't mind some hay and some buckets of oats."

Eliza said, "I'm guessing that's why Query keeps his eye out. They've got to do that when they're running wild."

"Sure enough," said the fellow, and Eliza did hope that he would spend the four bits on the horses and not on himself.

Although it was Sunday and it was Eliza's free day, she walked by Mrs. Parks's establishment. All dark, even Mrs. Parks's own chamber. She shivered and kept walking. It had never occurred to her to wonder where Mrs. Parks spent her time or ate her meals (it had to be somewhere, because Eliza had never smelled any cooking odors in the place). The thing she most wanted to do was to tell Mrs. Parks what happened. When she got to her boarding house, she even thought of telling Mrs. Clayton what they had found, but she didn't think Mrs. Clayton was prepared for such a thing, so she went to her room and rocked back and forth on her bed, trying, unsuccessfully, not to picture the details of what she had seen.

15

THE NEXT DAY, when Eliza showed up at Mrs. Parks's establishment around noon, Mrs. Parks was sitting on the veranda, gazing at some flowers she had planted that were now shooting up, with
her quill in one hand and her other hand lying across her notebook,
so that the page wouldn't flap in the wind. She said, kindly, "Good
morning, my dear. Do look at the shoots. Narcissus. Budding out. My
favorite. And do you know that Olive returned?" She chuckled. "A
relief, I must say."

Eliza said, quietly, with her eyes down, "Ma'am, do you remember the girl who was missing a finger?"

Mrs. Parks's eyes snapped in her direction, but she said, almost
calmly, "Of course, of course. That was . . ."

And then Eliza remembered, and they both said, "Mary."

Eliza said, "I was wondering how she lost that baby finger."

Mrs. Parks seemed to steady herself a bit before she said, "As I
remember, she herself didn't know. It happened when she was an
infant."

She went back to looking at her notebook, evidently wishing that
Eliza would continue into the establishment.

But Eliza said, "When was the last time you saw her?"

Mrs. Parks looked around, stood up, almost pushed Eliza into the front area of the building. She said, "My dear, why do you ask?"

Eliza was a little intimidated, but said, "I—I think she was one of the girls. One of the girls who were done away with."

Mrs. Parks closed her eyes, pressed Eliza farther into the front area, as if any window might contain a spy. She said, "I thought that. I thought that in the early winter. In the summer, after about a year with me, she decided to go up to San Francisco, thinking, well, I don't know what she was thinking, but in October, she returned, and told me that it was frightening and chaotic up there, and even though she had made some money and some gold dust, she felt ill at ease. I told her that she could take up our profession here again, and she said she would return, ah, on the following Monday, as we were having this conversation on a Saturday, as I remember. At any rate, she never appeared again. I didn't think about it for a few days, but, given her sincerity, I began to worry, and I did go to the sheriff. I went to him four times. And he put me off every time."

Eliza glanced around, whispered, "Do you think it was a customer who did it?"

"I hope not. I try to be careful. Carlos is good at spotting the angry ones and the drunks. I also listen to the gossip, if I can, about who around town is mistreating his wife or his children. If I hear something about someone, we put that fellow off."

Eliza said, "That is why my life here is more peaceful than it was when I was married."

Mrs. Parks kissed her on the cheek and said, "My dear, you aren't the only one."

"Do you think that Mr. Marvin really was the one who killed Mrs. Marvin?"

Mrs. Parks said, "Chances are. He drank a lot. My idea is that she got herself into a pickle, going after him when he was deep in the bottle. She had something of a temper, as I've heard, and I think she raised the rolling pin at him, and he grabbed it from her and struck her with it. Then she fell and hit her head, and he drank some more and passed out. By the time he came to himself, she was dead. He waited a bit, but he did go to the sheriff and confess. He said he couldn't really remember the details, though."

Eliza said, "There's a—what do they call it?—a big mesa, not too far into the mountains. Maybe an hour's ride, but a leisurely hour. You know how some of the trees around here have branches that droop to the ground? There was one of those on the west side of the meadow. She was under there."

Mrs. Parks put her hand to her forehead and said, "I will go to the sheriff and tell him that Mary Summers has been discovered. Did you touch it?"

Eliza shook her head.

Mrs. Parks said, "I will go right now. I will behave most respectfully, I will not insist, I will not pretend that this girl, our Mary, is of any importance at all." But her eyes were flashing and her cheeks were flushed. Eliza hoped for the best.

Mrs. Parks turned, but then turned back, as if reading Eliza's mind. She said, "You know, some Quakers, along with other women, held a convention almost five years ago now, in a town in New York, Seneca Falls, where they demanded that women be allowed to vote. That'll be the day. But we can hope."

For the next few weeks, everything took on that late-winter feel— too much darkness, not much to do, not even much to talk about. Three times, Mrs. Parks caught her eye as Eliza walked into the establishment, and then shook her head and frowned. Eliza knew each time that this meant that the sheriff, or whoever Mrs. Parks was talking to, had waved her off. Eliza stayed away from Olive, because she didn't want to be tempted to tell her about Mary, but she kept an eye out for her. Olive had paid attention to Mrs. Parks's warning, and was always in her room when Eliza showed up, waiting for her customer and working on her stitching project. Eliza and Jean talked about riding up to the mesa to check on the body, but it took a while for them to get there, and when they finally did, the remains were gone. No one had called them to the morgue or asked them any questions. The only events about town concerned the ships in the bay—whether they could make land or not, whether they could offload their cargo, whether the sailors could get a break from the storms and the surf.

During those weeks, Eliza did look at her customers with more suspicion, but they were all friendly regulars—even one of the sailors, who turned out to be the English fellow, Ralph, who had shown up three or four times in a row and asked her to marry him. When she reminded him of that, he laughed and said that he had found a wife who'd been willing to move to England from Nova Scotia—she still had relatives in Liverpool and was pleased to return to them. Of course, he now hadn't seen her in sixty-two days, but he would be there in the spring, the real spring, with blooming hedges, early roses, lavender. However, he was, indeed, "pleased ta say Miss 'Liza agane," and he left her not only a dollar coin but a book he had been reading on the ship, *David Copperfield*. It was much thicker and more intimidating than *The Scarlet Letter*, but Eliza expected to enjoy it, and then give it to Jean.

Another fellow who showed up, one night when the weather had been pleasant for almost a week, was Lucas. It had been so long since she'd seen him that Eliza had lost hope. She did believe that he liked her, but she did not believe that he had the skills to ride his horse from Santa Cruz to Monterey, or, indeed, to drive a gig. She walked into the front area of Mrs. Parks's establishment just before dusk one day, and there he was, standing by the door, evidently looking for her. He said, "Miss Ripple! I'm famished! Ten hours on my horse, and I lost my sandwich on the way!" He put his arm around her shoulders and turned her gently toward the door. Eliza looked back. Carlos was smiling. They went to a different eating establishment, farther up Alvarado Street, and ate a lovely beef pie.

Eliza said, "How's your dun?"

"Forever patient. I swear that, when I pulled out my sandwich and then dropped it, he glanced at me in disbelief."

Eliza laughed.

"I will say that I walk less and trot more. He's good at teaching me."

"Did it really take you ten hours to get here?"

"Well, let's say seven."

"And your uncle's rancho?"

"Prospering! He's doing dairy now, as well as beef. He bought six Jerseys from a fellow a little ways up from us, and I milk them in the evenings. Joe's son, Marcos, milks them in the mornings. It's rich milk, and he sells it, but what he wants to do is make cheese. He loves cheese and he misses all those types he used to enjoy back east."

Eliza said, "I do miss the curds. We ate those in Kalamazoo. My mother was very fond of whey."

Lucas gazed at her, and she knew he was expecting her to tell him something about herself, but she didn't want to say a word about her mother's letter or the girl—Mary—or her suspicions (and at this thought, she looked around the eating establishment, but saw no one who seemed odd or threatening). She said, "I wish I had more to relate. I enjoy my walks about town. My friend Jean and I go for rides when the weather is pleasant. The other day, I rode a horse who sports a question mark on his left side. The owner named him 'Query.'" She was sorry, given Lucas's open kindness, to have to keep so many secrets.

Lucas said, "My uncle is getting quite obsessed with this railroad issue."

Eliza said, "What is that?"

"They want to build a railroad all the way to California, but they can't decide whether to go through the Northern states or the Southern ones. They've been going back and forth for years, and my uncle knows this would help his business. But, of course, the slavery issue is standing in the way. Evidently, the fellows from the Southern states won't let the government hand out any funds if it isn't done their way. You know the Missouri Compromise, of course. They want to get rid of that as the price for incorporating the land the railroad would cross. This fellow—Senator Douglas, from Illinois—wants there to be a law that any state that comes in can decide for itself. New Mexico is a slave state and Utah is a slave state. It wouldn't affect California, but it might affect other parts of the West. I'm sure those folks who wanted to split us in two, right across this bay and then east to the border, would like us to be surrounded by slave states." Lucas's eyes flashed; then he said, "You know, the parallel, thirty-six degrees and thirty minutes, that divides the North from the South, runs right through this town. Look at us! That line could be crossing this very table."

Eliza said, "Do you mean latitude, what your friend Zeke was talking about that time we ran into him?"

"Exactly!"

Eliza tried to imagine such a thing, and then said, "But they failed in that, and now we have a lengthy border. It would be easy for slaves to escape into California, hide out in the mountains. Maybe that's a solution—lure the plantations to the Far West, and then welcome the escapees."

Lucas said, "My guess is that there's going to be a war."

"Between?"

"The slaveholders and everyone who disagrees with them. My uncle's ready for one. He's ready to take a ship back to Maryland and go stand on the balcony of the Senate or the Congress and scream bloody murder."

"Why is he so . . ."

"He's from Ohio. He saw and helped escaped slaves for twenty years before he came to California. Part of the reason he came was to get away from it all, no matter if he prospered or not, and now he's prospering, and he wants to make his feelings known, which isn't all that easy from the mountains of California."

Eliza thought of Peter, who had never said a word against slavery; he didn't want to own a slave, but it wasn't, he thought, his business. Her parents had said that the rewards and punishments for slave owners would be found in heaven. And who was that escaped slave? Ah, Josiah Grant. Her parents had liked him, liked his handiwork—he made shoes—more than they had liked Liam Callaghan. They had never termed themselves abolitionists, though.

Their server brought two lemon tarts, treats that Eliza had seen but not tasted. The conversation died down. Her tart was very good. After Lucas paid for their meal, they got up and walked back to the establishment, detouring for a look at the dun, who, as always, greeted Lucas with a nicker.

Their night in her chamber was by turns relaxing and exciting, and it had to be said that Lucas managed to present her with his prick three different times, and every time, she welcomed it. Still, when he left, he made no remarks about when he might return and said nothing about sending her a letter. Afterward, she didn't know if his visit made her sad or happy.

Nevertheless, that evening, she was in a good mood when another customer showed up. He asked for Eliza, and since her first customer was late and possibly would not come, Mrs. Parks brought him to her. He was that fellow she had seen in the Bear, who had looked her up and down in a judgmental way. He seemed pleased to see her, patted her on the hand and smiled. Eliza stepped back and glanced at Mrs. Parks, but Mrs. Parks left. Well, she did trust Mrs. Parks. The fellow sighed and said, "Ah, my dear. I need a bit of a rest. I have been talking all day. You never realize how tiring it is until you are not allowed to stop."

Eliza ventured, "Are you a lawyer, then?"

The fellow laughed and said, "I see that you understand lawyers." He laid down his bag, took off his jacket, hung it up, then sat on the bed. He rubbed the palm of his hand across his forehead and took a few deep breaths. After a moment, he said, "I am thankful you are healthy. The grippe is going around, as you may know. A lawyer can't come down with the grippe, or he will talk himself into a hoarseness that might never go away."

Eliza stood quietly. His demeanor now was calm and friendly, and she could not decide if he remembered her. Perhaps, she thought, it was just a habit he had as a lawyer, to seem to be glaring. She let him recover. At one point, she went to her pitcher and poured him a glass of water, which he took with a look of thanks. Finally, he slapped his chest, let out a couple of deep breaths, and said, "I suppose we should get on with it."

Eliza said, "Sir, if you have no appetite for this, Mrs. Parks will repay you whatever you have given her."

Now he surveyed her more carefully. In the eating establishment, he had seemed to denigrate her, to threaten her. But now she thought as she gazed at him, tired and depleted as he was, wasn't that the business of lawyers? And especially in California, where, she supposed, there were few lawyers and plenty of business.

She said, "Where did you learn the law, if I might ask?"

"Illinois. Chicago, to be exact. In a law office there." He sighed.

Eliza said, "You must know of this railroad issue."

"Indeed, if two lawyers argued about something as long as the Senate has argued about the railroad, they would be disbarred. Our legislators have never seen a calamity that they could not embrace."

"One of my"—Eliza paused—"other customers thinks there will be a war."

"Of course there will be. What would prevent it? I would think that, working in the business you do, you would see men for what they are."

"And that is?"

"Brutes! As soon as a man sees a rule, he strives to flout it, whether he sees it in the Bible or a constitution. That prohibition runs around in his head, and he can't stop it. Then there he is, transgressing, and you ask him why, and he says that something was unfair or he was provoked, but what he really means is that he kept having thoughts, and then those had to turn into action, and he could not stop them." The fellow looked out the window. It was dark, the trees were still, and the stillness seemed to enter the room. Eliza turned her eyes away from the lawyer and gazed at her taper, flickering, casting light and shadows, light and shadows.

He turned to her and said, "How old do you think I am?"

Eliza didn't know whether to be honest, but at last she said, "Forty, perhaps?"

He smiled, said, "How tactful of you! Almost fifty." And he did look it, Eliza thought, not much gray hair, no corpulence, but a lot of wear. He said, "You would call me restless. My parents did. I was born in Connecticut—New Haven. My father taught Greek at Yale College. But I wasn't satisfied with New Haven, so when I was fifteen I left for New York, to work as a bank clerk, and when I was nineteen I went to Philadelphia, and when I was twenty-five I took my wife and our child to Chicago, where I studied, then to Charlottesville, Virginia, but my wife couldn't do with a slave or without one, and we moved on to Indianapolis. When I set out for California, I thought the promise of this place would at last fulfill me, but it has not. My existence is still a round of one thing after another, the same one thing after the same other, and again and again."

Eliza said, "What does your wife think?"

"Who knows?" And that was all he said.

Now there was a long silence, and Eliza didn't quite understand what to do. The fellow was not threatening her, and she had no idea if he wished to get down to his business or not. Just then, she saw the door to her chamber open slightly, as if Carlos, too, was wondering what was going on. Thinking that Carlos might be looking to her for a sign, Eliza shook her head, then she heard him step away from the door, but he did leave it ajar.

Suddenly, the lawyer said, "Girl, sing me a song."

Eliza was surprised, but she had grown up singing songs (another of her mother's virtues), and so she began, "'Early one morning, just as the sun was rising, I heard a young maid singing in the valley below. Oh, don't deceive me, oh, never leave me, how could you use a poor maiden so?'"

When she got to the third verse, she saw that the lawyer was looking at her with a pleasant smile, and she began to undo her bodice and then her skirt. When she stepped out of her skirt, he was ready. He took her hand, brought her to the bed, and finished his business. Then he said, "If music be the food of love, play on."

She sang another, "The Bonnie Banks of Loch Lomond," and he nodded along as she did so. He said, "Your voice is light but clear, my dear. Thank you."

Just before the taper burned down, and so sometime in the middle of the night, he got up, put his clothes back on, and walked out. Eliza fell asleep singing more songs to herself. If she couldn't remember the words, she hummed the tunes anyway.

16

THE LAWYER TURNED UP again the next night. He asked for her specifically, and as soon as he entered her chamber, Eliza saw that he was in better spirits. He hung his jacket neatly on the hook beside the door, then set down his bag, also neatly. Eliza had seen this before, in some of her relatives—the desire for everything in a room to be proper. And then they exhausted themselves wiping down, dusting, setting things straight. The lawyer said, "My dear, that song was running through my head all night and all day."

Eliza said, "Which one?"

"The one about Loch Lomond. I know that one. But there is another version that the Irish made up. It goes this way. 'Red is the rose that in my garden grows, And fair is the lily of the valley, Clear is the water that flows from the Boyne, But my love is fairer than any. 'Twas down by Killarney's green wood that we strayed, And the moon and the stars they were shining. The moon shone its rays on her locks of golden hair.' " He reached over and touched one of Eliza's locks. " 'And she swore she'd be my love forever.' " He tossed his head. "There are other verses, but they always slip out of my memory."

Eliza said, "Sir, your voice is light but clear."

Just before he smiled, a look of annoyance flickered across his face, and Eliza saw that he didn't like to be teased. However, his spirits continued to be good. Eliza felt a slight uneasiness, as she sometimes did when a customer seemed to take too much of a liking for her. There were girls who, unlike Eliza with that English sailor, did welcome the repeaters and did end up married to some regular customer—that had been Olive's hope, after all. Often, the penalty for that was having to move out of Monterey to avoid gossip, which perhaps Olive would not have minded. Eliza did not intend to move out of Monterey. And, of course, it was well known that, however many fellows used the establishment for some relief from their wives, it was only in Jean's establishment that women got relief from their husbands. Eliza had never met a man who, she thought, might say, "Go ahead, my darling, continue with your profession and contribute your earnings to our resources."

The lawyer was less fatigued and more eager to get down to his business, though still more leisurely than sailors or young fellows. Just before they got started, he went to the basin and washed his hands—very kind, Eliza thought—and when he had dried them, he laid out the cloth neatly on the table. Eliza decided that he was pleasant enough—he didn't insist that she parade around the room unclothed or allow him to touch some odd place, like her foot, over and over. When they were finished, she sang another song, of her own accord, "Whiskey in the Jar"—one she had heard Liam Callaghan sing several times back in Kalamazoo. " 'As I was goin' over the Cork and Kerry mountains, I saw Captain Farrell and his money he was countin', I first produced my pistol and then produced my rapier, I said, "Stand and deliver, or the devil he may take you!" ' "

The lawyer said, "I've heard that one! Very tuneful melody."

When she was finished, Eliza waited. She could see no sign that the lawyer wanted to do his business again, but also no sign that he was about to leave. She sat down on the end of the bed and stared at the taper. He cleared his throat once or twice and glanced at the window. Eliza yawned, covered her mouth. He sighed. Eliza reached for her kerchief on the table, blew her nose. He didn't move. At last, she stood up, said, "I must go to the outhouse." She did not put on her gown, but she did put on her knickers and her chemise. She said, apologetically, "I should have remembered to do this before." The lawyer said nothing. But as she walked toward the door, she stumbled on a turned-up edge of the rug and fell toward the fellow's jacket. She grabbed it, righted herself. Fortunately, she did not rip it or pull it off the hook. When she regained her balance, she sorted the jacket so that it might hang just as he had left it. She did not look back to see if he was watching her. And then, as she opened the door, she realized that she had felt a dagger in the pocket of the jacket—straight, hard, tapering to a point, not sharp, no doubt encased in leather, but large. As she made her way in the dark toward the outhouse, she remembered Mary's stab wound, under her arm, between two of her ribs. Eliza lingered in the outhouse, wishing there was some way she could speak to Jean right then.

When she got back to her chamber, the lawyer was gone, the taper was burned out, and the front area was dark as well. Eliza wished to go to her boarding house, because that was where she was most likely to see Jean first thing, but even as she thought of making her way to her place, she imagined the fellow lurking around corners, waiting to stab her. It was the perfect time of night to drag her somewhere—down Pearl Street, perhaps, and toss her into the bay. How long was that walk? Fifteen minutes, if you were not carrying a body. She went back and forth for a bit, but even as she was doing so, she was putting on her gown and her shawl and her boots. Soon she was out on the street, making her way. She felt as though her ears were pricked, switching back and forth, like Query's ears. And, of course, she glanced here and there, too. But she got to her boarding house safely and quickly, went to her room, pushed one of the tables against the door, fell onto the bed, and slept in her gown.

In the morning, Jean was not on the veranda when Eliza looked out the door, but she was coming down the street, dressed in women's clothes and carrying a parasol. When she arrived, she rested her back end primly on the railing of the veranda, lifted her nose, and sighed a few times, as if this whole area was simply beneath her. Eliza, even given her mood, couldn't help laughing. Jean raised an eyebrow in her direction. Eliza said, "Darling, you need to go on the stage."

Jean said, "It would be cheap to have me, would it not? I could play any character, male or female, old or young, and perhaps two at a time. Did you ever see a play called *The Drunkard*? Our Temperance Society put it on back in Kenosha. There was one female character called 'the maniac.' I thought I could play her and ham it up quite nicely, but I was only fifteen when I saw it." She made a maniacal face. Then she said, "Or the drunkard himself. Watch this." She staggered down the street and back again. Eliza's mood improved, and she thought she might be overreacting to the lawyer, but when Jean resumed her pose, she said, "My dear, do you think a dagger is a common weapon around here?"

Jean's head spun around. She said, "Not as common as a pistol, or a rifle, or, for that matter, a club, I would guess. Easier to hide, but harder to employ."

Eliza said, "Especially if someone was attentive to your every move."

Jean nodded, then said, "You've found him."

"Perhaps."

"Did you tell Mrs. Parks?"

"I should. She would prevent his coming. But what good would that do? He would go somewhere else."

"But she could report him to the sheriff."

"She could, but she's told them about that girl we found—one of our girls, as it turns out—over and over, and they've done nothing besides take away the remains."

"They know who did it, then," said Jean.

"I *suspect* they do."

Jean straightened up and cocked her head up the street. Eliza went down the two steps. They walked along, as if relaxed, but Eliza knew that they weren't. She said, "He's a lawyer." Then she said, "He's come two nights. The first night he seemed exhausted; indeed, he said he was. But the main thing I remember is that when I asked him about what his wife thinks about this habit he has had of picking up and moving over and over, he said, 'Who knows?'"

"That's odd," said Jean. "Truly. What's his name?"

It was then that Eliza realized that, unlike many of her customers, he hadn't told her his name, nor had Mrs. Parks. She said, "I'll ask Mrs. Parks. But if she senses that I have a complaint, she'll turn him away. Or, rather, she'll tell him that she doesn't have anyone who suits him as well as she would like, and she'll get back to him when she has a new prospect. That's what she does with the local fellows who don't fit in. The sailors and the itinerants, she just has Carlos kick them out."

Jean said, "You're right. You have to lure him on, and we have to keep him to ourselves."

Eliza said, "Tell me what you mean."

"I mean that we don't know enough. The more he comes to you, the more you suit him, then the more he will reveal. He isn't going to threaten you in front of Mrs. Parks, or Carlos. He has to be secretive."

Eliza said, "He's a lawyer! He talks all the time!"

Jean glanced at her, then said, "All the more reason to think that he's well practiced in being secretive."

Eliza nodded. "Is he going to confess to me that he killed those girls?"

"No, he's going to be tempted to invite you somewhere."

Eliza instantly thought of Lucas, who had invited her somewhere both times that he had come, but she didn't say anything to Jean. Jean stopped walking right in front of Colton Hall—probably right where they could find the lawyer if they looked for him—put her hand on Eliza's arm, and said, "If he tries to lure you out, put him off. I will meet you every morning at just this time, and we will talk our way through this."

Now they went to the Bear to have their meal. It was not crowded, and Rupert pretended not to recognize Jean, to show her one seat and then another and then another, as if she was difficult to please, and then he showed them to a table near the window. He took her parasol, which she had hung from the back of her chair, opened it up, and held it above her. He said, "The roof at this end leaks a bit, madam." Then they all chuckled, and he went off to bring them their provisions.

Jean said, "Look around the room."

Eliza did. She did not see the lawyer, or, indeed, anyone she recognized. She counted nine customers, all men, some dressed for town, some dressed for the mountains, some neat, some rough, some with big mustaches and whiskers, some with nothing more than goatees. This reminded her to tell Jean that the lawyer's beard and mustache were neatly trimmed, as if he did it himself, possibly every day. Jean said, "That is telling, too. He doesn't act on impulse."

Rupert set their boiled eggs and hotcakes on the table, then put a plate in front of them that held orange wedges. Rupert said, "A ship brought these up from down south. Pueblo de Los Angeles, the place is called. Don't eat the rind." He smiled.

As they were not far from the window onto the street, when Eliza looked up from their breakfast, she saw that fellow walk by, the one with the limp and the Adam's apple—Zeke, it was. She watched him; his head bobbed up and down a bit. At one point, he grasped the brim of his hat because of the wind. She said to Jean, "I've suspected so many fellows. Remember the evangelical who wept and puked and passed out? The other night, I woke up absolutely convinced that it's him, thinking he's doing God's work, but also enraged that Mrs. Parks wouldn't let him come back, and then I fell asleep, and in the morning, I remembered when we met him on the street and he was a decent fellow. And, my goodness, I'd forgotten completely about one of the first fellows who ever came to me. Slammed me against the wall, and after I threw a candleholder at the door, Mrs. Parks came in, brandishing her pistol, and kicked him out. I don't even know if I've seen him about town, because I forgot him entirely."

Jean said, "It could be anyone. Look what happened to Mrs. Marvin."

Then Eliza told her what Mrs. Parks had said about the arguing the Marvins did. Jean said, "I guarantee you they were arguing about whether the sheriff was going to continue to do nothing about the girls."

These wedges of orange were especially flavorful, both bitter and sweet. Jean, of course, liked them. Eliza decided that it was best to squeeze the juice over her hotcakes.

Once they were out on the street again, Jean said, "I need to see the lawyer. I need to be able to watch him as best I can when you cannot." They walked over to Colton Hall, strolled about, watching the fellows going in and coming out of the doors. Eliza didn't see him. Jean said, "I have to get back to my establishment for the afternoon's customer, but I will come to Mrs. Parks's place this evening. We will see if he turns up."

She did come, dressed as a man, with that false beard on her face. Eliza was in the front area when she appeared. Mrs. Parks did not come out of her quarters. Carlos stepped over to Jean, and Eliza followed him. She said, "Carlos, my dear. This is my friend Jack. He's from San Francisco, and he's new to the area." Her glance strayed toward the entrance, but she made herself look at Carlos again. "He asked me if he might come and visit our establishment for a few minutes. He's somewhat indecisive. . . ."

Carlos shrugged and pointed to a chair, and Jean went over and sat down. Eliza went into her chamber, left the door open, started preparing herself. Her ears felt as big as hats—it seemed like she could hear every little movement outside the entrance. She saw Carlos walk over to Jean, tap her shoulder, point to the entrance, but Jean pretended to be sleeping (she actually snored), and Eliza went to Carlos and said, "Ah. A long day! I believe he made the trip all at once. He would have gotten on his horse before dawn. Please, be kind to him." She reached into her pocket and handed Carlos a dollar coin.

Carlos went back to his chair. Still no . . .

And then the lawyer showed up. When she saw him come through the door, Eliza wafted herself out of her room, greeted him in a friendly way, said, "Ah! You've arrived." As they passed the chair Jean was in (she was still relaxed, but her eyes were open), Eliza pretended to sneeze, paused, reached into her pocket for a kerchief. Jean sat up, said, in a deep voice, "Where am I?"

Eliza smiled and said to the lawyer, "I guess he will find out, won't he?"

17

T HEY WALKED to her room. He hung up his jacket, as before. The
first thing the lawyer said to her was "You aren't down with the
grippe, are you?"

Eliza put the back of her hand to her forehead, then said, "No
fever. I feel fine. Everyone in Monterey sneezes, as you no doubt are
aware."

He said, "Pollen."

Eliza said, "What's that?"

"It's that powder flowers give off. It floats in the air, lands on
nearby flowers, and makes the seeds. Look around. In a place such as
this, with plants and flowers all year, there's plenty of it."

Eliza could see that he was a moody fellow. Once again, as the
first night, he sat still, staring down at his feet. Eliza went about the
room, picking up this and that, setting the items neatly on her table
or the small chest in the corner. She glanced at his jacket. He hadn't
brought any sort of bag this time. He didn't move. Eliza said, in a
"light" voice, "Have you had a good day?"

"Same as always."

"The weather was pleasant."

"What difference does that make?"

"For me, a considerable difference. That's something I do enjoy about Monterey. Back in Kalamazoo, it was snowy all winter, rainy all spring, hot all summer. I did love it when the leaves were changing, but everything else rather fatigued me. Here, you never know."

He remained still and silent.

She said, "Perhaps, if I had had more cousins, or even brothers and sisters, things would have been more lively. At the very least, if you have three or four brothers, you can spend your youth watching them get into trouble."

No response.

She went on, "Do you have brothers? Sisters?"

He said, "Why is that your business?"

"It isn't. But all of my customers do seem to enjoy telling me stories, especially the sailors. Climbing the masts, that sort of thing. That's what makes my work here interesting. Going around Cape Horn—now, that stood my hair on end."

He looked up at her at last, and said, "If I talk all day and listen to others talking all day, then perhaps I prefer a period of silence."

Eliza said, "You could get that at home."

"How do you know that?"

Now she felt a bit daring. She said, "I don't, because you have told me nothing of your home."

But then she did fall silent. She went to the bed, sat down in a spot where she might continue to watch him, but do so tactfully, and she waited.

At last, he undid his boots, kicked them off, stood up, dropped his trousers and stepped out of them, then slid his drawers down and stepped out of them. Of course he paused and arranged his clothing, even going so far as to lay his trousers neatly over the arm of the chair. Then he came to her, said, "May I undo your gown?"

Eliza was used to this. She nodded her head and lay quietly on her back. He started at the collar, undid the hooks one at a time, rather slowly, sometimes touching her bosoms. When he had finished, he sat her up and slid her gown over the shoulders, stood her up, and slid it down over her hips. This in itself was not unusual, but his manner while doing it was—he was not unkind, caused her no pain, but at the same time, he did seem to be treating her like an object, perhaps a doll. He took her elbow, held her while she stepped out of her gown; then he picked it up and laid it neatly across his trousers. There she was, in her chemise and her knickers. He gazed at her, up and down. She remembered a fellow in the summer who had been so impatient (and his prick was oozing at the time) that he had ripped her knickers off (and then left her an extra dollar coin). But the lawyer didn't do that. He simply held the waist of her knickers open, pushed them down, helped her step out of them. Ah, well, for some customers, unclothing the woman was simply a necessity, whereas, for others, watching the woman unclothe herself was what they desired. A few were disappointed if they came into the room and the woman had clothes on. He undid her chemise, lifted it over her head. The activity of unclothing her seemed to relax him, and by the time she was sitting on the bed again, he was more as he had been the night before— happy enough, relaxed enough, ready to smile, or even sing a song, she thought. If Peter had never been shot and they were still living in some small house somewhere, Eliza knew she would be scratching her head and wondering about the nature of men and how to understand her husband. The great benefit of her trade was that, now that she had seen so many men, they had become more interesting to her, in all the ways they were alike as well as in all the ways they were different. He took off the rest of his clothes.

The lawyer turned her over, spread her legs, and entered her. This was not her favorite method, but, for one thing, she knew, as he was stripped bare, that he had no pocket and no knife, and she could also see the side table—no knife there, either. Fortunately, his prick was small enough so that this form of penetration didn't hurt. He slapped her buttocks lightly, let out a laugh, and finished his business. After he pulled out, she waited, and then he did turn her over. Now he was actually smiling. He pushed his hair out of his face and ran his hand down his beard. He said, "You see, Eliza, that if you are patient I will eventually emerge from my shell."

She said, "Peter, I do see that."

He grasped his prick, waved it, and laughed. He said, "That isn't my name, but I'll settle for it in this establishment." He laughed again. He took a few deep breaths, then lay down beside her on the bed, not touching her, but not pushing her away, either. Eliza was curious to see what he would say next. A clue, she hoped—was that what they were called? Jean often used that word. But he said nothing.

Finally, Eliza said, "Do you manage to get out and about much? I quite enjoy walking here and there. Sometimes my friend and I rent a couple of nags and ride up into the canyons."

He said nothing.

She made herself sound entirely conversational. "The horses we've ridden lately are said to have been caught as mustangs and trained. They are alert, but mannerly."

No response.

Now, she thought, was the time. She said, "I did have a friend who owned a lovely pair; Less and More, she called them. She'd bred them herself, and she took us for a long carriage ride here, there, and everywhere, but she was . . . Well, she was beaten to death by her husband. Very sad. He's locked up, and I have no idea what happened to those horses. They were like children to her."

Even though he wasn't near enough to be in contact with her, she could feel, through the mattress, that he stiffened. A moment later, he sat up. At last, he said, "I knew her. I knew them. Matthew Marvin was one of the first friends I made when I came here."

"Did I see you at her funeral?"

"You did not. No one told me of it." He sighed. Then he said, "I know I am a solitary person. I don't quite know how not to be. When the courts recess or there's a bit of time, I see my colleagues go out for a smoke or head to some spot for a bite to eat. No one thinks to ask me along, and I never push my way in."

Eliza said, "I would think in your business that men would take sides—"

"Ah, well, there's where you are wrong. We all know how to argue for and against one thing and another, and we all try to be as eloquent as we can, but when the gavel comes down, even for just a recess, we put the conflict away. You must do that, as you never know who is going to be your ally in upcoming cases, and who is going to be your opponent. For the parties to the contest, yes, it is life and death, but for us it is something like a game."

He glanced at her. The flickering light of the taper made him look old and worn. He said, "I don't sense that they dislike me. They forget me."

"And so you come here?"

"It's here or a saloon. I'm not fond of drink. Ah, well." He stood up, went over to the chair, brought her dress to her, then began clothing himself. Just before stepping into his trousers, he said, "What would you think of taking me about and showing me one or two of the spots you like to visit? That would be a change."

Eliza said, "Everything depends on the weather, but I will consider that."

After he left, Eliza sat up until daybreak, so unsure was she about whether she trusted the fellow or did not. Talking to him made her think of her father. She recognized that, whereas her mother was exact and decided in everything, her father went back and forth, so much so that she'd often heard her mother exclaim, "Quit waffling!" Once or twice, "Quit waffling! Fire the fellow!" He had inherited the lumber mill he owned from his own father. Eliza had never had a sense that he'd intended, or hoped, to do something with his life other than run the lumber mill and be saved, but maybe he had. There were no paintings or sketches of him as a young man ("idols," her mother called such things), and so she could not even picture him at the age she was now. Maybe she didn't even know how old he was, since her mother didn't celebrate birthdays, but as she thought of it, she remembered being told that he was twenty-six when she was born, and so that would make him forty-seven now, younger than this lawyer. And he acted in every way like an old man, older than her mother, who was, some relative had told Eliza at some point, five years older than her father. She thought of the people she knew in Monterey. Surely, many of them were as old as her parents, and here was another thing that Monterey did for you—it kept you young.

Jean was standing there in the dawn light when Eliza came out of Mrs. Parks's establishment. The fog was so thick that Eliza hardly recognized her, and they had to walk slowly, not because many people were out, but because the street was wet and treacherous. Normally, Eliza could see her feet, and where they were stepping, but this morning she could not. Jean said, "They call this a tule fog. I've never seen it before."

After planting a kiss on Jean's cheek, Eliza said, "I need to read one of those DuPANN stories again. I'm not sure how to understand the bits and pieces I am learning."

Jean nodded. She said, "I have about half a taper left. We should go to my place and read it, back and forth, until we know that the Bear is open. We can have our meal there. Then I need a bit of a nap before my day begins."

The walk wasn't long, though they did have to go slowly. Eliza went more slowly than Jean, but even Jean was careful.

All was quiet at her place. They went into her room, lit the taper by putting the wick against a red piece of wood in the fireplace. Jean set the taper next to the chair and began to read. Yes, Eliza remembered the first part as being slow. The title of the story, "The Murders in the Rue Morgue," had pushed her, the last time she read it, to see and understand the murders. But this time she was impressed with how Mr. Poe was thinking, how he understood "analyzing." She made herself pay attention to the part she had found boring before, where he shows his friend how he watched what he was doing, heard what he was saying, and then understood ("analyzed") how one thought led to another. When Jean got to the scene of the crime, she handed the book to Eliza and closed her eyes while Eliza quietly read the gruesome parts. When they got to the witnesses, who "deposed" what they had seen or heard, they passed the book back and forth for each witness. Eliza was the one who read what the last witness said, the physician who described the injuries. As she read, "The face was fearfully discolored, and the eyeballs protruded," she remembered how horrified she had been when she first read it, but now, even though she imagined what Poe was depicting, she was more intrigued than put off. And then there were the possible weapons—a club, an iron bar, a chair. As she read about them, she pondered what injuries each one might produce: "Separated head." "Razor." She thought, "Dagger. Pistol. Arrow. Throttling."

Then Jean read a part that Eliza had forgotten entirely, where DuPANN talked about the larger picture, about looking away from the body to the valley, the mountain, the stars in the sky. She said, "It sounds like he's visited Monterey." Jean laughed and set down the book. As they walked through a much lighter fog to the Bear, she tried to think of the larger picture.

One aspect of the larger picture was that every person she thought of now, including herself, was complex. Her father, her mother, Mrs. Parks, this lawyer, perhaps even Jean, given how she loved to portray herself as so many different types—not only a man and a woman, but sometimes a rough man, sometimes a dapper fellow, sometimes a haughty woman, sometimes an amusing pal—even Rupert, even Mrs. Clayton, perhaps even Lucas. And no doubt Eliza's mother thought Eliza was complex, too, as well as damned. She thought of the boy who wanted to become a doctor, of the sailors who came from everywhere and went everywhere. She thought of the dead girls, each of them different, each of them found in a different spot. Then they sat down at their table, and Rupert brought them each a boiled egg and a fresh biscuit. Jean said, "Make yourself not think about it for as long as it takes to enjoy our meal."

Eliza nodded. She fell quiet, ate with pleasure, saw a few bits of sunlight begin to hit the front window. And then, for no reason that she could understand, she remembered that the girl with the missing finger, Mary Summers, was also the girl that Mrs. Parks had once told her was Mr. Marvin's preferred girl. And so she began to follow Poe's trail—the lawyer liked Mr. Marvin, Mr. Marvin's preferred girl was Mary, Mr. Marvin and Mrs. Marvin got into a violent argument about something and he killed her, Mrs. Parks went to her funeral and muttered to herself, "Least said, soonest mended," the lawyer was a friendless, fearful, aggressive man who seemed drawn to her, the lawyer had a dagger, not a pistol.

She walked Jean to her place. They hugged. Jean said, "Maybe I'll dream of something. You'll see me tonight."

The sky was now clearing, and the streets were busy. Eliza turned and headed down Pacific Street toward the bay. She went past the house where the Zeke fellow lived and noticed that the front garden was healthy, if not yet blooming. Then she wandered past Colton Hall, twice around the building, looking for the lawyer, but nothing. By this time, the midday meal was being served there, and she peeked in as many windows as she could, in spite of the sunshine, but she never saw him. She went back to her place, took off her gown, and slept deeply, without dreams, so deeply that she didn't even remember any of her concerns until she sat up and saw her gown hanging from the hook. She glanced at the window. It was getting dark.

When she met Jean at her place, Jean said, "I have a plan." Eliza surprised herself by saying, "I do, too," and they walked around the block one time. They conversed back and forth, as they so often did.

Jean said, "You should tempt him."

Eliza nodded. "Out of the establishment."

Jean said, "Sunday would be the best day."

Eliza looked up at the puffs of clouds floating in the brilliant sky and said, "When the weather is pleasant."

When they turned the corner, they both noticed a fellow whose pocket had a long bulge, indicating a pistol. And then he smiled, and stepped aside. Eliza and Jean both tipped their heads. When they had passed him, Jean said, "Tell him you will show him a couple of spots if he shows you a couple, too."

Eliza glanced back at the fellow. He was striding away from them with something of a determined air. For all she knew, he could be the one. She looked at Jean and said, "The lawyer might take me past his house."

Jean was so intent on their plan that she didn't seem to care a bit about that fellow with the gun. She said, "Wander in the direction of the spot where the girl was under the tree."

Eliza said, "But don't show any sign that I've been to the spot before."

Jean stopped, stared right at her, said, "Keep your eye on his visage."

Eliza nodded. "At all times."

Jean leaned slightly forward and lowered her voice: "Nutmeg and I will be about twenty yards behind you."

Eliza said, "You'll be dressed as a fellow."

Jean looked thoughtful for a moment, then nodded. "An idle fellow. A fellow with good intentions who can't find employment."

Eliza said, "Chewing a strand of hay."

Jean said, "How else would I pass the time?"

They both laughed.

Eliza went inside, and Jean continued around the block. Eliza watched her gaze intently at all the buildings, especially at the one directly across from Mrs. Parks's establishment. In their endeavor, it was her role to be the temptress and Jean's to be the protector. No surprise in that.

Her customer was not the lawyer, but someone new, which was fine with Eliza, as it was Wednesday, and she needed some time to practice being a temptress, and also some relief from the lawyer. The fellow was youthful—maybe five years older than Eliza—but experienced, and also graceful, good-humored, and kindly—not in a way that made it seem as though he was making an effort, just in a way that made kindliness seem like an ingrained habit. He had an excellent gelled mustache that swept up into points that seemed to mimic his smile. He told her his name was David, said her name aloud, carefully, and then addressed her in a friendly manner as they did their business. He knew what he wanted, and how to get her to do it, and even though what he wanted was entry from the back, she didn't especially mind. When he was done, he turned her over, raised her up, and gave her a gentle hug, a rare thing. Then he lifted one of her locks and set it behind her ear. When he got up and began putting on his pants (leaving a good-sized coin on the table), she dared to say, "Where might you be off to now?"

"My friend and I are going to get the horses and ride down the hill. Do you know that spot off to the left, where the meadows are? We have a ranch there. Well, it will be a ranch. We just came here from San Francisco. It's harder to find a spot for a ranch up near that bay than it is here."

Eliza said, "How long were you in San Francisco?"

"Three years. That's where we met. It was odd, because we both came from Pennsylvania. He's from Bellefonte and I'm from Williamsport. And it turned out that we're related! My grandfather and his brother had a falling-out. My grandfather left in a huff and didn't even tell us about the Bellefonte relations. And then I was chatting with this fellow, and it turned out we had the same last name, and there we were." He was now neatly dressed. He came over and took her hand in a gentle way, actually said, "Thank you!"

Eliza said, "What is your last name?"

The fellow said, "Harwood. Another one of my great-uncles lives in this town."

Eliza couldn't help it that her eyebrows popped up into her forehead, but she said nothing. David said, "I might as well let you know that it was my great-uncle who sent me to this establishment. When I first came here from up north, and my cousin and I were staying with him and Aunt Ruth, I saw a girl come out of his room one morning, and I asked Aunt Ruth about her. She told me about their arrangement." And then he walked out the door. Eliza washed herself, got dressed. The Harwoods! She hadn't thought of them in ages, and also had not included them in the trail of logic. She now remembered how spooked she had felt that morning, looking out the window into the Harwoods' back area at some odd trees, the like of which she'd never seen then. Now she had seen those over and over and loved them.

She went with Jean, who was loitering across the muddy street, back to her boarding house. The fog had thinned to only a mist, and saloons were still open. They walked in a leisurely way, but once again, they saw nothing. Eliza decided she would stroll past the Harwood place and see what she could see. One thing she could see already was a bit of a resemblance between David Harwood and old Mr. Harwood. The chin and the cheekbones, and the eye color, too—greenish blue, what her mother had called hazel. And, yes, Mr. Harwood was still a regular customer, and Mrs. Parks said that Olive and a new girl, Nell, didn't mind going there and spending the night, as their own accommodations were rather spare.

But even as she thought these thoughts, she felt David Harwood, young and kind as he was, turn into a suspect. It seemed as though, if the lawyer could be, if the fellow who wept and puked could be, then anyone could. As long as no one did a thing about the killings of the girls, then everyone who could have done it (therefore, everyone around Monterey at the times of the killings) might have done it. And it didn't have to be one fellow—it could be as many fellows as there were killings. It could be that someone heard about a killing and was moved to try it himself. Hadn't every girl with brothers and cousins and neighbors who were boys seen how they prodded one another to do this or that? In Kalamazoo, it was all about ice—the cold would set in, the lakes would ice over, and the boys would be out there, daring each other to go farther and farther toward the center of the lake, where the ice was thinnest. The same boys would be at it again in the spring, as the ice melted, having learned nothing about the pains and the dangers of falling through the ice when the winds were howling and the temperatures were well below freezing. Or they would climb trees, higher and higher, taunting each other as they eased out to the end of the limbs. One boy—his name was Leon Something—had fallen from a very tall tree, landed in a pile of leaves. Fortunately, he'd only broken his arm. If the girls went along, which they did sometimes, they knew it was their responsibility to at least say a word of caution, but words of caution had no effect—a boy who showed caution would be sneered at by the other boys. If a dare could persuade a boy to fall out of a thirty-foot tree, then perhaps a killing was possible, too.

The afternoon mist came in early, but there was no wind. Eliza wrapped herself in her shawl and walked up Jefferson. Once she got past the Harwood house, she turned the corner and went around the entire block. The Harwood house was the only one surrounded by trees. It rather surprised her that they could have constructed it in such tight quarters. But it was not intended to look like a California house—wide and open, with pleasant verandas. It was intended to look forbidding or, perhaps, imposing. And it did. Still quiet. The leaves weren't even fluttering. She continued up Jefferson into what had been a wooded area but was now being built up. Some spots had only been cleared; in others, materials, wood or adobe, lay in neat piles. One house was nearly built—a crew of fellows had put together the two floors and were working on the roof. Several houses were completed, and the gardens had been planted. As she walked past those spots, she imagined having a house of her own, but such a thing, she was willing to admit, did not seem likely. At the top of the street, she could smell the scent of the pine forest up the hill. She stood there for a while, taking in the fragrance.

She began her walk home. It was as she was approaching the corner of a short street—only one block—off to the right that she saw the door of a small adobe open and the lawyer emerge. He paused, tested and retested the locking mechanism on his door, then turned toward another new neighborhood that was still mostly woods. She crept along the short street, watched him turn left and hurry off, neatly avoiding the dips and the many tree limbs that were hanging over the path. When she was sure he was well on his way, she went back to his place.

It was modest, and, more important, unfenced, the door and the front wall right along the street (such as it was). A small path led toward the back, but she could see no barn and no horse pen. There were two windows, one to the left of the door and one to the right.

She glanced nervously in both directions, then went over and peeked into them. Of course, they were washed clear (the stoop was clean, too). Perhaps the lawyer would have said that he had nothing better to do than to make sure everything was perfectly maintained. When she looked in, almost afraid of what she might see, she was reassured in a way. The front room was well lit—skylights—and sparsely furnished—two chairs and a table. The wall to the left was lined with bookshelves, and there were stacks of books on the floor. Some were very thick, some thin; some looked new and glinted in the sunlight, others looked dusty. No doubt, many of them were law books, but Eliza didn't think that they all were. She herself had never bought a book—that would cost her at least a day's wages, or possibly two days' wages. But she enjoyed the ones that some of her clients or Mrs. Parks gave her. Still, even in her parents' home back in Kalamazoo, she had never seen so many books in one place. Elegant attire and books—these were the lawyer's luxuries.

She kept peering through the window to the right of the door. She saw papers on the table, and two or three envelopes that appeared to be unopened. She stepped off the stoop and eased around the house to the right, not without checking for passersby. There was another window on the side of the house, which looked into the front area from a different angle, and then there was another window past that one, which looked into the lawyer's bedchamber. There was no skylight, and the sun had dipped, so she had to wait a bit in order to see anything. What she then saw was a narrow bedstead, a small table with a short taper, a row of hooks across the far wall with apparel neatly hung, no wardrobe, no rug.

In the back area, there were some tubs, evidently for washing, as well as a small outhouse (also locked), a well, and another window. She peered through that one, into a room that had formerly been used for preparing food, but now looked abandoned—no wood or coals or even ashes in the fireplace, no jugs or kettles or empty plates. She kept staring, and then saw, laid along the table, a collection of knives, not all of them daggers—some for preparing fish or meat, others perhaps for chopping vegetables, but several too small to be of any use that Eliza could understand. All of these knives—ten of them—were also well taken care of. She squinted, and saw a whetstone next to the largest of the knives. And so the lawyer was a collector—of books and knives and jackets.

When Jean met her at Mrs. Parks's in the evening, the knives were the first thing Eliza mentioned.

Jean said, "Have you ever asked Mrs. Parks if maybe the customers should put their weapons in a bin or a box before they come in to you?"

"I don't think fellows in Monterey would do that."

"Ask Carlos if anyone has ever threatened him with a pistol."

And so Eliza did. It was still a bit early when she got there. Carlos was not sitting on his stool but, rather, in a chair by one of the front windows. He was eating some beans and rice from a bowl. Eliza saw a couple of tortillas on the table. When she approached him, he turned his head in a kindly manner, and Eliza said, "I was wondering, Carlos, whether any of the customers ever threaten you."

Carlos nodded. He said, casually, "Some of the drunks wave their pistols around. Occasionally, I've removed them from their grasp. It isn't difficult. When they lift them up to wave them, you stick two fingers under the handle of the pistol and pry it out. Then you catch it. I used to worry that one would go off if I did that, but it's never happened. Sometimes they drop to the ground, and then I kick them away from the fellow."

"Why doesn't Mrs. Parks ban the pistols?"

"She tried that, but the fellows who had them brought them anyway, and tended to brandish them about even more. It works better to banish the customer than to banish the pistol. And you know to keep your door ajar."

Eliza nodded. Then she said, "Do you worry about knives?"

Carlos shook his head, ate the last of his beans and one of the tortillas, wiped his lips with his kerchief, and took his bowl to the washing area. Eliza had thought of telling him about Mary and her stab wound, but she didn't. She sincerely hoped that the lawyer would not show up this evening.

For some reason, the chat she'd had with Carlos not only did not reassure her, it made her feel more in danger than she had been feeling, even while walking around town, even while discussing the killing with Jean and Mrs. Parks, even, indeed, while gazing at Mary curled toward the trunk of the tree. She had already folded up her shawl and laid it on the table when she grabbed it again, wrapped herself in it, and ran outside. A customer was climbing the steps. He jumped out of the way when she stormed past him. Jean was across the street, dressed as a fellow, leaning against the side of the opposite building, some sort of woodworking business that made kegs out of the local oak.

Eliza exclaimed, "Why is it that we're the ones that have to do this? We know nothing about these things! Does everyone else really not care? At least Kalamazoo wasn't like this! At least they had constables!"

Jean turned toward her, said, "Ask me how I got to Wisconsin."

Eliza took a deep breath. "How did you get to Wisconsin?"

"In my mother's belly. She was a slave in Kentucky who escaped across the Ohio, and found her way to Wisconsin Territory. She actually hid out for a while among some Indians, or said she did. She took up with my father just before I was born. They moved to Kenosha when I was a year old, and pretended that he was my father."

"He wasn't your father?"

"My father was the fellow who owned her in Kentucky. Her sister had two children by him, she said."

Eliza stared at Jean.

Jean laughed. "Where did you think I got the dark hair and the brown eyes?"

Eliza said, "I assumed you were Black Irish."

"I don't know what that is. Anyway, 'MacPherson' isn't an Irish name, it's Scottish. It means 'the parson's son.'"

Now they both laughed.

"That fellow, Liam Callaghan, that I loved back in Kalamazoo had dark hair and dark eyes. He said that there was a battle between the English and the Spanish some hundreds of years ago, and a lot of the Spanish sailors ended up in Ireland."

Jean said, "My mother was rather pale-skinned. I'm suspecting that her father was a slaver, too, but she didn't know." Then she went on, "Why do you think I came to California? I fit in perfectly here. You look around. No one stares you up and down, wondering about you. If they do, they are wondering if you are Spanish. Wisconsin is not a slave state, and doesn't want to be, but there are plenty of white folks in Wisconsin that are ready to speed up your trip to Canada if they suspect you are an escaped slave. My mother noticed that, too."

Eliza glanced across the street. Mrs. Parks was looking toward her—perhaps she could see her, certainly she was looking for her. Eliza kissed Jean on the cheek and said, "Thank you for telling me. I'll see you in the morning."

She crossed the street. Mrs. Parks saw her, said, "Your customer is here. I'll tell him you've gone round back to prepare yourself."

Eliza did as she was told.

The customer really was an old fellow—white hair standing on end, raspy voice, thin. He wanted to do his business more than he *could* do his business, but he was clean and decent, so Eliza spent a while with him, doing this and that. At one point, she noticed that his neck and shoulders seemed stiff and painful, so the thing she did the longest was rub him there until he felt better. She kissed him a lot, fiddled with his prick. Eventually, he did the thing that she suspected that he really wanted to do, which was to fall into a deep sleep. She covered him, quietly put on her gown, tiptoed out. She waved to Carlos, mimicked a snore, and, a little surprised, found Jean sitting outside on the top step.

19

As they walked along, Eliza saw Jean gazing at her. Finally, Jean said, "Did my story shock you?"

Eliza shook her head. "I would expect anything of you. Remember when we first met, and you took me down to the Mission in Carmel, and then we walked back up the hill, and you were practically prancing while I was heaving and pausing and trying to decide whether it might be easier to kill myself? That was the day when I decided just to wait and see what the next thing you might do would be. I must say, I do not know much about the lives of slaves. In Kalamazoo, everyone we knew deplored slavery, but no one said much about it."

"I haven't told anyone but you. I do pay attention to abolitionists, but many of the ones who want to get rid of slavery also want to get rid of the slaves. To ship them back to Africa."

Eliza said, "That's a terrible idea."

Jean nodded.

Eliza said, "So here is our plan. If there is some sort of war and, God forbid, the slaveholders invade California, we can start a congregation, and you can be the parson."

Jean said, "I will show them the way to eternal damnation."

Eliza said, "May they find it."

At Eliza's boarding house, Jean gave her a hug, then said that, as tomorrow was Friday, she was likely to be busy all day, but she would be sure to show up at Mrs. Parks's establishment at the proper time. Eliza said, "I guess I will spend the whole day tomorrow figuring out how to be a temptress."

Jean said, "Flare your nostrils. That should do it."

They laughed again, and Eliza watched Jean walk off. It was another truth of life, she thought, that until you got away from your parents and your youthful self, you didn't really know what a friend was.

Late the next afternoon, perhaps two hours before she was due at Mrs. Parks's, she walked back up Jefferson, keeping her eye out, but seeing nothing. At the top of the street, she once again occupied her time by enjoying the fragrance of the pines, and she sincerely hoped that Jefferson Street wouldn't get so far into the forest that the folks building houses would cut the pines down. She watched birds flit here and there, and saw at least two hawks floating on the currents of air. She could hear seagulls in the distance and also see the fog rising off toward the ocean. Then she made her way along the street, slowly and observantly. Sure enough, when she was about a block above the side street where the lawyer lived, she saw him round the corner and head down Jefferson, walking steadily but slowly, not looking around, evidently without any suspicions. Eliza followed him. He entered Colton Hall through a back door. Eliza turned to the right, walked over to Madison and then Pacific, where she watched to see where he might emerge. It was almost dusk when he emerged from the front. He walked down Pacific Street to Pearl. He was evidently on his way to Mrs. Parks's establishment. Eliza was not far from her place. She trotted over there, changed into her warmest and most worn gown, threw on an old brown shawl, and walked rather quickly to Mrs. Parks's. Today was not the day to tempt him—best to put him off somehow, though exactly how, other than wearing these drab garments, she wasn't sure. She thought she might get there first, but he was already in the front area when she stepped onto the veranda.

When he looked at her, she thought of his fear of illness, coughed three times into her shawl, and glanced in his direction. She saw, with relief, that when he noticed her coughing, he began to look alarmed. She stepped inside, cleared her throat, gave him a friendly smile, held out her hand. He did not take it. Mrs. Parks, who was standing in the doorway of her room, looked at them. Eliza said, "Ma'am, do you remember the gentleman last night, the older man? He was coughing a lot, and I am wondering if I picked up the grippe from him. I have no idea. I haven't got a fever." She put the back of her hand to her forehead. "I've sneezed a few times, though."

The lawyer started shaking his head, which Mrs. Parks noticed, and then Mrs. Parks stepped up to him and said the perfect thing. "Sir, I suggest we wait a day. I will send her home with some honey tea, she can stay quiet all day tomorrow, and then we can see if anything has developed."

The lawyer nodded.

Mrs. Parks cleared her throat. "Perhaps another of the girls? Olive Breeze—"

But the lawyer seemed anxious to get out of the building, and he shook his head.

Eliza put her shawl over her mouth, cleared her throat.

Mrs. Parks said, "I assure you, sir, that I take good care of my—"
But he was gone.

Mrs. Parks sighed. She did not look angry, but she did not look pleased, either. She waved Eliza out the door. Eliza went onto the veranda, then down the steps. Mrs. Parks came to the doorway and said, "I have no honey tea, but at least take care of yourself. Plenty of water. Open the window of your room."

Eliza nodded. In fact, she wondered if she had gone too far, and chased the lawyer away forever. She walked down the street, and at the corner actually touched her forehead with the back of her hand again, just to reassure herself. Cool as could be. But she had made up her mind. Even if the lawyer did not come back, she knew where he lived and she knew his habits. She and Jean could not put away their investigation. They would simply have to come up with another plan.

The next evening, Eliza saw the lawyer walking about on the street outside Mrs. Parks's establishment. She paused, watching him. He saw her at once, came toward her, then stopped in the middle of the street, looking right and left to see whether a horse or a carriage was hurtling in his direction. Eliza could hear some shouting from maybe a block down the street, near one of the saloons, but that was all. She approached the lawyer. He looked calmer and in a better humor, and said, as if he cared, "How are you feeling today, my dear?"

"No coughs or sneezes at all. I don't know what that was yester-day, but it seems to have gone away. Shall we go in?"

"I regret it, but I'd rather not. However, I do have another thought. Tomorrow is Sunday. I know this establishment is closed for the Sab-bath, but I thought we might make use of the good weather and go for an outing. I can bring along a basket of provisions. It's something I like to do on a Sunday, and I customarily do it alone, but I would be pleased if you might accompany me."

Eliza maintained a pleasant look on her face, but did roll her eye to the right. Jean was there, in the shadow of the building. Eliza said, "Perhaps," and Jean stepped closer. Eliza said, "Which area might you be thinking of?"

The lawyer said, "It depends on you, my dear. You know the town better than I do. Usually, I take my basket to the wharf or one of the plazas."

Jean moved a step closer.

Eliza said, "I do love one spot, but it is a long walk."

He said, "I don't mind that."

"A lovely high ground between two canyons. East of town."

He said, "Fine. I will meet you here, and you may lead me there. I need something new."

He turned and walked up the street. When Jean came over to her, Eliza said, "I am thinking that this fellow is the least likely suspect of all of my customers. I am actually coming to feel fond of him."

Jean said, "Indeed. Well, we'll get a picnic out of it. My plan is to get one of the horses, go as a fellow, and be ambling about when you arrive. That chestnut mare—Nutmeg? She's one I can rely on. She ground-ties very nicely. I'll keep an eye on you."

"And him."

"And him."

Eliza went into Mrs. Parks's establishment.

Mrs. Parks came out of her room. She said, "You seem well."

"I am, indeed."

"Hmm. No sign of the lawyer, but you have another customer later. One of the sailors you've seen before. Small fellow. Not out of his teens."

Eliza said, "The one who loves to climb the masts? He's amusing."

"Perhaps. He said that the ship is leaving at dawn, so he is sleeping early and coming after midnight. I know you don't mind that."

Eliza nodded.

Mrs. Parks softened her demeanor, and Eliza realized that her employer had gotten a bit harsher lately. Mrs. Parks said, "His name is Caleb."

Eliza said, "Well, I look forward to hearing about some of his adventures."

When Caleb entered, she did recognize him, but he was no longer a boy. He had grown two or three inches, was now taller than Eliza, and had put on a good deal of muscle. He smiled pleasantly, and Eliza said, "Are you still climbing masts day and night?"

Caleb laughed and said, "No. Only if I have to. Sometime in the summer, I was up one of the masts, rolling down the sail, when the ship listed so far to the lee side that I thought I was going to get dunked. I was well tied, but I also learned a lesson."

"Which was?"

"All boys eventually learn that death exists, even for themselves."

Eliza said, "Indeed, you do not look like a boy anymore."

"Nor do I feel like one."

But Caleb's prick was still youthful, and he did plenty of business. When he was dressing to leave, Eliza said, "Where is your ship off to this time?"

"Australia. And we are stocked with goods. It's a lucrative voyage. And I do like it there. The folks you meet are always bragging that they were criminals in England and sent to Australia as a punishment, and then it turns out that the crime they committed was stealing a pair of shoes, or mistaking someone else's goat for their own." He shrugged. "Great wits, they are. I might get left behind someday when my ship leaves without me."

Eliza said, "That's amusing. Around here, there are a few black-legs who say they're from Australia. Behind their backs, some folks call them Sydney Ducks."

Caleb laughed. After a bit, he departed and Eliza took a nap.

When she woke up, she instantly thought of the trip they were taking, and Mary under the tree, and the row of knives in the lawyer's house. The thoughts filled her with dread—it felt as though they were pinning her to the mattress—but then, of course, she had to fetch her piss pot, and once she was on her feet, pulling on her garments, her dread was replaced, bit by bit, with curiosity, and even eagerness. The odd thing, she thought, was that she was both more afraid and more eager to see what would happen than she had been before she had set out for California. It was as if, for her whole life, she had been dumb and patient, like a milk cow. Now she reminded herself of Query, flicking his ears this way and that, but trotting on. She felt her fear slip away, rather like the morning fog bank receded into the bay and the sunshine lit up the sky.

The day was well begun, and everyone was out and about. Eliza went to the Bear. Rupert pointed her to the table where Jean was already eating some hotcakes. Jean said, "It will be Nutmeg. I've already handed over my money. When you head for the meadow, walk past the stables. I'll get on and stay about a block behind you. Wear red."

"I don't have anything that's red."

Jean handed her a bandanna that was, indeed, red. She said, "Put this around the back of your neck."

Eliza nodded. Rupert brought her hotcakes. After he left, she said, "The trick will be getting him to reveal himself. I don't know if I should be friendly or seductive. Sometimes one way works with him and sometimes the other, depending on his mood."

Jean leaned across the table, looked her in the eye, and said, "I believe you will know. Look at it this way—every day, you have to figure out how to get some fellow's prick to wake up. I can't imagine such a thing. When my ladies come to me, almost all they want is affection, and time and relief from their daily round. Not one of them stares at their lower regions and gets disappointed or angry."

Eliza said, "Yes, that can cause a bit of tension. So I take it that, at your establishment, you don't have anyone like Carlos keeping an eye out for misbehavior?"

Jean shook her head.

After they left the Bear, Eliza went to her boarding house and opened her wardrobe, stared at the apparel. She chose her walking boots, the silvery-blue gown that Mrs. Parks had given her four dollars to buy. It had a somewhat higher hemline, which was better for getting about, and a sturdy crinoline that gave her feet room to move. The dress also had a rather loose bodice, so she could get more air, and narrow sleeves that could not be easily grabbed. The blue color contrasted nicely with the red bandanna. The hat she chose was also light-colored, made of straw, with no string. She glanced around the room, looking for some weapon, but she had no pistol or walking stick. She felt her nervousness rise a bit, then she noticed her hat pin—six inches long. She set it beside the hat, then picked it up again and touched the point. Not exactly a weapon, but it would do in a pinch, she thought.

20

W HEN SHE MET the lawyer, outside of Mrs. Parks's establishment, he was very neatly dressed. She actually stared at his jacket, and then said, "I don't think I've seen that before." He lifted the sleeve and looked at it. He said, "It's herringbone. Perhaps too elegant for this, uh, town." The next thing she noticed about the jacket was that it had large pockets. He carried a basket covered with a cloth that was tucked in around the edges. He lifted it toward her, said, "Let me say for myself that I've brought along some good provisions. No sardines! You shall see, my girl. You shall see."

Now she led him up Pacific. She glanced about and walked along at a leisurely pace, as if to show him how to enjoy himself, but really so that she would have more time to pass Jean. Sure enough, Jean had the chestnut mare saddled up, was pulling on her gloves. To all appearances, she didn't even look their way as Eliza and the lawyer passed, but of course she noticed. They turned onto Pearl, kept veering left. By now there were some horses and carriages in the street, but for the most part, Eliza knew, those who had gone to church were setting up their midday meal. She said, "I always wondered why my mother prepared so much food on Sunday. There were only three of us. A beef roast would be the least of it."

The lawyer said, "Our family ate Sunday dinner at about two. Then my brother and I were sent out with bowls and platters of the remains to the more impoverished neighbors down the street. We'd leave the provisions, and then those boys would bring back the pottery the next day."

Eliza said, "What was the weather like in, where was it, New Haven?"

But he didn't answer.

Now they were passing the Casa Munras. Eliza pointed it out. She said, "There are some handsome buildings in Monterey. They do say the Casa Munras is haunted."

He glanced at it, evidently uninterested, and said, "Our house in New Haven was a block from the cemetery. That's where we played when I was a boy. My mother didn't like it, but my father said it was good for us to understand the workings of life and death." Eliza saw that, even though he had been perky, he was now rather down.

They walked past the cathedral, then toward the cemetery. The lawyer switched the basket of provisions from one hand to the other, but he wasn't breathing hard. Eliza thought they had walked about a mile. She said, gesturing toward the green area, "Have you visited this place? The town cemetery?" She did not say that that was where Peter was buried. She heard the clip-clop of horseshoes behind them, but she didn't look around. The cemetery was lush with grass and lovely, as it had been before, the empty paths running around the graves and among the oddly shaped trees. Even so, she truly didn't want to end up there, and so she couldn't help glancing back. Jean was idling along. The lawyer said, "A client of mine is buried in that place, but I don't know where. Couldn't afford anywhere else, as he had lost all his money on some foolish investment." He sighed. "Never paid our firm, either." Eliza decided to keep him talking, so she said, "I would guess that is not uncommon around here. I've known several fellows who came here thinking that whatever they did would be like turning over the ace of diamonds, and they would be set for life.

But look around! You have to give it some thought if you are going to make use of this place. I do know a fellow with a decent-sized ranch, but they didn't have the funds to build a fence, and several of their cattle slid through the mud into a ravine."

The lawyer didn't respond to the story, but he did do what Eliza thought he might—he turned up the dirt road that led to the place where they had found the girl as if he knew where they were going. Eliza stayed a pace or two behind, her heart fluttering with the growing suspicion that, after all, he was the killer. She watched to see what he would do next. He continued for two strides, then stopped and looked around. He said, "Where are we? Have you been here before?" Perhaps his difficulty as a lawyer was that he faked his beliefs so poorly.

Eliza coughed, said, "Once or twice. It's a lovely spot. If the weather is right, folks like to bring their horses here and stroll around, but perhaps it's a little far out of town for those who don't have horses. The walk doesn't seem to have affected you, sir."

He said, "At least there's a good breeze. I don't have to remove my jacket."

"There's always a good breeze," said Eliza. "Shall we go up to the open area? This is a decent path. Not too steep." Eliza picked up the hem of her gown, adjusted her straw hat, fingered the hat pin, and walked briskly ahead of the lawyer. He didn't try to stop her; rather, he followed her. She glanced here and there at the trees, as if she was admiring them, but really she was looking for a sign of Jean and Nutmeg. All she saw was a young doe with huge ears and a long, thin neck. As soon as Eliza looked at her, she turned and walked away. Maybe, Eliza thought, that was a sign that nothing was going to happen. Or that Jean and Nutmeg were nowhere to be found.

The forest opened up, and they were standing in the moist grass. The sunshine was brilliant, and the sky was as blue as she had ever seen it. A hawk floated above them, then lifted its left wing and swept away. She could see its shadow on the grass. She glanced at the lawyer, to see if he noticed it, but he was switching the basket from one hand to the other and then rotating his shoulder, as if it hurt. She kept walking, pretending to explore, but also exploring. Then, knowing that she had to keep her eye on the lawyer, she whipped around. He was about three paces behind her, now casting his glance here and there. She said, "Did you see the hawk?"

"I did not."

He gazed across the mesa, then looked to the right and the left. He set the basket of provisions on the ground and rotated his shoulder again. Eliza wondered if this was when he might pull the dagger out of his pocket and come after her, but nothing about his posture suggested he was ready to do so. The breeze dwindled, and she listened again for any sound that would indicate that Jean and Nutmeg were somewhere nearby. All she heard was her own heart pounding. She stared at the lawyer again. He picked up the basket and started walking along the edge of the trees. After a bit, he pointed to one of them—beautiful, but not the tree that Mary had been curled under. This one had spreading limbs and plenty of rustling, spring-green leaves that stretched upward, into the blue. The lawyer said, "I am quite hungry and perhaps a little warm. I think we need some shade before we"—and there was the slightest of pauses—"go about our business."

Eliza couldn't help herself. She said, "I never view walking about as a business, but, rather, as a pleasure." Just then, she did hear something, behind them, some kind of crack or thump that sounded like a tree limb breaking. The lawyer didn't react, and when she looked back, she didn't see anything. And it was true that the wind suddenly picked up, jostling her hat and blowing some of her hair. Thinking something might have happened to Jean or Nutmeg, she grabbed her hat pin and adjusted her bonnet. Instead of taking off his jacket, the lawyer huddled into it.

He glanced at her, then took the basket over to the tree.

The wind died. Eliza lifted her arms, making herself pretend to be enjoying the landscape. She said, "You look a bit glum. Look at these trees! And the flowers!" She spun around as if she was happy, but really she was quite nervous, and looking for Jean. She heard no clip-clopping, and didn't see her anywhere. She thought, "Nutmeg! Give me a whinny!"

She reached up and touched her hat pin again. She went over to the tree, put her hand on the rough bark, then forced a smile onto her visage and turned around.

The lawyer was uncovering the provisions. He had evidently gotten them at the Bear—she recognized the pottery they were in. But they were all items that she could never have paid for—no salted fish, no boiled potatoes, no muffins. Rather, some beef stewed with onions, some baked apples, a small loaf of bread. To one side were some crisply fried potatoes. She walked carefully toward the lawyer, gazed at what he had brought. The stew was so fragrant that she could smell it even in the fresh air. A thought occurred to her: why would he spend so much money on such luxurious provisions if he intended to . . .

And then she sensed something, a rustle in the grass, even something about the ground beneath her feet, and looked to the left, to the path that had brought them to this spot.

It was the Zeke fellow. His arm was raised, and in his hand there was a dagger. The look on his face was intent and ugly, and his eyes were squinting, as if he could see only her. Her right hand jumped away from her, as if it was looking for something to steady her—the trunk of the tree, perhaps.

Eliza gave the lawyer a fleeting look. He was staring at Zeke, but he wasn't doing anything. Eliza began backing away, holding her skirt up, panting. Zeke stumbled—evidently having stepped in a gopher hole, or what they called, in Monterey, a ground-squirrel hole. But he did not drop the dagger, and regained his balance. Eliza continued to back away. Perhaps the open area would be safer—she had no idea, but if worse came to worst, she thought she might run.

She reached up and pulled the hat pin out of her bonnet, and her bonnet fell off her head. She picked up the hem of her skirt. Zeke straightened himself up and limped, a look of pain crossing his face, but his gaze remained intent upon her.

She glanced at the lawyer. He was staring at the ground, his hand on the basket as if he had left it there and forgotten about it. She tightened her right hand around the hat pin and waved it, tightened her left hand around the bunch of fabric that she was holding, and took a couple of steps. She looked down, checking for holes, and Zeke jumped toward her.

And then it happened: rhythmic thumping sounds, followed by Jean on Nutmeg, galloping toward them. Jean was leaning forward, reins in her left hand and a tree branch in her right. Eliza backed away; the cliff was nearby, and she didn't want to fall over it, but she also didn't want to be stabbed. Nutmeg continued to gallop. Zeke looked around, his dagger still in the air. When she got to Zeke, Jean didn't club him over the head; rather, she pointed the tree limb into his back like a spear and knocked him down. The dagger flew out of his hand. Jean pulled Nutmeg to a halt, dropped the reins, and jumped off, right onto Zeke, who was attempting to roll over. As always Jean was fit and adept. She jumped up and down on Zeke, avoiding his flailing arms. She kicked him in the face and in the crotch, and he cried out; then she jumped up and down. He cried out again. Jean gave Eliza a look, and Eliza ran toward her, picking up the dagger. Jean bent down and throttled Zeke, and then Eliza planted the dagger in his breast.

Zeke gave out a muted moan. It was followed by a long silence.

Eliza closed her eyes.

Jean said, "Let's drag him to the cliff and toss him into the ravine."

They were both panting. For some reason that Eliza never understood, the next thing she did was walk into the open area and fetch her bonnet, put it on, and use the hat pin to secure it. Then she came back. Jean was still staring at the body. Eliza picked up one foot, and Jean picked up the other. The brush rattled as they pulled him through it. They pushed him over the cliff, and he disappeared.

When they turned away from the cliff, Nutmeg was still standing calmly, and the lawyer was still sitting by the basket, though now he had his eyes closed, as if no time had passed and nothing of consequence had happened. Eliza shivered.

Jean marched over to the lawyer and gave him a kick. She said, "Stand up!"

The lawyer got to his feet.

Jean exclaimed, "How many did he kill?"

The lawyer said, "Five, after I got here. I don't know about before that. Not all of them were whores like you."

Eliza said, "Was one of them that girl? That girl I heard screaming outside his house?"

The lawyer said, "He told me about that, about seeing you, seeing the look on your face, and then listening to the tone of your voice when you asked about her. As far as I know, she left town, so she wasn't one of the five. The story he told you about the tarantula? That did happen."

Now there was a long silence, and it was Eliza who broke it. "Why did he push her? And slap her?"

The lawyer said, "I don't know. He never mentioned that."

Eliza said, "Why did he kill them?"

The lawyer looked at her. He said, "I told you. He couldn't help himself."

Eliza said, "What do you mean?"

"That night, when I first came to you. I told you that there were fellows who couldn't stop thinking about committing evil. They would try to stop themselves, and the more they tried to stop themselves, the more they wanted to do it." Then he said, "He sent me to you. He knew you were onto him. He told you about the tarantula and tried to be friendly, but every time he saw you, some look on your face made him want to do you in. I told him that he had gotten away with too many killings, that things were changing around here, but . . ."

Eliza waved her hand toward the drooping tree and said, "Why Mary?"

The lawyer glanced toward the tree. He said, "I gathered that she took a liking to him. At any rate, she kept coming by his house and knocking on the door. His housekeeper tried to shoo her away, so she would come late at night and stare into his bedroom window. She said that she loved him."

Eliza said, "How could she?"

The lawyer said, "I wondered that. But you told me that when you saw him that time and asked about the woman who screamed, he seemed cheerful and easygoing. Perhaps he was that way with her, too, and everyone knew that he had plenty of funds." The lawyer put his handkerchief to his nose; then his head dropped. In a low voice, he said, "You never know about love. At least, I never have."

Eliza said, "But it's you who have all the daggers and knives. I saw them through the window, in your house."

He glanced at her, then said, "Those were his. Too many people in and out of his place. And he knew his housekeeper would be suspicious. She's always in a sour mood, and I think he was a little afraid of her."

Eliza said, "And he hasn't killed her?"

"I tried to explain . . ."

Jean exclaimed, "You helped him! Why did you do that?"

The lawyer now looked her in the face for a moment, then dropped his head again.

Eliza said, "And the girl in the river! What about her?"

The lawyer said, "You mean the first one. She wasn't here long, no one . . ."

Eliza said, "Did Zeke kill her?"

"She was always in a rage."

"What about?"

"She thought . . . She'd worked in a brothel back in St. Louis, and she came here thinking she would find a wealthy fellow in a week or two. She saw that Zeke built houses for men with means, and she pestered him all the time to set her up with one, preferably someone elderly. Zeke got fed up, and told her he'd bought a rancho—would she like to see it? I gathered that she considered this some sort of marriage proposal. At any rate, we took her out there. I had no idea he was going to stab her. I thought he was going to leave her out there as a bit of a lesson. Then we just left her in the river, upstream from the bridge. He thought it was the safest place to dispose of her. He was not pleased when her remains were discovered." He glanced at Eliza. "I was. I *was* pleased. I hoped . . ."

Jean said, "She wasn't the first one."

He said something else in a low voice.

Jean pushed him with her fist. "Speak up!"

"She was the first one I was involved with. He never told me about others. But I couldn't report him. I didn't dare. Zeke was . . . was there when I . . . when I . . . when I strangled my wife in Indianapolis. He was at our place. We'd had too much whiskey, and she came down the steps and began yelling at me. I just grabbed her." He cleared his throat, then said, "After our son died, she wasn't the same person. She raged about everything. I . . ." Then he paused again, and said, "If I were defending myself in court, I would say that I didn't know what I was doing, but maybe I did. I didn't black out. I do remember the incident. We carried her up the staircase, and then pushed her corpse down. It was a steep staircase. No one doubted me when I said she had gotten up in the night and stumbled, broken her neck. I didn't know why—they didn't even look for marks. Zeke then left town. I thought he'd gone to gold country, but when I got here, I saw him at a saloon. He knew he could use me, and he did. I should have gotten out, but I hadn't the funds." He shook his head. "Please don't think I took pleasure in this. Please don't." Eliza stared at him. She did not think he was lying. Perhaps, she thought, what she was feeling toward him right at this moment was sympathy. She did not ask how the son had died, but whatever it was—cholera, drowning, falling out of a tree—losing a child did happen to most people.

Jean glanced at her. Eliza knew that Jean was wondering what was next, what they should do. Eliza thought that maybe, since the lawyer had confessed to them, he would confess to someone else, too—a judge or even a priest. She opened her mouth, but, as yet, she had nothing to say.

The lawyer sighed, and after that he smiled—well, it was not a smile, but, rather, something more rueful, more resigned. He looked at the basket of provisions. Eliza saw Jean tense up, as if she thought he might attack, but Eliza didn't see that possibility at all.

And then the lawyer turned, walked straight to the cliff, and jumped. The only sound he made was the sound of brush cracking and rustling, no screams or even moans. Eliza and Jean stared at one another for a long moment. Even Nutmeg pricked her ears.

The first thing Eliza said was "Did you see tears on his cheeks?"
Jean said, "I did."
Then Eliza said, "You saved me."
Jean said, "We saved each other. I doubt that just jumping around on him would have worked."

As they were gathering the remnants of the meal and everything else that might show they had been in this spot, Jean said, "The killer saw me following you just after I saw him hiding behind a tree. I don't think he knew who I was, or why I was here, but he ran at Nutmeg, waving his arms, and she spooked me off. We were still in the woods. Then he whipped around, and I knew he was running toward you. I saw the broken branch and grabbed it."

"Did the fall hurt?"

"Not really. She's short, and I let myself crumple to the ground. At least I didn't have a skirt to catch onto the saddle somehow. I jumped back on her. I knew she could get to him. She wasn't afraid."

They threw the basket over the edge, too, and Zeke's hat.

THE WALK TO Jean's boarding house was quiet and strange. They didn't have to talk, and they didn't. They both knew that Jean really had saved Eliza, and they both knew that neither of them could ever say a word about what had happened. The only witness was Nutmeg, and she seemed to be on their side. They both wondered if anyone in Monterey would care whether Zeke or the lawyer had gone missing. The gossipers would assume these newcomers had gone back east or down south or up north. They always did.

21

T HE SENSE OF UNEASE didn't come to Eliza for some time. She
was happy to have done what she had done, and she knew that
Jean was, too. As she thought back upon that logic trail, she saw that
the fellows who deserved suspicion were the ones who had acted sus-
piciously. As a result, her suspicions of her customers, or the fellows
in the street, faded away. She wondered if her customers noticed that
she was more easygoing and willing. Perhaps they did, because they
left her significant funds. At one time she had had fifty dollars in the
bank and counted herself lucky. Now she had almost five hundred.

What she first sensed, maybe a week after the deaths, was her
own enhanced alertness. She had always kept her ear out for gossip, but now her ear could understand almost every word she heard,
almost every conversation. The lawyer had said that he was solitary
in Monterey, and maybe he was. Zeke had said that his buildings
were prized, and maybe they were, but the first mention of the disap-
pearances, which she heard at the market when she was purchasing
some soap, was about the lawyer. A woman with a child on her hip
was saying to another, older woman, "I don't know what will happen
to our case, now that Jenkins has skipped town. We thought he was
reliable!"

The other woman said, "Who is, around here? At least he didn't take your money. Remember that fellow who talked my husband into investing in his clipper? So many trips they could make from this lovely bay. Turned out he didn't know a thing about wind or fitting out a ship. He just saw George as a sucker, and ran off to Mexico."

Eliza wondered what the case was about, but the woman didn't say, and Eliza didn't want to linger near her for very long.

The first time she overheard anything about Zeke, it was essentially the same thing. Two men were talking in the Bear, not about themselves but about someone they knew. The older one said, "The place was about finished. All they had to do was put the tiles on the roof, but Cornish said that the tiles hadn't hardened enough, so they were waiting."

The other guy said, "Well, if the place was almost done, your friend had paid up, right?"

"I think so."

"So Cornish took the money?"

"My friend says so. He's going to claim the house, but he has to find the tiles, and he hasn't been able to do that."

Eliza wondered if this was the house up Jefferson. She walked past the one she had seen, but the roof was wooden shingles, not tiles.

In other words, whoever cared about the lawyer or Zeke figured they had absconded.

Until the first of May, when some sailors, hiking about for a little respite from their ship, went up the trail along the ravine, and maybe because they were sailors, and observant, one of them saw the brim of a hat, so they pushed aside the coyote brush and saw the corpses, not far from one another, as well as a few remnants of the pottery. Then the sailors did what Eliza knew they should not have done—they carried and dragged the corpses into town, thus destroying whatever clues there might have been about the causes of death. How had the corpses looked? Eliza didn't hear anyone talk about that, but, remembering Mary, she suspected that they were basically skeletons with some leathery skin here and there, maybe with their jaws wide open. No doubt the lawyer's herringbone jacket had lasted longer than he did. No one mentioned the knife she had plunged into Zeke's chest.

Eliza thought she should be relieved at that, but, somehow, she wasn't—she realized that her wish had been that the turkey buzzards would take care of the remains.

Even so, she heard no gossip about the deaths, other than that they must have been drunk, they must have stumbled over the cliff, and that cliff—what was it, twenty feet high? How high did a cliff have to be? Well, that depended on whether you broke your leg or your neck or cracked open your head, or were so drunk that you landed smack on your face and couldn't turn over.

In mid-May, Eliza and Jean went up to the open area for the first time, walked around. They saw nothing—the grass was rich and thick, and when they looked down into the brush, there was no sign of the knife. As Jean said, their tracks were covered.

But Jean, too, had become edgy. When Eliza tried to ask her questions about that, Jean shook her head. They were still friends, but they didn't spend as much time together, and that night when Jean had pretended to be Eliza's customer, and then slid into bed with her and slept so comfortably, seemed long gone. In fact, Eliza had more conversations these days with Olive, which Mrs. Parks didn't seem to mind. But Eliza wasn't going to prod Jean, or even reassure her—she knew Jean was her own person, and would do things her own way.

David Harwood showed up again, at the end of May, and was as handsome and charming as he had been the first time around. When she asked him about the ranch, he said that it was in better shape now—there was plenty of grass, and old Mr. Harwood had financed a fence, so the cattle were safe from the ravines. Mr. and Mrs. Harwood had taken him and his cousin Daniel aside and said that, since they did not have any offspring, their wealth would go to David and Daniel—well, not exactly to David and Daniel, but to fix up the ranch itself. They said that they did not want the ranch to wait. They were going to set up some kind of arrangement whereby Mr. and Mrs. Harwood would retain enough to live on, and invest the rest in the ranch. David suspected that this was Mrs. Harwood's idea.

Eliza said, "She is a strange one."

David said, "Other members of our family have thought that, but my aunt, who knew her fairly well back in Pennsylvania, wrote me a note about her. She said that I was to not take Aunt Ruth at face value, because she is very secretive about some condition she has suffered from for twenty years. Whatever it is—maybe gout, but no one knows—stiffens her joints so that she can barely move. That's why she had no children, and also why she allows my uncle to solicit services from this establishment. I do believe that she blames herself for her condition, some sin that she thinks she committed that made her deserving, but my aunt says that she never heard of a single bad thing that Aunt Ruth might have done." David shrugged his shoulders, smiled. "I will say that she always looks as though she would like to do you in, and then turns around and gives you something you never expected."

They did their business with ease and, Eliza had to admit, mutual pleasure. He stayed all night, then went off, after giving her a kiss, when the sun was up and the weather was pleasant. He did not take her for something to eat, as Lucas had done, but even so, there was something about him that she was drawn to. She had a thought that she had never had before: how might she notify him that she wished to have him back, that she would service his needs for free, if not here, then at her boarding house?

But then Eliza again considered the killing and wondered if she should have a sense of guilt. What was a sense of guilt, anyway? Was it refusing to think of the killings? Obsessively thinking of the killings? Hardly thinking of the killings at all? This was another thing she could not converse about with Jean. It was odd to her, though, that what stuck in her mind was not the sight of Zeke storming toward her with that knife raised, but, rather, that moment when she and Jean pushed his crumpled body over the edge of the cliff. She imagined being defended in court by the lawyer—Jenkins, she had to remind herself—and his case would be self-defense, would it not? When she imagined the jury declaring her not guilty, she thought that she should declare herself not guilty, as well. But she didn't know how. Ah, well, life had turned out to be more complex than even she, in her business, had expected.

The gossip subsided over the summer, and Eliza continued to make money. Then, in late August, Mrs. Parks came to her and said, "My dear, I do believe that you should find yourself different employment."

Eliza was alarmed. She said, "Are my customers complaining of me?"

Mrs. Parks said, "Far from it, but it is my belief that I need what you might call turnover. This establishment has only a small number of rooms, and most of my customers do like novelty." She paused, then said, "And, I also believe that it's best for you, for all of you, to learn another trade, or, perhaps I might say, another set of skills. Everyone knows that this is a risky business, and I do my best to make sure that you girls are safe not only from the rough ones, but also the, shall I say, infected ones. However, in some ways, the odds are against us. I worked in this trade myself before I came to Monterey and set up this establishment, and it was evident to me when I got here that I was no longer a salable commodity, you might say. At any rate, I will give you a few weeks to think of something."

Eliza knew that Mrs. Parks knew that she, Eliza, had plenty of funds, but they didn't say a word about that. She said, "What about Olive? She's older than I am."

"Olive is planning to go to work for the dressmaker—you know, the one you like? She told me that she has more customers than she can handle, so I brought her by and showed her that fire screen Olive made."

Eliza imagined a gown with a bird embroidered on one shoulder and a horse embroidered on the other. Then she dared to say, "Please tell me, are you really Mrs. Parks?"

Mrs. Parks's only response was a smile, and then, "Are you really Miss Ripple?"

For a few days, Eliza walked about town, peeping down the street and into doorways and windows, trying to see what women were doing with their time. Yes, she saw what she expected. It was mostly the same things that women were doing back in Kalamazoo—cooking, dusting, walking to the store, gossiping, carrying babies on their hips. Yes, working for Mrs. Parks had given her liberties that were rare here, rare in Kalamazoo, and, she suspected, rare everywhere. The next time she saw Jean, which was for a morning meal at the Bear, they talked in a friendly way about this and that, but the main thing she wondered, as she ate her hotcakes and gazed at her friend, was whether she might do as Jean did, wear what she wished, pretend to be whoever she wanted to be. Thinking of this, she said, "You know when you mentioned taking to the stage?"

Jean laughed, then said, "I would join a traveling company, if they would have me, but I suppose I'll have to go to San Francisco to do that. They don't come through here very often. No doubt that's because that theater on the corner of Scott Street is so small. Have you been there?"

Eliza said, "I've passed it."

Then Jean said, "I am itching to get out of here, though." They exchanged a glance, and Eliza couldn't help but nod. Jean sighed, then leaned forward and said, "Ask me what I want to do."

Eliza lifted her eyebrows. Jean said, "I am going back east, and I am going to work with the Underground Railroad."

Eliza said, "I will miss you so!"

Then they both looked around, to see if anyone had heard them, but it didn't look as though anyone had. Once they were outside, they could talk more freely. They walked toward the rocky point that overlooked the bay. Jean said, "I didn't understand that I was rehearsing all along for this! I thought it was amusing to deck myself out in all sorts of clothing and play at being all different sorts of men and women. I thought I, we, had been pushed into finding the killer because no one in authority cared enough to do it. But now I feel that there was some aspect of fatedness about it. If I was going to do what, perhaps, I am meant to do, what I must do, there were things I had to learn."

Eliza nodded. She didn't know whether she believed in Fate, but she did understand that what Jean wanted to do had to be done, and that Jean was perfect for it. They climbed up onto the rocks, scaring off a few seagulls as they did so, and then, with the breeze rising, and the birds calling, and the puffy clouds floating by, they hugged as they had never hugged before. Eliza said, "Do you have the funds?"

Jean said, "Maybe. I don't really know."

Eliza said, "I do. Whatever you need."

THE NEXT DAY, Eliza walked up Jefferson. She was curious about the lawyer's place—if anyone had done anything about the books or the clothes (or the knives). And then, as she was walking along, she thought of David and the Harwoods, and there she was, opening the Harwoods' gate and knocking on the front door.

Eliza didn't know who she expected would answer—of course she hoped it would be David, expected it would be Mr. Harwood. But when the door finally squeaked open, there was Mrs. Harwood, standing up as best she could, looking forbidding and stiff. Eliza, thinking of what David had said, smiled in a friendly way and ducked her head a bit. Then she warmed her voice and said, "Mrs. Harwood! I am pleased to see you. I am wondering if I might come inside and ask you a question."

Mrs. Harwood's facial expression did not change, but she did back up and pull the door open. Eliza entered. Mrs. Harwood pointed to one of the chairs near the fireplace. Eliza set down her bag and went to the chair, sat down. Mrs. Harwood made her way to the other one. Her gait was stiff and slow, but she was not limping, and she didn't look to be in pain, exactly. Mrs. Harwood put her hands on the arms of the chair and eased herself into the cushion.

Eliza took a deep breath. "I must tell you that I am leaving my place of business." She paused. "However, the last thing I wish to do is leave Monterey. I have some funds, and so I could stay here for a while, but I feel that I would have nothing to do except think of the weather, and so I am wondering if I might . . . if I might come work for you. I feel that I could learn . . ." She looked around the room. "I could learn a good deal about living in a proper way. I mean, of course, about maintaining a clean and healthful home, but also about making a home attractive and beautiful, as this place is." Then she said, "Indoors and out."

Mrs. Harwood did not smile, but her face seemed to relax, and the expression of her eyes changed to something soft, perhaps even amused. Then she said, "Girl . . ." in that old harsh, even scraping way, but as she did so, she coughed, shook her head, and tried again, lowering her voice. She said, "Miss." She took a deep breath, shook her head again, then nodded. Out of her mouth came some soft words in a low tone: "I could use some help." Eliza smiled, smiled perhaps even more brightly than she thought she was going to, because her own pleasure surprised her. She also saw that it was her job to ask, to speak before she was spoken to, to save Mrs. Harwood the effort. She said, "Shall I return tomorrow?"

Mrs. Harwood nodded, and her face was so soft that her look almost constituted a smile. Eliza said, "Ma'am, I can let myself out. I will be sure to close the door firmly, and I will appear tomorrow morning, shortly after I eat my morning meal."

Mrs. Harwood nodded, took a deep breath, leaned back in her chair. Eliza let herself out the door.

She said nothing of this to Mrs. Parks. She was exceedingly

pleased with her plan, though, as she knew she would actually learn something, and she would also see David Harwood from time to time. What would happen there she had no idea, but if Monterey had taught her anything, it was to make the best of things. Every ship that sailed into the bay had to do what the winds demanded, whatever the captain's plans might be.

Acknowledgments

With thanks to Dennis Copeland for his help in aligning this fictional story with the facts of Monterey history and geography.

A NOTE ON THE TYPE

This book was set in a type called Baskerville. The face itself is a facsimile reproduction of types cast from the molds made for John Baskerville (1706–1775) from his designs. Baskerville's original face was one of the forerunners of the type style known to printers as "modern face"—a "modern" of the period AD 1800.

Typeset by Scribe,
Philadelphia, Pennsylvania

Printed and bound by
Berryville Graphics, Berryville, Virginia

Designed by Cassandra J. Pappas